THE BLACKSTONE RITUAL

The Blackstone Ritual is a work of fiction. Names, characters, places and incidents are either the product of the author's imagination or are used fictitiously, and any resemblance to actual persons, living or dead, business establishments, events or locales is entirely coincidental.

Published in the United States by Literary Wanderlust LLC, Denver, Colorado. www.LiteraryWanderlust.com

ISBN Print: 978-1-942856-57-3
ISBN Digital: 978-1-942856-62-7

Cover design and map: Gabriella Bujdoso
Printed in the United States

THE BLACKSTONE RITUAL

Swearingen Durham

Literary Wanderlust | Denver, Colorado

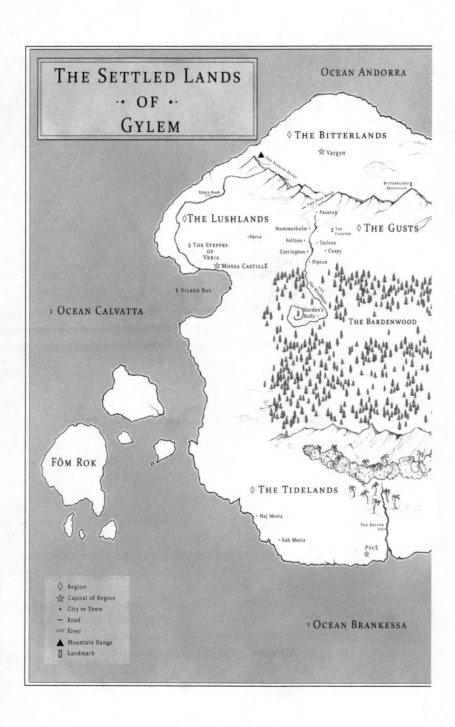

N

THE BILLOWS

◊ THE
CLIFFLANDS

FLITSTEN

CHANNEL D'GRAZA

THENDERLAND

TRISTAKALL PASS

◊ THE SUNLANDS

THE
CLEFT

☆ ASHAR

W•   •E

◊ SALDA ASHARI

□VAIDA ASHARI

S

• BRAN MOTTA

THE FERALS

I dedicate this, my first printed work, my debut novel, and the beginning of my hopefully many tales, to myself.

"Dare to live the life you have dreamed for yourself."
- Ralph Waldo Emerson

1

The Stableboy

Ard looked the bird in his beady eyes. "Now," he whispered. "When Lord Herman steps out from under the roof, I want you to jump on him. Preferably his face, but anywhere you land will work fine. Rustle around a bit too. Don't just scurry off. Try and land a peck or two around the ankles. Got it?"

Keeping a fully-grown turkey quiet on a roof might have seemed difficult for most, but not for Ard. Most of his pranks involved a fair bit of forethought and planning, but sometimes he liked a more simplistic approach—like dropping live fowl onto the bird-fearing village lord first thing in the morning. The turkey looked down at the bread in his hand and let out a small gobble.

"Shhh!" Ard hushed, breaking off another crumb. "Look, we had a deal. You can't have all payments upfront. You hold up your end, and I'll hold up mine."

The bird gobbled up its bread and pecked around for more. The loaf Ard had was running low, but he still had enough to finish. Lord Herman always took his early morning strolls before sun up. He usually scouted for traps Ard had set, but would never expect an attack on the home front. Feet shuffled from inside the house. He was putting his shoes on, probably ready to walk out the door any second.

"Alright," he whispered to the turkey. "That's your cue. Get ready."

The bird bobbed its head about, completely unaware of its instructions.

"You turkeys are all the same," he said, shaking his head. "You never listen."

Ard could hear Lord Herman approach his front door. It was now or never. He picked up the ever-confused turkey and held it over the edge of the roof. As soon as he saw the gleam of Lord Herman's balding carrot top, he released the bird, who made sure to give him a wide-eyed look of betrayal the entire way down.

A glorious landing. Square on top of Lord Herman's head. He let out Ard's favorite high-pitched shriek straight away. "Agh!" he squealed. "Beast! Beeeaaast!"

There wasn't a sound in the Cluster that filled him with more joy. Ard let out a fulfilled sigh. Without wasting a second, he climbed down from the roof and darted home for his alibi. The road was dark this early, but he knew the way. Across the still air, he heard Lord Herman's yelps of terror carry on without end. It seemed the turkey could follow instructions after all. Dashing down the road he almost didn't notice that someone had stepped out of an alleyway in his path. He tried to slow himself down, but the slight downhill of the street made it hard to stop. To avoid careening into the innocent bystander, he stumbled around them costing himself his typically sure footing. As he prepared himself for a good rocky spill, the figure snatched his wrist and caught him just before he hit the ground. The early morning light was too dim to see the details of their face, but it looked like that of an older woman.

"Beg pardon, ma'am!" he apologized as she lifted him up. "I didn't see you there." The woman quickly turned and walked up the road without a single word. An odd exchange, but Ard had no time to question it. The sound of her footsteps faded and Lord Herman's screams picked up again. The shouting would surely wake the whole village. He needed to get back home. If he got there in time, he could start on his morning chores and remain innocent as a lamb. He just had to make it. Watching for any other unexpected early-risers, he picked up his pace down the road. He could still hear the sweet sound of Lord Herman's terrified squeals. *Seriously never gets old*, he laughed to himself.

He ran down the main road toward his home, which sat at the very edge of the village, trying his best to stick to the patches of grass that had grown in between the gravel. He'd learned to escape the scene of a prank as quickly and quietly as possible, but the crunch of gravel was always a tough obstacle to get around. As he approached his home, he slowed down to catch his breath. There was no better giveaway than heaving from a sprint. He fixed his hair and brushed it out of his face. He stopped to listen for any commotion down the road but heard nothing. No more screams and no sign of the strange woman. He was in the clear. Time to get started on his alibi. But just before he made it to the doors of the stable, they burst open to a familiar, plump frame accusingly barring his way.

"Where ya been, boy?" his grandmother croaked in her Old Clustish accent.

He had planned for this. "Nowhere, Gran," he lied. "Just checking on the lodger's horse is all." He made sure not to look her in the eyes. She could always see the truth if she saw his eyes. He even added a sniff and a scratch of his nose to give the fib weight.

Gran crossed her arms with a skeptical brow raise. "Master Baylard left early this mornin'. Took the 'orse with 'im. Even left you some metals for the good brushin' you gave it last night if you can imagine."

An unexpected volley. No matter. He was quick to respond, "How nice of him! Well, I guess I better go sweep out the stall then."

"Already done," she retorted with a sly smile. "Do you 'fink I was just in there breafin' all them gaggin' fumes for me 'ealth? No, sir. So, where were ya? Let's 'ave it."

She had him cornered. "I was...out for a morning stroll," he tried.

"Unlikely."

"Hm, morning jog?"

"Doubtful at best."

"Morning...swim?"

She rolled her eyes at him, disheveling her messy, reddish-gray bun on top of her head. "Arden Ford," she sighed. "If I 'ave to flirt with that lordly buffoon to get you out of trouble again, I'll deal ya a smackin' so good, it'll be sung about in songs 'til the end of your days. You 'ear me? If you don't 'fink I know the cause of all that screamin' and shoutin' down the road, you're sorely mistaken, m'boy. To the inn wif ya. Go on."

He'd tried his best, but she knew his every move. He shuffled toward the house, sure to kick a pebble or two while pouting along the way.

"At's right," she jeered. "Everyone in this town knows o'your antics and you 'fink you can pull a fast one on your own grandmother? Pff. Not today, boy. Not ever, in fact. The only 'fing that ever escaped me—"

"Was your husband," he interrupted knowingly.

Gran held her head high, adding, "And truth be told, I let 'im go. Now, go on into the kitchen. I made breakfast for Master Baylard but there should still be a few nibblins left."

Ard was growing suspicious. Had she forgotten what today was? Surely not. Gran never forgot a thing. She always made sure every guest that came into Sore Swallow Inn had everything they needed when they needed it. She knew it all and all knew it well, so she certainly couldn't have forgotten. Certainly.

He was not wrong. When he followed her into the kitchen, he expected to find half-eaten biscuits or some other reminder that he was the poorest kid in town, but he entered to fresh hot rolls, boiled eggs, beef sausage, bacon, and an entire unopened jar of blackberry jam—a birthday breakfast fit for a king. He looked at his grandmother with a quizzical smile. "That fancy man left all this nice and fresh, did he?"

"Well," Gran replied coyly, "I guess he wasn't 'ungry!"

Ard smiled and thanked her with a tight hug. Her face nestled right in his chest, like it had since he was ten. As it turns out, it wasn't very difficult for a growing boy to pass four and a half feet. Her hair smelled like rosemary, how it always smelled when she had been cooking. She always stuck the herb sprigs in her bun for easy grabbing. He adored that smell. It was far stronger than usual this morning, so she must have used a fair bit of spice in the food. Regardless, he ate everything his stomach could hold. He always ate this much on his birthday. Usually, Gran would have to break an arm or two in town to convince anyone to give food to a notorious prankster, but every year she managed to rally together a magnificent birthday breakfast for him. The town's adoration for Gran was probably the only reason he still had a home in their village. His constant practical jokes were not well received by the townsfolk. Gran always said they were just a "tough bushel," but he knew it was him they disliked, not his pranks—which made them all the more fun.

After breakfast, Ard planned to stir up some more trouble before the rest of the town woke up, though the food was definitely making it harder to leave the table. He couldn't remember his previous birthday breakfasts tasting this amazing, but he wasn't about to argue after seventeen of them. Every bite was bursting with oddly incredible flavor. Maybe the other villagers decided to let up on him and actually provide some quality food this time around.

"Lords, Gran," he slurred between chews. "You trying something new with your cooking?"

"Same as I've always ma'it. Perfect down to the last crumb," she boasted. "Somefin' wrong wif' it?"

He shook his head. "Just the opposite," he smiled, taking

another enormous bite. Gran fixed herself a small plate and sat down next to him.

"Well," she said, "I can't imagine why anyfin' would taste diff'rent, but I'm glad ya like it. Hurry now, there's still chores ta'be done."

"Yes, ma'am. What are your plans for today?"

"Not too much, pup," she said affectionately. He loved when she called him that. "I'll 'ave to get the linens from Master Baylard's room washed 'n' dried. Washin' linens—seems like ages since I've 'ad to do that. Need to run to the square sometime today as well."

Ard could barely listen to her. He couldn't keep his mind off of the food. Why was it so delicious? It was hard to focus on anything else. Feeling hoggish, he pushed his plate away and sat back in his chair, still chewing on a mouthful of bacon.

"You 'ad enough?" Gran asked curiously. He nodded with an exhausted look. It was all he could manage.

"Well, 'appy birthday, Arden," she said with a cheeky smile. A smile that instantly turned to a stern grimace as she ordered, "now, go grab the mop."

He laughed. "Aren't you a predictable one?"

"Too right yar, pup," she said with pride. "Our dear lodger obviously didn't know the purpose of a doormat. Poor dolt."

"Who? The Baylard chap? First lodger we've seen in ages, that one. What was he doing here anyway? He looked lordly enough for castle halls."

Stacking empty plates, she replied, "Bringin' news from Mossa Castille to Lord Herman. Member of the queen's messenger brigade, he was. 'Cordin' to 'im, there's rumors of trouble brewin' eastward."

"What?" Ard asked fearfully. "Eastward? Like...Ashar eastward?"

"Dunno," Gran shrugged. "Wouldn't say much, the 'ole bloke. Back when my hips were wider I might've been able to rustle out a bit more words."

Ard rolled his eyes at her. "Gran, be serious. You don't think the Ashen Horde would come this far west do you?" he asked, ignoring her joke. "What could they want here? Lumber? Got plenty of that."

"Kolbran and his lot haven't set foot in these parts since before you were born," Gran assured him. "I'm sure if he were ever 'eaded this way, we'd know about it. Lord Herman may be stupid, but he'd never put us in 'arm's way."

"You think Herman will call a gathering about it?"

"*Lord* Herman," she corrected him, hands on hips. "Let's 'ave a bit of decency, boy. The man does run this town. I'm sure he will. I doubt he'd keep anythin' from us if it were important. Now, are you gonna' mop or do I 'ave to do everythin' m'self?"

"Yes, ma'am." He swallowed the last bit of biscuit in his mouth and started clearing his spot at the table. Gran was drying plates near the sink when he thought he heard her say something. "What's that, Gran?" he asked.

"What's what?" she replied, confused.

"You just said something."

"I did not."

"You sure?"

Gran turned and glared at him. "You 'fink you're funny, do ya? You 'avin' a laugh?"

"What?" he asked with his hands out.

"Boy, I'm old," she groaned. "And I'm the last person in these parts you can make a fool out of. So why you tryin' to pull somefin' on me, eh?"

"Honest," he pleaded. "I'm totally innocent!"

"Pff," she scoffed. "A fib if there ever was one. So 'elp me if I catch wind of any of your devilry, Arden Ford, it'll be your backside." She balled her hand into a playful, shaking fist.

Ard was bewildered. He knew he heard her say something. Or he heard someone say something. He decided to let her believe he was playing around. Gran was getting old. She may have said something then instantly forgot she said it. He hoped that was not the case. Either way, he made himself forget about it. He left the kitchen to retrieve the mop and bucket from the storage closet near the front door. As he was grabbing the mop stick, he heard her whisper something again from the kitchen. He walked across the entrance back toward the dining table and leaned his head in.

"Gran?" he called. Only she was nowhere to be seen. There was no one in the kitchen. He walked over to the sink and peered out of the window to see her outside working in her garden. The whisper came again, this time from behind him. He whipped around to find nothing but an empty kitchen. He thought to himself what people did to folks who claimed they heard voices. "Clearly I should have gotten more sleep."

He looked out the window watching her work and smiled. He loved to watch her sometimes. He loved seeing her wipe the sweat from her brow or throw garden tools about in frustration. His Gran was the hardest working woman in Pipton and she had been raised that way. Her grandfather was one of the first people to settle in the town. He built the entire inn with his own hands. When he died, he passed it down to her and she always made sure to remember him for it. She had the original drawing for Sore Swallow framed and hung above the hearth so that everyone passing through could see the work he did.

As Ard went to retrieve the mop, he passed by his great-great-grandfather's drawing and ran his fingers along the frame. After all his years of seeing the drawing, it still made him proud. Coming from such strong people made him feel better about being so scrawny. It also made him proud to be the inn's only stableboy. Where most people would never lower themselves to cleaning horse manure, he was happy to. At least happy to do so for Sore Swallow anyway. Plus, he enjoyed the company of horses, creatures he found much more agreeable than people. Smiling to himself, he looked at the drawing one last time before returning to his chores.

Suddenly, a third whisper came from behind him. He

whirled around, startled, but again—there was no one there.

Nothing but the empty foyer of the inn...

He couldn't hear what the whisper said, but he knew he heard it. He had a strange feeling someone was trying to get his attention. He dug in his ears curiously. Maybe he *was* going crazy.

2

The Gathering

After finishing his chores, Ard decided to stroll through town in search of a worthy victim. A well-deserved morning prank was his favorite way to begin the day. He spared no villager when it came to practical jokes: children, elderly, rich, poor. The only thing he looked for in a target was obliviousness. The more unwitting the better. All the people of Pipton were flitting about like ants on an anthill, all of them chatting about how nice the weather was, completely unaware—just how he liked it.

Pipton girls were a favorite target of his. Especially since most of them teased him for his size and for working in the stables. The other boys in town were large and strong since all of them were taught to swing axes straight out of the womb. Too bad that's all they were ever taught. With them out cutting wood from dawn to dusk, the other boys rarely showed up at school, so Ard was left the only boy among a sea of condemnatory teenage girls. But, at least he could read and write..

Strolling down the main road, a perfectly oblivious group of girls headed in Ard's direction. Reaching into his pocket, which he always filled with random pranking equipment, he pulled out a wad of black cloth with a string of yarn hanging from it. He furtively dropped the cloth in the girls' path and waited. As they passed, he jumped and shouted, "Rat! It's a rat!"

The girls stamped their feet squealing at the top of their lungs. He covered his mouth to stifle the laughter, but one of them noticed. "Arden Ford!" she shouted. "You rotten, smelly—"

"Careful now," he called back. "Yelling like that draws the real rats."

"Very funny," the girl huffed, but before she could retort, he pointed down to the ground where a real rat was conveniently perched on a small stone. The girl's eyes went wide and she and the others ran off down the street squealing hysterically.

Ard nearly choked from the laughter. As the rat scurried off, he called to it, "thank you, my friend! You, sir, have impeccable timing." Satisfied with his joke, he continued through town. Noon wouldn't approach for hours, but the sun was just high enough to where the morning rays took away the crisp chill of the night before. Being in peak autumn season, the streets were littered with fallen, yellow leaves. The light fell on the gravel road warming the stones as all the stores prepared to open their doors and shutters. Although he always thought village life was droll, he called Pipton home, and it had its merits.

The whole village was built down one road with shops on either side. Homes and huts were set up on side streets as well as spread across hills and pastures on the town's outskirts. The village square where everyone met for gatherings was in the center of town. It also housed most of the shops. Gran would frequently send Ard to the square to get various items for the inn and its guests when Sore Swallow housed any. Business was never great for an inn built at the end of the road near a forest feared throughout the entire kingdom – The Bardenwood.

Named for the hundreds of bards that spew stories of what lies between its pines, the whole wood was off-limits to anyone except the woodcutters, though even they never ventured far past its edge. Some villagers say the trees uproot themselves every night and rearrange so that travelers become lost inside, ending up easy prey to the array of dark creatures said to roam freely among its floor. Ard had never experienced anything close to these legends and always remained skeptical of the forest's reputation, but even he never dared to pass under its canopy. However, it did offer him a fair bit of material when it came to terrifying young children.

As he continued on his morning stroll, he greeted other townsfolk with a smile or friendly nod. Eyerolls, scoffs, and the occasional curse were the only responses he ever got. Not that it bothered him. If anything, the town's keen distaste for him just made his pranks all the more unpleasant—for them anyway. Nearing the square, he stopped off to see one of the only people in town who actually enjoyed his company, Mr. Temmus Brinkley, Pipton's one and only cobbler.

Every boot, shoe, and sandal in town was made by Mr. Brinkley, in his own shop, by his own two hands. Any chance Ard got, he would be at his shop. Along with tolerating, and possibly enjoying, all of his pranks, Mr. Brinkley was one of the only people in town, along with Gran, who had lived in Pipton since it was founded. He loved hearing the two of them ramble on in their heavy accents, telling their Old Clustish stories. It humbled him.

It made no difference to him that his best friend was one of the oldest people in town. He preferred the company of Mr. Brinkley over any of the kids in Pipton his age. Ard passed under the weathered, swinging sign above the front door that read *Brinkley Feet* and almost bumped directly into the old cobbler who was on all fours searching for something.

"What're you doing down there, Brinkley?"

The cobbler sat up, pushed his spectacles up the bridge of his scrawny nose, and said, "Arden Ford, m'boy! Sorry, I've dropped a button fer the slippers I was makin' fer the baker's wife. What'ser name again?"

Ard thought for a moment. "Mrs. Nilda?"

"That's the one!" he exclaimed, pointing a knobby finger.

"Nilda Fletcher. She'll 'ave my 'ead if I don't 'ave these slippers to her come this afternoon."

Ard stooped down to the cracked, wooden floor of the shop. He could see dusty footprints glazed over the floor panels in the glare of the light from the front door. "I'll help you look," he said, patting Mr. Brinkley on the back.

"Thank you, m'boy," the old man sighed. "What brings you inside me shop on this fine day? Shouldn't you be pesterin' our Lord Herman or otherwise wreakin' havoc somewhere?"

"I had an early start," he boasted.

"Ah," Mr. Brinkley realized. "Of course. I thought that might've been you this mornin'. What bird did you drop on the poor fool?"

"Turkey," he answered. "Incompetent turkey. How'd you know? Am I really getting that predictable?"

The cobbler nodded with an apologetic look. "'Fraid so, lad."

"Ferals!" he cursed. "This town only has so much material to offer, Brink."

"Amen to that. What other mischiefs you got planned? I could use a bit of entertainment. Who's next on your list today?"

Ard crossed his arms with a grin. "Questions I'm not at liberty to answer, I'm afraid. A proper jokesmith never reveals his targets. I should get going though. Big day ahead of me, you know."

"Is that right?" Mr. Brinkley said, looking under the doormat.

"Mhm. *Really* big day. One might even call it 'special'."

"A 'special' day?" Mr. Brinkley said quizzically. "Gracious. What day is it, lad?"

"Just my birthday, you coot!" he laughed.

Mr. Brinkley gasped sarcastically. "Well, pardon me, m' lord!" he exclaimed, waving his hands. "Must've slipped past me tiny little old man brain! What with being a sorry ol' coot and all."

Ard laughed again. "Oh, cut it. I'm only joking."

The cobbler's hazy eyes crinkled into his cheeky grin. "Happy birthday, lad," he winked.

"Thanks, Brink. Got any plans today other than making shoes for bakers' wives?"

"Nothing, in particular, I can recall." Eyes wide, he looked down at Ard's feet. "Boy!" he scolded. "What in the Ferals 'ave you done to your boots?"

Ard groaned. "They're fine, Brink."

"They most certainly are not!" he snorted as he poked his finger into the side of his peeling sole.

"Stop that!"

Mr. Brinkley stood up. "I'll 'ave you a new pair soon as I can."

"No thanks, Brink. I'm fine!" he protested. "Don't go through all that trouble. Honestly. Finish Nilda's slippers before she takes your head off."

"That old grackle can wait," he scoffed. "It's your birthday after all! Besides, you've been needin' new boots for at least two years now seems it."

"So, I procrastinate."

"Well, you'd best hope your grandmother doesn't catch wind 'a this," Mr. Brinkley warned. "If Flora sees the condition 'a those leaf crunchers we'll bof' be gutted."

"Well," he sighed, "if you don't have anything else to do today then I suppose I could use a new pair."

"You'll have 'em, lad," Mr. Brinkley grinned. "On me. So, 'fink there'll be a town gatherin' near noon. Beautiful, beautiful day for one, eh?"

"I'm sure," he said, disinterested. "And it'll be just as grand as the last one. A whole town gathering called just to talk about a sick cow. I mean really."

Mr. Brinkley laughed, "Well, it was either that or Farmer Albert's missin' garden 'oe. I s'pose we 'ave to talk about somefin' now don't we?"

"I wonder if it'll have anything to do with the fellow we put up at Sore Swallow last night," Ard thought out loud.

"What fellow?" Mr. Brinkley asked distractedly, looking

under the entry table for the still missing button.

"Baylard, I think," he answered. "According to Gran, he was bringing news from Mossa Castille. She said he wouldn't say much, but it was about rumors of trouble eastward."

Mr. Brinkley sat up, suddenly interested. "Trouble eastward, eh? What kind of trouble?"

"No idea," he shrugged. "Like I said, Gran couldn't get much out of him. He headed back west early this morning."

Mr. Brinkley scratched his scruffy chin, puzzled. He took a breath to respond but was interrupted by the ring of the town bell. He walked to the front door and stepped outside to take a look. Everyone in Pipton was scuffling to the square. The old cobbler grabbed a small boy that was running by and asked, "What's the word, lad?"

The boy, with a head full of hay and dirty trousers, replied. "Town gathering, sir!" Before Mr. Brinkley could say anything else, the boy darted off to the square, eager to hear some news. Any news in Pipton was interesting news. Mr. Brinkley turned back to Ard and motioned for him to head out of the shop saying, "Be a good lad, Ard, and let me know what our good master has to say. If I don't get these slippers done before long..." Mr. Brinkley shivered and motioned his hands toward his neck, pretending to be strangled.

"You got it, Brink," Ard laughed, patting his shoulder on the way out. He moved down the street through the crowd of townsfolk who were shuffling about looking for good spots to hear what Lord Herman had to say. He moved past two women fighting over a seat for their children and shook his head. He hated how people acted during gatherings; pushing, shoving, and scuffling around each other in a hot, sweaty mess.

He never blamed the people for being excited about them though. For most of the villagers, this was the only interesting thing to happen throughout their day. Most of the people in Pipton were lumberjacks, or family to lumberjacks, or worked for lumberjacks...

Wood, wood, and more wood. Then, a bit of wood on top for good measure.

That was all Pipton meant to its kingdom and it was all its people cared about. As loathsome as Ard found it, most lives in Pipton revolved around the production of lumber. Many villagers were okay with this notion but never missed a chance to hear about things happening in the town or, on rare occasion, matters of the kingdom. These gatherings kept them going and were their only connection to their capital of Mossa Castille. So, naturally, they had to have the best seat.

Ard knew a better way to witness a gathering. He had a usual spot above the blacksmith forge on the roof. The forge was built in the back of the square, so on the roof none of the other villagers noticed him. There, he was able to enjoy space, privacy, and not to mention a good view. Plus, being away from the smell of people stuffed together in a tiny square was always nice. He snuck his way behind the forge, climbed the water barrels, and hoisted himself up onto the roof. He slid carefully down the shingles onto the edge letting his long legs dangle over the side. He looked down into the crowd of people and noticed the baker's son, Dail Fletcher, walking around selling fresh cookies. Dail was tiny, but his shrill voice still rang out over the bustling of the town. "Fresh cookies! Freeeeesh cookies! Buy one, get another for the same price because I don't got time for anyone who's cheap! Fresh cookies!"

Ard dug around in his pants pocket for some spare metals. Passing up fresh Fletcher cookies would be an offense to the Lords Above, no doubt. After a fair bit of digging, he managed to pull out a single dusty coin. Once Dail got closer, he whistled softly to catch his attention. Putting his finger over his lips to make sure he didn't give away his secret spot, he flicked the coin to him. Dail turned, caught the coin, then tossed him a cookie as quickly and quietly as he could. Ard winked at him as he continued making his rounds. He and Dail had never been close, but the boy was one of the only villagers Ard had a soft spot for.

He had a witty sense of humor, something rare in children his age. This paired with his delicious cookies kept him safe from Ard's pranks—for the most part.

Ard scanned the crowd for Gran but couldn't find her. He didn't worry though. She never attended gatherings anyway. She did all she could to avoid exchanges with Lord Herman who fancied her ever since they were young – another reason Ard hadn't been banished from Pipton. He had always hoped she and Mr. Brinkley would end up together, but Mr. Brinkley was far too shy to ever approach the feisty baroness of Sore Swallow. Ard gave up on trying to find her when all the chattering of the villagers dulled slowly as Lord Herman approached the podium. Giving his red beard a tousle, he cleared his throat and spoke with his typical, monotonous drone. "Good day, Piptonians," he called.

"Good day, m'lord," the crowd repeated in the usual fashion.

"I hope you have all been enjoying this fine day here in our town," he beamed. "It's rare to get days this lovely and warm so far north this time of year. I pray you will not waste it as I will, slaving away at a desk swimming in parchment."

The crowd responded with soft laughter.

Lord Herman cleared his throat again and said, "Now, there are a few things I must go over with you today. Please refrain from any questions until I have finished explaining all of them." He squinted at his notes on the podium. "Firstly," he called. "As you all may have heard, last week The Buttered Bum Pub in Cuspy caught fire and is in need of rebuilding. It's, of course, unnecessary for me to point out how important The Buttered Bum was. Without it, there would be nowhere to celebrate our annual harvest celebration, nor would there be any place for you men to hide from your wives at week's end."

The men in the crowd laughed while the women scowled.

Herman went on, satisfied with his small joke, "Only joking, madams, only joking. Lord Shain has asked us for more lumber to aid with the rebuilding, so we must be diligent with our output over the course of the next few days."

The crowd settled then nodded in agreement.

Herman continued, "Secondly, there are rumors swirling about trouble in the East, particularly concerning Ashar." Whispers immediately filtered through the crowd as Herman continued. "Master Baylard of Queen Leonora's messenger brigade has brought a declaration from Mossa Castille as of yesterday and it reads as follows." Lord Herman shuffled at his podium, waved the declaration so that everyone could see, then squinted his eyes and recited:

To Lord Herald Herman and the People of the Village of Pipton—

It has come to my attention that there are rumors of King Kolbran of Ashar moving west across the Sunlands and possibly into the borders of our blessed Verdamaïn. Through the many sources I have stationed throughout our kingdom and the kingdoms nearest to us, I have determined this rumor to be utterly false. King Kolbran and his Ashen Horde have not been seen or heard from in the Lushlands for over two decades. Any movement by the Burnt King and his army of scoundrels would have first been detected by our Thendish friends in The Gusts, from whom I have been informed of no such action.

However, I do not take the spread of such falsities and lies lightly. Whosoever is caught spreading these rumors will be apprehended and held accountable for fear-mongering and for slander to the word of the Crown. Those who disobey will be punished under the full extent of the laws of this kingdom and judgment for their crimes shall be swift and final.

I bid you all the best of days from your shining capital and hope that this declaration is of the clearest and most transparent understanding.

May the Lords Above grant you blessings.

Queen Leonora Veleno

Ruler and Protector of the Lushlands, Chief Magistrate of the Steppes of Veria, and Grand Sentinel of Silber Bay

Lord Herman folded the parchment and placed it back onto the podium, scanning the crowd for any confused looks. Everyone seemed in accordance and looked to have understood the declaration entirely. Although talk of the Ashen Horde was not a common occurrence, most people liked to stir it up every now and then, but no one dared test the words of the queen, whose reputation for harsh punishments had spread even beyond the Lushlands.

"Moving on," Herman said, clearing his throat for one final topic. "Late last night, the Busby family discovered their eldest son, Gell, to be missing."

More whispers and gasps spread through the now worried villagers. Everyone knew Gell Busby, the shy boy of fourteen who always walked alone everywhere he went. The boy who never took off his musty blue cloak for even a single wash. Ard always tried to be nice, but even he couldn't deny the stench of that blue coat when Gell walked past. The poor boy never said much to anyone and was the usual target for other kids in Pipton who were always making jokes about his weight. Ard scoffed at the villagers. None of them ever cared about "Smelly Belly Gelly" before they knew he was missing. He tried imagining all the people who would suddenly act kinder to the Busby's now that their son was possibly in trouble. He imagined that Gell probably left Pipton because of how awful people were to him. Even Ard himself had thought about leaving Pipton before. Still, he hoped Gell was all right.

"If anyone," Lord Herman implored, "has any knowledge of Gell Busby or his whereabouts, please come forward immediately. In the meantime, I will ask for volunteers to gather up a search party this evening. We will need plenty of lanterns and a few good hounds from whoever would like to aid us in looking for him."

People in the audience began raising their hands to volunteer for the search party. Conversation now swirled about Gell and where he might be. Just as Ard was preparing to descend from his spot on the forge, a frightened voice reverberated in his ears.

"Leave me be! Please!"

Someone sounded like they were in trouble. The shouting startled him so much he nearly fell off the roof. He whirled around looking to see who was shouting for help. Nobody in the crowd seemed to notice. The voice shouted again, this time louder and more frightened.

"STOP! Help!"

Ard's breathing quickened. Someone was in danger and it sounded like it was coming from the Bardenwood, but that was impossible. The Bardenwood was at least half a mile back down the main road. How could he possibly hear from that far? Still, none of the other villagers seemed to notice the shouting. Suddenly, the voice turned into a blood-curdling shriek that shook Ard down to his boots. Alarmed, he climbed down from the roof and sped toward the crowd. He grabbed one of the villagers, barely verbalizing, "did you hear that?"

Recognizing who he was, the villager huffed at him. "Nice try, Ard."

"I'm serious!" he protested. "Someone's in trouble! I think it might be Gell. How did you not hear it?"

"How disgraceful," another villager added. "Playing a joke now of all times. Haven't you anything better to do, menace?"

"I'm telling you!" he pleaded. "I heard him!"

The commotion had caught the attention of Lord Herman who now glared at him from the podium. "Arden Ford!" he boomed across the crowd. "That's enough out of you, pest. The Busby's are going through enough as it is. Shame on you!"

Ard tried to speak again but was silenced by the villagers.

Lord Herman stroked his mustache and concluded. "That is all for today, everyone. May the Lords Above grant you blessings." Everyone began shuffling out of the square and onto their daily tasks, glowering at Ard as they passed. Shaking and still recovering from the screams, he looked around to check once more if anyone seemed to notice anything unusual, but no one believed him. Not one villager was alarmed. He was baffled beyond measure. What could it have been? He'd heard stories of people going crazy by hearing voices in their head, but he never thought he would be one of them. He regained his composure and tried shaking it off, but to no avail. He needed someone to believe him.

Mr. Brinkley. He'd know what to do, he thought. He started back down the road to Brinkley Feet, but as he walked onto the street, the horizon slowly began to sway back and forth causing him to stumble to the ground. His vision started to blur and everything seemed to keep moving past him even though he was completely still. He rubbed his eyes in confusion, trying hard to focus on the ground in front of him. He could make out other townspeople walking right past him without a care. They probably thought he was playing another ridiculous joke, but he wasn't joking at all. He became violently nauseous, fearing that he would vomit at any moment from the world swimming around him. Out of nowhere, he was blasted with a strong scent of rosemary, the same scent he'd smelled in Gran's hair earlier that morning. Something was wrong. He couldn't gain control of his senses. He stumbled down the road choking on his own breath, barely making it into Mr. Brinkley's shop.

When he burst through the door, he startled the old cobbler so much that he dropped the slipper he'd been working on, popping one of the buttons off. As the button bounced invisibly across the floor, Mr. Brinkley grumbled, "Confound you, boy! I'll never get these slippers done on time."

"Brink...B-Brinkley," he murmured, trembling.

The old man's face shifted. "What's the matter, lad?" he

asked, moving toward him. "You don't look s'good." Ard tried to speak, but before he could, the world spinning around him went black as night and he fell to the floor.

3

The Toadstool Path

Ard opened his eyes and found himself staring into a gray, clouded sky. His head was still pounding, but he managed to slowly sit up, rubbing his temples. Wincing, he focused his eyes and found himself sitting at the edge of the Bardenwood. He'd never been this close to it before. A childlike fear came over him as he stared into the endless darkness of the infamous forest. He scrambled to his feet and put some space between himself and the ghostly trees, afraid he might be dragged in by their branches. Dusting off his pants, he turned to get a look around and saw Sore Swallow behind him. He was home, but something gave him the uneasy feeling that he'd never been here before. The grass around him bent in the wind and a distant, low thunder reverberated through the field, bouncing off the trees which stood only a few feet away from him. He rubbed the back of his head, trying to figure out how he ended up here. He remembered bursting into Mr. Brinkley's shop but after that— nothing.

He looked back toward Pipton. The whole town seemed empty and quiet as if no one had ever lived there. It looked almost...abandoned. The storm above seemed to be growing stronger as another thunderclap tumbled across the sky. He started back to Pipton, but the sharp crack of a twig behind him froze his feet to the ground. A shuffling sound came from the woods and he whirled around to find the strangest sight he'd ever seen.

It was a girl no younger than himself. She had rich, auburn hair that fell straight as a sewing needle. Her cream-colored dress rippled across her thin frame and her bare feet hung like dainty, weightless ribbons three feet off of the ground. She was levitating.

Ard blinked his eyes over and over, making sure he wasn't imagining it. He couldn't see how this was a trick. He'd been a prankster his whole life and could think of nothing that would allow this girl to pull off such a hoax, especially one so convincing. She continued swaying in the wind, floating with barely any effort. He stared at her with his mouth wide open, unable to speak. The girl looked around her then leaned forward as if to tell him a secret. "Come and find me," she beckoned. Her voice sounded like multiple whispers speaking at once. It echoed through the trees, fading into the distance. Before he could respond, her ghostly figure started sinking back into the dark of the Bardenwood as the storm rumbled once more.

"Wait!" he managed. "How? How do I find you? Who are you?"

Before slipping out of view, the girl's voice echoed again, "The Bardenwood awaits you, stableboy."

He moved to follow her into the woods, eager to ask more questions, but a deafening clap of thunder and flash of lightning snapped him out of the dream.

Ard awoke in his bed in the loft of Sore Swallow. It was still storming outside his window. He sat up, still weakened from his spill in Brinkley Feet. His brain was rattling from the unusual dream. He felt like he'd been in bed for hours unable to move.

Before he got a chance to get out of bed, he noticed Gran walking up the loft stairs carrying a small candle to light her way. Her familiar gait warmed his heart. She didn't notice him wake up because she was preoccupied with watching her steps. She never came to the loft because the old stairs made her nervous.

"Hey, Gran," he announced, smiling.

Gran looked up in shock and gasped. "'e's awake!" she called downstairs. "Thank 'eavens! Ard's awake!"

"Wait, how long have I been asleep?" Ard asked. "Who's here, Gran?"

Gran scuffled excitedly across the floor and sat on his bed hugging him tightly. "Never you mind that, pup. Are you alright?" she asked worriedly. "Are you 'urt? 'Ow do you feel?"

"I'm fine, Gran," he laughed lightly.

"You 'ad me worried sick!" she exclaimed, letting go of her constricting embrace. "You've been out cold for three whole days, you 'ave!"

His face went white. "Three days?" he asked, looking around the room.

"Temmus barely made it to you before you cracked your noggin on the floor," she went on. "Gave 'imself a few good bruises savin' your neck! You ought to thank your lucky stars for 'im."

Just as Gran finished talking, Mr. Brinkley's wrinkled face appeared in the stairwell. He adjusted his spectacles and smiled at Ard. "'ow are ya, lad?" he asked warmly.

"Fine," he replied with a smile. "I'm fine. Just a little woozy is all. I have no idea what happened." He paused. "Wait. The screams."

Gran and Mr. Brinkley looked at each other confused. "What screams?" they asked.

Ard restarted, trying to sound as rational as possible. "The screams," he repeated, "at the gathering. I think it was Gell Busby. No one else heard it. They acted like I was making it up."

Gran rubbed her hand on the back of his head and hushed,

"There, there, pup. We believe ya'. We'll look into it, alright? Right. Now, you'd best take it easy. The healer downstairs says it could 'appen again anytime."

"I'm fine," he repeated. "I'll be fine."

Gran nodded her head and pulled gently at the strands of his black hair one last time before walking out of the room with Mr. Brinkley. "We'll give ya some privacy, lad," Mr. Brinkley said, putting his hand on Gran's back. "Just shout if ya need anythin'."

Ard nodded his head and they both made the careful tread downstairs. He looked out his window to see the storm had lightened slightly. Thunder was still bellowing through the sky, making the inn tremble. He stood up out of bed, scratching his hair which had grown stiff and oily from being pressed against the pillow for three days. He felt unusually lighter like he'd lost a lot of weight. He shrugged it off and walked toward the window where he was able to make out the hazy border of the Bardenwood through the sheets of pouring rain. He thought about his dream of the levitating girl. It felt so real to him, unlike any dream he'd ever had.

The Bardenwood awaits you...

What did she mean? And why did it feel more like a memory than a dream? Ard fought with himself. What if she was some kind of omen? What if she was the one who was screaming during the gathering? He was desperate to know more about her, but right now he needed food. He suddenly realized how hungry he was. It was like he hadn't eaten for weeks. He supposed that was why he felt like he didn't weigh as much. His stomach turned inside out and made him feel like there was a hole right through his middle. He started for the stairs to head down into the kitchen.

Gran had lanterns and candles lit all throughout the lobby of the inn. The storm took most of the light away, but Ard could tell it was late afternoon. He shuffled down the stairs and into the kitchen, where Gran and Mr. Brinkley were enjoying some fruit, cheese, and hot peppermint tea. The smell of the apples filled his nose so much that he almost sneezed, but apples had never smelled to him before. At least not this strongly. The cheese was so robust it felt like it was plugged into his nostrils. The peppermint from the tea tinged the air so heavily that he could practically see it. While the scents swirled together in the kitchen, his mouth began to water.

"Would you like somefin' to eat, lad?" Mr. Brinkley asked, chewing on an apple rind. Ignoring him completely, Ard tore into the fruit as if he'd been starving. The apple burst with flavor in his mouth. He could feel the water from its soft core run down his throat like a river. Without a doubt, this was the best apple he'd ever eaten. He gobbled it down, following it up with a few good cuts of the cheese and some slices of bread that Gran had baked. It was as if he'd never enjoyed food before in his life. He groaned with delight as he tore through almost the entire tray of comestibles.

"Slow down, Ard!" Gran exclaimed. "You'll make yourself sick, you will!"

He realized how much of a pig he was being and slowed his chewing. He took one last bite of his third apple and wiped his mouth clean. He looked out of the kitchen window and saw that the rain had lightened to a drizzle. Now that his hunger was satisfied, it was time to figure out what happened to him.

"I'm going into town," he announced as he went to pull a coat out from the closet in the foyer.

"You sure that's a good idea, pup?" Gran asked nervously as she stood up from the table. "The 'ealer said—"

"I'll be fine," he called, still chewing on bits of apple and cheese. Shutting the door behind him, he pulled the hood of his coat over his head just as the droplets of rain were catching in his hair. He wanted to retrace his steps and see what had happened to him three days ago. He couldn't believe he had been out for so long. As he walked down the street, some of the other villagers stared at him—stares that were somehow different this time. Before his episode at the gathering, the villagers always looked at him with disgust or disapproval. Every now and then he'd receive a scoff or two, but now they just stared at him emptily. Worried wasn't the word, but they all seemed more or less concerned for him. Maybe they were afraid for him. Ard pulled his hood closer to his face, uncomfortable with the feeling. When he reached the square, it was almost completely empty save for a few people. The storm had pushed everyone back into their homes early for the evening. As he approached the blacksmith forge where he first heard the screams, he was intercepted by a familiar, vexing group of peach dresses beneath frilly umbrellas.

"Hello, Arden," the head of the clique said.

Ard looked up to find the only three girls in all of Pipton who chose to speak to him, albeit never on good terms. "Hello, Madsyn," he replied. "Nelia. Jonna."

Nelia and Jonna stared blankly at him, looking at his clothes as if they were rags. "We thought—sorry, *hoped* you might be dead," Madsyn said with disdain.

"And leave you three maiden fairs behind for the taking?" he laughed. "I shudder at the thought. Never fear, m'ladies. I'm afraid I'm not so easy to rid."

"Heartbreaking," Madsyn replied sarcastically. "Truly. I don't know how we would live on with all the peace and quiet."

Ard countered, "I'm glad to see someone would miss my handiwork. Who would I strive hard for every day to cultivate excitement in this pitifully boring town if not for you three?"

"That was a rotten prank you pulled the other day before the gathering," Jonna cut in. "My aunt got sick and nearly died from a rat once!"

"Was that you three?" he asked. "Hm. Sorry about that. You Pipton girls are tough to tell apart. It's like none of you own anything unless it comes in peach or pink."

"Forgive us for having a sense of style," Madsyn spat back. "Though what would you know about fashion? Not all of us enjoy rolling around in horse manure all day. Must be a trend from...

actually, I can't imagine where that would be a trend."

"Thought it might keep you from bothering me," he volleyed. "Clearly I was wrong. I'll be sure to use garlic next time. Or is it a circle of salt? I can't quite remember which one keeps away—"

"You are foul and rotten, Arden Ford!" Nelia cried, cutting him off. "We could be hanged for being called—"

"Witches?" he finished with a devilish smile.

The word alone could quiet even the most blustering clamor. *Witch.*

The girls had a right to fear such an accusation. Everyone knew what happened to witches in the Cluster. It wasn't many years ago that the Village of Cottington hanged a girl of thirteen on counts of witchcraft. The rumor was that she held seances in the cotton fields that grew behind her family's home, but no proof was ever brought forward. Though it made no difference. An accusation of that sort was enough to set loose suspicion in the heart of any town—even enough to wrap a noose around a child's neck.

Nelia and Jonna gasped, but Madsyn just narrowed her eyes, unfazed. "Girls, please," she said, shaking her head. "As if anyone in their right mind would believe Arden Ford, the notorious village liar."

"I like to think of myself as more of a purveyor of the pranking arts," he corrected with a dramatic twist of his hand. "I'm no liar."

"Really?" Madsyn said raising her eyebrows. "That's not what everyone else is saying. Going on about screams at the gathering? Fainting in the street like a lovestruck damsel in distress? Honestly, Arden, you really must be dying from lack of attention."

"I did hear screams," he said defensively.

"Oh, I don't doubt it," she prodded. "I bet you hear all types of voices, don't you, Ard?" She spun her finger in a circle next to her head followed by laughs from Nelia and Jonna.

"Very funny," he said. He pushed past the girls, careful not to show defeat on his face, but Madsyn wasn't ready to give up.

"You know," she continued, "I bet everyone in town would believe me if I told them you were hearing voices in your head. That would explain all your desperate cries for attention. Forgive me, *pranks* as you call them. Lords Above, they'd lock you up for sure!"

Ard turned and scowled at her. She stood with her arms crossed and a smirk painted on her rosy lips. Madsyn was the prettiest girl in all of Pipton, there was no doubt about that. Her family, the Wickwyles, were arguably the wealthiest in the Cluster and Madsyn made sure no one forgot it. Her flaxen blonde hair and blue eyes would easily be wed to one of the woodcutting boys. They would have a huge wedding in the square and make a million little woodcutting babies. Had she not been so hateful to Ard growing up, he may have thought her attractive in ways. He could even remember as a boy desperately wanting her to talk to him, as he was sure most boys did. Now she was nothing but an entitled brat prowling the streets for someone to pick on. Somehow unable to think of a decent counter, he muttered a meek, "That's not funny."

"It's a bit funny," Madsyn jeered. "It would be even funnier if you were actually telling the truth like a scared little boy crying wolf. I'd be the savior of the whole town. Madsyn, the girl who finally got rid of Arden Ford the Pipton Menace. I'd be known far and wide!"

"I thought you were already," Ard shot back. "Madsyn, the dullest and most useless girl in the Cluster? No?"

Madsyn gave him a glare. She knew how to make him hurt. She knew which sword would push past his armor and into the folds of his heart. She'd only been waiting to unsheath it. "Honestly, how poor Ms. Flora got landed with a burden like you is beyond me."

All Ard could manage was a teeth-gritting scowl.

"Ooh," she grinned. "That one stung, I can tell. My father says she was a different woman before you came along. He said—"

"Your father is an ass," Ard cut her off. "And so are you."

Madsyn put her hand over her heart, acting like the insult hurt her, then burst into laughter. Jonna and Nelia giggled along with her as Ard walked away from them. He'd get them back. He just had to figure out where to get a jar full of cockroaches. Although he had developed a pretty thick skin, somehow Madsyn always found a way to get under it. He let the girls' laughter fade away into the raindrops as he approached his spot on the roof of the blacksmith forge.

What had happened to him? He knew he heard the screams, but what concerned him most was the falling unconscious for three days. He thought of the strange girl swaying in the wind. Maybe if he went to the spot where he saw her in his dream he could find some answers. He made his way down the main road and ducked into an alley to head toward the fields.

Ard knew he couldn't let Gran and Mr. Brinkley know that he was going near the Bardenwood. They, along with all of the other villagers, were terrified of the forest. He rounded the last building on the road and came face to face again with the Bardenwood's gray veneer. Only this time it wasn't inside a dream, it was real. *Real terrifying*, he thought. The forest swayed lightly with the post-storm wind and he could see a hazy fog begin to creep out from its canopy. He imagined the strange girl standing there among the trees. An unsettling thought. He scanned left and right as far as his eyes would let him before saying under his breath, "I must be out of my mind." He readied himself and crept across the field to the forest's edge, crouching low so no one would notice him. A single, shuddering chill shot down from his neck to his ankles as he passed the painted wooden sign.

BEWARE THE BARDENWOOD!
Some trails need never be trodden.

The rain had completely dissipated when he reached the line of sentry trees. The sky was still dark and distant thunder rumbled high in the sky. All he could hear was the pattering of water droplets hitting the bed of fallen leaves on the forest floor. He looked once more into the dark woods, then back at Pipton where he could see a small line of smoke floating from the chimney of Sore Swallow. He took the deepest breath his lungs would allow, pulled his hood closer to his face, then stepped into the Bardenwood for the first time in his life.

Nothing happened. His inner child would have Ard believe that the forest would swallow him whole as soon as his foot passed across the tree line. Everything inside the forest was gray with mist and rain. The droplets falling all around him echoed off of the pines and the whole wood seemed still and peaceful, aside from a few leaves falling weightlessly to the ground. He pressed further in, making sure to keep a watchful eye on every tree he passed in case they were rearranging like the stories said. He kept looking back so he wouldn't lose sight of the forest edge, promising himself he wouldn't go so far that he couldn't see the exit. The wet, dead foliage on the ground crushed and crackled under his boots. He focused on every sound he could, even the sound of his own breathing. His eyes never rested on any object for more than a second, darting back and forth like a scared animal. Until now, the Bardenwood had never truly frightened him. Looking up, he could see the gray pines stretch so high they disappeared into the sky. The light fog fell lower and lower, giving the woods an eerie, sinister presence as if he were unwelcome where he stood. He looked around one more time, then decided to head back. The forest had lived up to its reputation and the girl from his dream was nowhere to be found. He could've spent more time searching for her, but the woods sent unrelenting chills down his spine and he couldn't bear being among the trees for a moment longer.

Just before he turned around to return home, he noticed movement on the ground near his feet. A tiny, white mushroom sprouted out of the ground right in front of his eyes, growing bigger by the second. It grew to the size of his palm then stopped. Ard was bewildered. He'd never seen a toadstool sprout so abruptly. He knelt down to get a better look only for another mushroom to sprout a few feet from it.

"What the—" he started. But before he could finish questioning his sanity, another mushroom sprouted, this time farther away from the second, forming what seemed to be a path. He took a few cautious steps toward the third sprout, and sure enough, a fourth sprung from the soil. He looked back to the forest edge, swallowed hard, then followed the mushrooms deeper into the forest.

The mushrooms weaved themselves around stumps and under logs, but Ard was agile enough to follow them wherever they sprouted. Adrenaline rushed through his whole body as it surged with energy. All the climbing and leaping was easier than it had ever been for him, but he was too busy enjoying it to even notice the difference. Light as a feather, he continued following the sprouts, making sure to keep his eyes and ears open for anything. The toadstool path stopped abruptly at the trunk of a large tree entangled in colorful ivy. He tried looking around it but couldn't see anything. The undergrowth was hazy with fog, making it difficult to see much of anything. The trees of the Bardenwood grew so thick here they formed a barrier of branches and vines that stretched right and left, like a wall of some sort. He looked hard to see where the mushrooms had continued sprouting but found nothing. He turned around, puzzled, then started heading back with a defeated sigh. Out of nowhere, a wooden crackling sound whirled him around to the wall of trees.

Ard's eyes widened with fear. The bark of the large tree where the toadstools had stopped was ripped open, revealing an open door to the other side of the tree wall. He could see a dim light coming from the other side. He looked around nervously. He couldn't bring himself to move. He waited, still as stone, but nothing came through the door. He peered inside but could only see a flickering glow reflect on the inside of the tree. Jaws clenched, he slowly wedged himself through the door.

On the other side of the tree wall, there was a beautifully tended garden. There were lush, green trees everywhere, bearing the ripest and most delicious looking fruit he'd ever seen. The ground, which was normally ridden with dead wet leaves, was glazed with an emerald mixture of soft moss and grass. He was greeted by fluttering fireflies that zipped in and out of the bushes and saplings. Their glow mimicked the tiny flames of ornate, wooden lanterns dangling from the low-hanging tree branches. The firelight cast flickering, warm shadows across the greenery, giving the whole garden an orange-tinted glow. He crept further in, looking all around him. His boots made no sound as he made his way across the mossy floor, his footsteps masked by the rippling of the Witchfoot on the other side of the tree wall. Still, he was certain not to step on any fallen twigs or branches so as not to alert anyone or anything in the garden.

As he made his way deeper, he came across an enormous, dead oak tree which stood in the center of a clearing. The ground around it was muddy with dark soil, unlike the green floor elsewhere in the garden. As he got closer, he could see the trunk of the dead oak was charred as if it had been burned or struck by lightning. Its branches hung low, practically scraping the ground, and its giant roots dove in and out of the muddy soil. The branches had lost all of their foliage, leaving the boughs to look like elongated, spiny fingers. As he gazed at the enormous tree, a shuffling sound came from behind it.

Eyes scanning vigorously for danger, Ard waited for the sound again, but he could hear nothing but the soft buzzing of insects flying in the fruit trees. His hair stood on end as he grew suspicious, his breathing softening to a slow pace. He perked up his courage and softly uttered, "Hello?" The sound shuffled again, and from behind the dead oak tree peeked the girl from his dream.

She seemed worried and scared at first, but as her eyes collided with his, the girl's face softened into a smile—the same smile she had given him the night before in his dream. She stepped out from behind the dead tree and began crawling on all fours down its giant roots, avoiding the moist soil near the base. Her hands and bare feet were muddied from treading the forest floor, but her skin was white like fresh hail and her hair flared a bright auburn red. A red even brighter than before in his dream. Her cream-colored dress extended down to her knobby knees and was cloaked by a hooded shawl made of dead leaves, pine straw, and bark sewn together with some type of fiber. The cloak was torn and her dress was stained with dirt near the bottom, but her small frame maneuvered lightly beneath it unseen. She moved like a squirrel, quick and cautious, but her silvery, gray eyes stayed locked to Ard's, wide open with excitement even as she crept down the tree. Her tattered cloak eerily scraped against the blackened bark of the oak roots while the flames from the lanterns reflected off of her eyes like some ghoulish wild animal. As she got closer, Ard thought she might be blind. Her eyes were fogged over completely, showing nothing but a hazy pupil in their center—but she couldn't have been blind. She was staring right at him.

Intensely.

She reached the end of the roots and hopped lightly down onto the ground right in front of Ard who was rigid with fear. "You came," she breathed, still smiling. Her voice was like a soft, exotic fabric. No frays, no rasp, just pure silk, light and pleasant. His reflection disappeared in her white eyes as they swirled like the fog outside the garden.

"Y-yes," he muttered. His body tensed with anxiousness.

"I'm so glad," she said. Her piercing gaze finally broke and she looked around her. "Do you like my garden?" she asked with an excited grin.

Ard swallowed, "It's—"

"Wonderful?" she interrupted. "Spectacular? Magnificent? Yes?"

"Sure," he breathed nervously. "Yes. Like nothing I've seen."

"I'm so glad," she repeated. "I lit the lanterns for you just in case. It's dreadfully dark during storms here."

He agreed half-heartedly with a slow nod. The strange girl locked her foggy eyes with him once more, still smiling. Seconds passed nearly to minutes yet her haunting stare held without a single break. Tense with awkwardness, he introduced himself. "I'm...Arden Ford," he said, "of Pipton. Everyone calls me Ard."

"Are you nervous, Arden Ford of Pipton?" the girl asked quizzically, cocking her head to the side.

"Just 'Ard' is fine, thanks," he said. "And yes, a little. It's not every day you follow a trail of mushrooms into a secret garden hidden inside erm...forbidden woods."

The girl chuckled. "It's not so strange for me."

The awkwardness grew as strong and intense as her stare. With every cautious step back he took, she took a confident step closer. She was so close that he could see the hazel of his own eyes reflected in hers. "You're the girl from my dream," he said. "Are you the voice I've been hearing? The whispers?"

"Why, yes! Who else?" she said plainly. Her gaze held as the uncomfortable silence again fell between them.

"Well...what do I call you?" he asked to alleviate the quiet.

Her stare broke and she crinkled her nose. "How improper of me!" she exclaimed. "So, so rude. My name is Emagora."

"Emagora," he exhaled less nervously. "And what are you doing out here in the Bardenwood? Are you lost or something?"

Emagora clapped her hands over her mouth and jumped around with glee. "No, you silly thing!" she laughed. "I'm a witch."

4

The Hound Queen

As the sun descended slowly below the horizon, sinking into the waves like a burning ship, a queen let the last of its warm rays kiss her face from her chamber window, drawing deep, focused breaths. As she opened her wintery green eyes, a knock came at her door. Her expression tightened as she instructed for them to enter. A member of her council and trusted advisor stepped inside. He was a lean man in his forties with thin, receding, white hair. His face boasted a neatly trimmed salt and pepper goatee and he was adorned in black leather boots, an emerald cloak trimmed in gold, and a number of medals and badges attached to his silver vest.

"My queen," the man said, bowing low. "Pardon my interruption."

"Sir Ellys," she responded formally. "Is it time already?"

"I'm afraid so, Your Majesty," Ellys said, motioning for her exit. The queen took a final meditative look at the cyan waves crashing against the cliffs of her castle, straightened the ruffles in her gown, and glided out her chamber door. She greeted the guards Sir Ellys had stationed to receive her and was escorted through the dazzling, polished, limestone halls of her castle to the main hall. There, a prisoner apprehended by her men awaited her majesty's judgment.

She entered the great hall preceded by her escorts and strode to her throne, hands delicately clasped together at her waist. A crowd of nobles gazed at her beauty as she was introduced. "Presenting Her Royal Highness, Queen Leonora Veleno, Ruler, and Protector of The Lushlands, Chief Magistrate of the Steppes of Veria, and Grand Sentinel of Silber Bay."

The people in the court bowed gently as Leonora passed while her lavender and verbena perfumes filled the throne room with a besotting aroma that clung to the air flowing behind her every step. She was a stunning monarch. Regal, fair-faced, and ripe in her prime. Everyone in the kingdom and even lands afar coveted her lush, glistening gowns made from the finest fabrics Mossa Castille had to offer. She dressed in colors some in the Lushlands had never even heard of. Cloaks of chartreuse, juniper, and sage drifted behind her steps giving the Castillian queen a couture all her own. From her head flowed the purest ebony hair that bore a black so deep it seemed a nightmarish hue of blue. Her skin was a light olive that paired perfectly with the inky brown of her brows and lashes. Without a doubt, Leonora was a sight to behold. A sight that burned forever in the darkest parts of a lusting heart.

She stepped up onto her throne made of shining gold ornamented with emeralds, sapphires, and rubies. As she sat down, she adjusted her glittering crown which formed a ring of pure silver maple leaves across her temples. Her hand rested on the head of her most faithful servant and feared counterpart, an enormous black dog with devilishly pointed ears that sat statuesque beside her throne. The dog was so large, its head stood level with its mistress's while lying down on its stomach. Its incredible paws hung menacingly over the stone dais upon which the throne sat. While stroking the dog's shaggy, black fur, Leonora inhaled softly then commanded. "Bring forth the accused."

From the crowd of onlookers in the court, a man in muddy clothes was forcibly dragged and brought to his knees at the foot of Leonora's throne by two armored guards. He looked beaten and worn but bore an unwaveringly vengeful face. He looked as if he had been plucked from the fields harvesting crops only minutes before the hearing. As the guards stepped away from him, he glared viciously at the queen.

"State your name," Leonora directed him.

The man remained silent and his glare endured unbroken.

"*State your name*," she repeated, this time with a slight growl.

"Markis," the man uttered reluctantly. "Markis Kindleton of Cuspy."

Leonora sat back in her throne and lightly turned up her chin. "Markis Kindleton of Cuspy you have been hereby accused of fear-mongering and of slander to the word of the Crown," she recited. "Do you deny these crimes?"

"Yes," the man grumbled, still glaring. "Yes, I deny them."

Leonora looked to one of the guards who apprehended the man for an explanation. "We traced the talk of Kolbran straight to him, Your Grace," the guard said. "He claims to have seen riders in the east. Riders of Ashar." A soft gasp came from the people of the court followed by flitting whispers. Leonora raised a hand to calm them.

"It's true," the man growled. "It's the Ashen Horde. I've seen them with my own eyes. They're in the Cluster, killing and burning everything. From what I can tell, I was the only one to make it out of my village alive."

"My sources," Leonora said, "confirm this to be a lie. We received word from Cuspy just this morning. Nothing but a burned down pub in need of repairing. The Village of Pipton is even helping to rebuild it."

"Then your sources," the man mocked, "are wrong."

The dog tensed next to Leonora, focusing on the man with intense poise. One of the guards stepped forward and barked.

"You will address your ruler with respect, old man."

The man looked to Leonora, who awaited his apology stone-faced. He scoffed, growling, "You're no ruler of mine, *Hound Queen!*" Jerking forward, he spat onto the dais near her feet.

More gasps echoed from the court followed by a low grumble from the giant dog. Leonora stood slowly. "Brave," she hissed. "Very brave of you. An admirable attribute, undoubtedly. However, as I said, I do not take the spread of such mistruths lightly. Markis Kindleton of Cuspy, you have hereby been found guilty of fear-mongering, dishonesty in a royal court, slander to the word of the Crown, and now malicious intent upon your queen."

Markis lunged, but Leonora's guards seized him before he could reach her. He fought violently against them, but they were strong and fiercely dedicated to their queen. The people in the court all tensed with silence. Leonora continued unwaveringly, stepping down from her throne. "As stated in my decree, judgment for these crimes shall be swift..."

She approached the thrashing Markis Kindleton, cupping his muddy face in her hands. He ceased his struggling but glared at her through furrowed brows.

"...and final."

CRACK!

With a mighty twist of her arms, Leonora lethally snapped his neck and let his body crumple to the ground, lifeless. Both men and women in the courtroom cried out in shock. She shut her eyes softly and inhaled a slow, deep breath, regaining her composure. She strode back up onto the dais and the crowd gasped once more as the guards lugged the body of Markis Kindleton away. Leonora turned slowly to face the court, resting her hand softly on the neck of her snarling hound. "Let this be a clear and transparent lesson," she called, "to those who would not believe the truth of their queen. A more violent end awaits the next citizen who deems it wise to spread falsities throughout my Verdamaïn. This hearing is hereby concluded. May the Lords

Above shine on your paths home." She dismissed the court with a wave of her hand.

The nobles scurried out of the throne room and back into the streets of Mossa Castille followed by a moaning, guttural howl from her giant dog. Leonora melted firmly back into her throne and motioned for her guards to leave her. Sir Ellys gave a polite bow to his queen and followed the guards out. As Leonora sat in her throne of jewels, running her fingers through the fur of her hound, a small and fearsome smile spread across her face. Looking into its frozen eyes, she cooed, "Hello, my treasure."

5

The Witch and the Stableboy

A rd was frozen.

A witch. A *real* witch.

He had no weapon. Defending himself wasn't an option. Even having a weapon might not do him any good. Who knew what this creature was capable of? She entered his dreams while he was unconscious. She could have him under a spell right now for all he knew. *Why is she staring at me like that?* he thought. *Does she want to eat me? No. She doesn't look hungry. Is she after my soul? My skin? My fingers and toes? Stop thinking about it. She can probably hear your thoughts, idiot.* He tightened his jaw to try and stifle his fearful imaginings.

Emagora stood there smiling at him with her ghostly gray eyes. Her feet shuffled on the ground nervously as she sensed his discomfort. "Have you ever met a witch, Arden Ford of Pipton?"

Ard took a cautious step back, careful not to ensue her wrath. "No," he said quickly.

"Don't be frightened. I won't hurt you. I'm not what you think."

"You're a witch," he argued. "Witches—"

"Can't be trusted?" she finished. "Steal your children and

boil them into a stew? Live in houses with gingerbread walls? Turn you into a toad or maybe even put a curse on you? Yes...that sounds appropriate. Curse you for all eternity." She made herself look menacing by hunching her back and pointing a shaking finger. "I, Emagora," she croaked, "hereby curse Arden Ford so that he may never use his legs to stand AGAIN!"

Ard shut his eyes tightly, waiting for the feeling in his legs to vanish for all eternity—but it didn't. He opened one cautious eye and saw her loose a coy chuckle. He was definitely one for pulling pranks, but he was not one to *be* pranked. He straightened his shirt and embarrassingly said, "That's not funny."

"Oh, Arden Ford of Pipton," she smiled, "you make me laugh. I like you."

Ard refused to be made a joke out of. "If you're a witch, then why aren't you hideous? You don't look like a witch at all."

Emagora placed her hands on her hips and feigned offense. "So, since I'm a witch I should be ugly?" she huffed. "I should have green skin and warts? Oh! Let's not forget my toad minions or my enchanted, flying broomstick."

Ard all of a sudden felt slightly foolish. Emagora crossed her arms, but sent an endearing smile his way, beckoning for an apology. "Alright," he admitted reluctantly, "I'm sorry. I suppose all witches can't be hideous."

"I suppose not. Unless I've got you under a spell right now that makes you believe anything I say," she joked. His face turned nervous and the witch laughed with delight once more.

Ard gave into a small smile. "Still not funny." Unconvinced that he could trust her, he interrogated her further. "How did you end up living all the way out here?"

Emagora plopped down at his feet, crossing her thin legs together. The way she acted was incredibly bizarre. She acted more like a wild animal than a person. Staring intensely, abruptly sitting and standing, jumping around like some sort of mad rodent, even the way she spoke was quick and nonchalant. "Some witches," she explained, "learn to use magic. Others are born knowing what it is. My family abandoned me as a child when they found out I was a witch. A bornwitch some call it. They turned the whole town against me, and I was chased out of my village." Ard slowly sat down across from her, keeping his distance and situating himself comfortably on the mossy ground. She continued. "With nowhere else to go, I went to the next town, where word had already spread of my being a witch. They tried to kill me. I was chased into the Bardenwood for the same reasons you don't trust me now. Fear. They didn't know who I was on the inside. The only thing they knew about me was that I was a witch—and witches must be killed." Even though her story was dark, she sat on the ground flapping her knees up and down happily, without uttering a single tone of sadness.

Ard, suddenly feeling embarrassed, asked, "How did they know you were a witch?"

"All witches whether born or not have a tell," she explained. "They never really *knew* I was a witch. But that didn't matter. It never seems to matter anyway."

"A tell?" he asked. She raised her head and opened her eyes wide for him to see. The fog in them sent chills down his spine but he found himself strangely enchanted with them. Now he understood. "Your eyes."

Emagora looked back down, twisting a blade of grass around her finger. "For some it's different. Sometimes it's a scar, or sometimes it's the color of their hair, and for some it's —"

"Warts?" he interrupted.

She laughed loudly. "Yes," she smiled, "I suppose that's where the tales come from."

Ard smiled back at her. He felt it safe to take his eyes off of her now and get a good look around. Looking up, he could see the bluish, twilight sky peeking through the trees. A crystal-clear spring bubbled nearby and birds fluttered in and out of the tree branches, preparing for evening's end. The fireflies had ventured to him again and were zipping around his face like tiny stars falling from the leaves. He reached his fingers out to touch them, but they would buzz right out of reach every time he tried. The garden really was quite a spectacle.

"Do you really like it?" Emagora asked.

He nodded with a small smile. He couldn't lie.

"I'm so glad," she grinned. "Are you a gardener?"

"No," he answered. "My Gran is though."

"Is she? Has she a green thumb?"

"I'd say so," he said with a nod. "Yeah, sure."

"A green thumb like me?" she asked, curling her fingers toward the ground. To his astonishment, a bright yellow sunflower sprouted slowly from the soil, blooming right in front of him. The petals unfurled like butterfly wings and blazed into a brilliant, golden yellow. She cupped the bud in her dirty hands and took a loving whiff.

Ard could barely find words. All he could muster was a hushed exhalation.

"Oh! Do you like it?"

"Yes," he grinned. "I love sunflowers. Haven't seen one since the summer months."

She pulled the tall stalk out of the ground with a quick tug and passed it to him. "I hear you're supposed to give flowers to people you like. I can't imagine why killing something so pure and then giving its limp corpse as a gift would be considered a gentle gesture, but it's yours. Keep it, keep it."

He took the flower from her with an awkward smile. "Thanks. I'll...keep it, keep it."

"I'm so glad," she repeated. "Well if you aren't a gardener, then you must be a woodcutter."

"No," he scoffed. "Definitely not."

"A baker? A blacksmith? A cobbler? A tailor! You look like a tailor. I do enjoy tailors. Such a wonderful trade. Yes, you must be a tailor."

"I'm a stableboy," he stopped her. "Just a stableboy."

"Oh! Horses! I dearly, dearly love horses. Such agreeable creatures those."

"Do you?" he asked, grateful to come across common ground. "Me too."

"Oh, yes! Much better company than unicorns."

Ard's mouth hung open. "Unicorns?"

"Well I've never met one personally," she went on. "But I hear they're insufferable snobs."

"Yeah," he said, bewildered. "I can...imagine."

"Well, Arden Ford, stableboy of Pipton," she said, "I'm happy you like my garden. You do like it, don't you? Ooh, please don't lie. I work very hard to keep it this way for guests. Very hard work indeed. Your Gran would surely agree."

"Yeah," he said. "I definitely do. More and more by the second."

"I'm so glad," she said. Only she wasn't. She was looking at the ground emotionless, giving a half-hearted smile. It looked like something was upsetting her and she was trying to hide it. She noticed Ard's perceiving eyes watching her so she repeated, "I'm so glad!" This time with a beaming smile and a toss of her fiery hair.

He had caught on. "Is there something wrong, Emagora?"

The witch bit one of her nails shyly. "No, no!" she said, trying to make herself seem fine. "Goodness, no. I'm alright. I promise. I'm so glad!" She stood up and walked further into her garden, nervously avoiding his presence. He followed her gently. When she heard the step of his boots behind her, she turned to face him. She seemed as if she were about to cry. "It's...dying," she whimpered.

"What's dying?" he asked.

"My garden. The forest. All of it," she said, brushing her hair out of her face.

Ard was confused. "It's just autumn, that's all," he said reassuringly. "Forests die this time of year, Emagora, but they always come back in the spring."

"The pines here are always to be green," she corrected. "Year-round. Now they've turned gray like cold stones on a mountain. The whole wood once looked like my garden, so full of life. Green, green, green."

Now that she mentioned it, the pines of the Bardenwood had always been gray. The fields and shrubs near Pipton grew green in the spring and summer, but the forest edge always looked the same. "What happened?" he asked, interested.

Emagora darted over to one of her fruit trees, pretending to inspect its bark. "Are things...easier for you?" she asked, abruptly changing subjects.

Ard scrunched his face with confusion. "What? Wait, what do you mean?"

"Are things easier for you?" she repeated. Ard was stumped, unsure of what she meant. Seeing how perplexed he was, she went on. "Do scents seem stronger? Sounds seem louder? Foods taste sweeter? Do your feet feel lighter on the ground?"

He was shocked that she knew this was happening to him. He hadn't told anyone about those things. The rosemary, the food, the weightlessness. All of them were happening to him. "Sure," he admitted. "I suppose they have, but what does that even mean?"

Emagora smiled and locked her hazy eyes to his. "It means you could be...special." Ard looked away, still unsure of what she was talking about. *Special?* he thought. How was he special? He was just a stableboy from Pipton. He'd never been anywhere or done anything interesting in his life. Aside from meeting a witch in the woods, he didn't feel special at all. Emagora looked up through the branches of the fruit trees and noticed that the day was coming to a close. "It's getting late," she sighed. "You should be heading back."

Ard, still eager to know more, pressed further. "Hold on. What do you mean *special*?"

"Another time," she smiled. "The forest becomes quite dark at night and you won't be able to see the toadstools soon." She began walking back to the entrance of her garden with Ard following reluctantly behind. When they reached the door, she grabbed hold of his hand, startling him. She looked up into his eyes and he could see the fog swirling in them again. He stared at her beautiful, silky hair that fell weightlessly against her dress. Now that he was face to face with her, he noticed how alluring she was. She was vibrant, young, and full of life. She was nothing like the girls in Pipton. He noticed tiny flowers and leaves that were caught in the deep red strands of her hair that he hadn't seen before. He suddenly found himself entranced with her.

"Ahem...it's late," she repeated conclusively, snapping him out of his moment.

Clearing his throat bashfully, he asked, "Would it be alright if I came back tomorrow?"

"I'd be tickled," she beamed.

"How do I know I can I trust you?"

"How do I know I can I trust *you*, Arden Ford of Pipton? Should I expect torches and pitchforks at my garden door tonight?"

He laughed. "Lords, no! I won't tell anyone about you. Even though now it all seems a bit silly to be afraid of witches."

"Well, I suppose all witches can't be as wonderful as me," she said with a wink.

He stood for a moment longer then stepped through the door of the giant tree trunk. He looked back to find her eyes staring back at his, glistening in the flames of her lanterns. "I'll be back tomorrow," he promised.

"And the next day I hope." She tugged at her hair.

"You should be so lucky," he said smoothly. He looked into the Bardenwood, which was darker and even more sinister now. He gripped the stem of Emagora's sunflower and strangely he wasn't frightened anymore. He looked back at the door of the garden and saw her shutting it softly. He took a deep breath, trying to make sure he wasn't dreaming. Was all of this real? Had he still not awakened from Mr. Brinkley's shop? Was he dead? Either way, he felt happy. Nothing interesting ever happened to him in Pipton and now everything was happening to him all at once. Eager to sleep and return the next day, he set off down the toadstool path and through the insidious Bardenwood with an excited smile spread from ear to ear. Probably something no one had ever done—smiling in the Bardenwood. If he had any inclination that he was going insane, that was it.

By the time Ard reached the edge of the Bardenwood, it should've been dark. The light of the sun was long gone and the moon was hidden by leftover clouds, but he could see clear as day. Only it was as if everything was stripped of color. He rubbed his eyes praying he wasn't going blind. When he opened them again, he saw the same. No shadows, no color, just the field and the edge of Pipton clear as a crystal spring. What was happening? He turned to look back into the forest, expecting to see darkness, but he could see every tree. Just like Pipton, there were no shadows or colors. He was able to make out the details of every trunk, shrub, and creeping vine as if it were right in front of him. He turned back around scratching his head. The conversation he'd had with Emagora flowed back to him.

Are things easier for you? Do scents seem stronger? Do sounds seem louder? Foods taste sweeter? Do your feet feel lighter on the ground?

Ard slowly realized—he could see in the dark. He blinked a few more times and looked at the moon. It blinded him like the sun. It was like everything was bathed in cool silver. The moon had never shone like this. He let out an excited laugh to himself and looked at his hands. Even in the dark of night, he was able to make out every line in both of his palms. Every tiny hair on his fingers tingled, sending shivers up his arms and into his shoulders. His whole body began seething with energy and suddenly, he felt a deep need to run.

Just...run.

As fast as he could with no destination in mind, he bolted off toward Pipton, dropping Emagora's sunflower to the ground. He crossed the field in no time at all, kicking up dust and grass onto his coat tail. When he reached the main road, he looked around for any sign of people. All the villagers seemed to be inside their homes for the night, probably lighting their evening fires to combat the slight chill of autumn. Barely out of breath, he took off past Sore Swallow and down his normal route through the alleyways. He leaped over hedges, vaulted over troughs and woodpiles, and slid under fences with exceptional fluidity and grace. His legs burned, but not with a sense of overexertion. They were teeming with vigor and vivacity. Whooping with excited laughter, he continued his race through town, letting the chilly night air wisp through the holes of his coat and across his bare skin. It was like he could feel everything around him. The air, the vibrations in the ground, everything. He felt as if he could run all the way to Mossa Castille going like this. He reached the town square and looked to his spot above the blacksmith forge. The overhang was about twelve feet up. Without hesitating, he leaped from the ground straight toward the edge of the overhang and hoisted himself onto the roof.

Twelve feet. Ard had jumped twelve feet into the air without so much as a running start. He was too excited about these new abilities to even question them. On the roof, he was able to see all the tops of the shops around the square and the main road. Normally all out of reach, with his new strength he could leap from rooftop to rooftop with ease. He took two paces back on the forge roof, braced himself, then took off over the edge. As he soared over the street, he was made frighteningly aware of how high up he was, but he landed on the adjacent rooftop without fail. He was invigorated beyond belief. Although his breath was starting to catch up with him, he continued blazing across the rooftops of Pipton, careful to avoid the puddles leftover from the rain. While running on the edge of a building, he noticed a lantern was lit inside Brinkley Feet. Mr. Brinkley must've still been awake. He aligned himself on the building across from the old cobbler's shop and leaped down, landing in a crouch. Where his feet would've normally made a large crunch in the gravel of the street, there was only a soft thud. He smiled to himself. He could get used to this. Creeping across the street, he peeked into the window of the shop.

Just as he suspected, Mr. Brinkley was working on a shoe. He sat completely fixated in his chair with his unsightly large magnifying spectacles on. Though, across from him, Gran sat at a table with her face in her hands. She wasn't crying, she just looked terribly worried. He shamefully realized that he'd been gone for hours. He was so busy enjoying himself that he'd forgotten all about his poor grandmother. Ard was all she had, and for all she knew, something could've happened to him. He could've been dead. He felt a sharp sense of selfishness. With a sigh, he opened the door to Brinkley Feet and stepped inside.

Gran looked up immediately, eyes red from staying awake. Mr. Brinkley didn't even notice that someone had walked in. He continued fiddling with the shoe. Gran stood slowly, wiping her face. Her expression quickly went from worry to anger and she glared at Ard from across the room.

"I'm sorry, Gran," Ard said helplessly.

"Sorry?" she repeated with sarcasm. "You're sorry, are you? D'you 'ave any idea what I've been 'finkin'?"

"I just lost track of time, Gran, honestly," he pleaded innocently. "I didn't mean to worry you."

Mr. Brinkley finally stood up, shoe in hand, as his magnified eyes gawked between Gran and Ard. He stepped over to Ard and patted his shoulder with a smudgy hand. Smiling, he said, "Glad you're back safe, lad." His small frame walked to a room in the back of the shop. As he went to shut the door behind him, he murmured, "Leave a bit of the poor boy for winter, Flora."

Ard closed his eyes and sighed, dropping his gaze to the floor. His only defender had abandoned him in his time of need. He'd make Brink pay. The old cobbler may find his shoeshine replaced with ink soon for this one. Gran's eyes held their intense glare. Through her teeth, she scolded, "I've been goin' out of my mind, Arden Ford."

"I know," he sighed. "I really am sorry." Gran let out a huge sigh of relief, stepped out from around the table, and walked over to him, wrapping her arms around the middle of his back. The rosemary scent of her hair filled his nose again as he laid his head on hers, hugging her back tightly. Suddenly, she released the hug and stepped back from him raising a bundle of gray pine needles she'd gotten off of his coat. With a suspicious look, she inquired. "Now, where've you been, boy?"

"Nowhere," Ard tried, sighing helplessly. He was caught red-handed. There was no way he was pulling out of this unscathed. Gran was too sharp. Despite her age, she had a quick mind. A mind that Ard himself got honestly. Her eyes narrowed, beckoning him to speak truthfully. With a held breath and sigh of defeat, Ard confessed, "I was...in the forest."

Gran was shocked. Ard could tell she suspected it but didn't want to believe it. With a gaping mouth and widened eyes, she breathed. "The forest? The Bardenwood, Ard? That forest?"

A guilty nod. Not nearly enough to save him.

Gran almost choked on her words. "Lords 'ave me, Ard! I 'fought you'd been out doin' sumfin' normal. Normal 'fings. Boy 'fings! Peekin' into girl's windows, 'frowin rocks at front doors'n such. Not trudgin' about in the ruddy Bardenwood! Lords Above!"

He tried to explain. "But, Gran—"

"Ard," she interrupted with a concerned sigh, shaking her hands in his face, "it's dangerous out there! You know it, I know you do!"

Knowing he couldn't destroy the foundation of his grandmother's sanity, Ard decided to leave out the bits about Emagora and her garden. A witch in the woods? She'd either faint or beat him senseless. Most likely the latter. As quick as he was, the lie rolled off his lips with ease, "I was looking for the Busby's boy."

"What? Gell?" she asked.

"Yes, ma'am."

"Oh, Arden," she argued, "there weren't any screams, boy. Temmus'n I been askin' all afternoon if anyone had 'eard or seen anyfin'. Not a 'fing, they said. Even the search party couldn't find a trace of the boy. Gell's just run away is all."

Ard knew he heard screams, but thinking of his new heightened senses he could've been overhearing it from somewhere else. Maybe it had been Gell, but either way, he didn't want to fight with Gran or worry her anymore. Choosing his battles wisely, he pretended to agree. "Sorry," he said, "you're right. I'm sorry, Gran, honest. Must be this fainting business happening to me. I haven't exactly...felt like myself."

"It's alright," she assured him. "I'm sure it'll pass. In the meantime, you promise me you won't go meddlin' in those woods again. 'Fings happen betwixt 'em trees. Unnatural 'fings."

"Yes, ma'am," Ard lied. "I promise." He felt bad about lying to her, but how could she be expected to understand his current situation? The only one who knew what was happening to him was Emagora. He knew he couldn't move on without knowing more about these abilities and she was his only hope. He also knew he couldn't worry Gran especially with her fear of the forest. He decided what she didn't know wouldn't hurt her. Besides, Emagora wasn't dangerous and neither was the forest. Both were unnerving at times, but he was beginning to feel as if witches, monsters, and even the Bardenwood itself were all just misunderstood. He knew what that felt like.

Gran put her hands on her hips and gave a heavy sigh, letting her worries wash away. He could see a small smile crinkle at the sides of her lips. The smile he loved seeing. The smile that told him no matter how much he got into trouble, he would always be forgiven and loved just the same. "Come on, boy," she said playfully. "Let's go 'ome 'fore I smack you good."

Ard nodded his head and called to the back of the store, "Goodnight, Brink!"

Gran added, "G'night, Temmus!"

"Yes, yes," Mr. Brinkley responded from behind the door, probably still captivated with the pair of shoes he'd been working on. Gran grabbed her lantern from the table and walked out the door followed by her grandson. Ard laughed to himself knowing he didn't need a lantern to see the path home anymore. Nevertheless, he walked with his arm resting around Gran's shoulders all the way back to Sore Swallow. When they reached the steps to the front door, she stomped her feet on the doormat to get rid of any dirt. Before going up the steps, she stared out into the dark toward the Bardenwood, something she did every time she walked in for the evening. Her face was still. It was as if she were waiting for the forest itself to cross the fields and grab her. Ard wished he could tell her not to be afraid of the woods anymore...that all the stories she told him as a boy were just stories. Just tales of the Bardenwood. But, she was set in her ways. After a good, long look, she hobbled up the steps to go inside. He stopped on the porch behind her.

"You comin', pup?" she asked.

"Just a minute," he answered.

"Careful, boy," she warned. "Stay out too long and you might freeze off what little arse you got left."

Ard giggled then fired back. "Well then, I suppose I'll just have to borrow some of yours. Got plenty to spare, seems it."

Gran laughed his favorite laugh then shut the door. Through the window, she made a fist at him. Of course, he made one back. He looked out toward the fields one last time watching the grass stalks sway back and forth in the chilly autumn wind. The trees of the Bardenwood sat stoically as the breeze whistled between them. He looked up into the sky and noticed that he could see the stars better than he ever had before. They weren't tiny specks of light scattered across the darkness like usual, it was like they were twinkling diamonds floating in a shimmering sea of colored dust and light. They seemed larger than usual too. He smiled. Mouth agape, he wondered if this was what the world was missing out on. What normal people were missing out on. Did the night sky always shine this way? He began to pity his former self. Whatever was happening to him was exposing him to things countless people would never experience in their lifetime. Was this what the world really looked like? Were these feelings and abilities he had buried deep inside of every regular person? He had so many questions and he knew he needed them answered. For now, he took one last look at his new view of the sky, then stepped inside, filled to the brim with a new purpose.

Ard awoke the next morning with stinging regret. His muscles ached so much it was hard to even sit up. He rubbed his head, feeling like he'd been trampled by a raging stallion. He stretched his arms up to the ceiling and arched his back trying to relieve the soreness. *Better.* He pushed too hard last night. Blowing air and wincing, he slid on a shirt and moved slowly down the stairs to find his grandmother waiting in the kitchen with a breakfast of fresh blueberries and cinnamon porridge. His unusual hunger had returned and he gobbled every bit down as fast as he could. Even after his last meal, he still felt like he was starving.

"Goodness, Arden!" Gran said as she sat at the table. "Your appetite's been beastly lately. You feelin' alright?"

Ard nodded with a mouth full of food, shutting his eyes reassuringly. "I'm fine. How have the horses been?" he asked.

"I let them all starve to deaf'," Gran joked.

"Ha, ha," Ard snickered. After swallowing the last bite of his breakfast, he could feel his strength coming back. Snagging one last handful of blueberries and stuffing them in his pocket, he sped out of the kitchen to do his chores.

First, like most mornings, he began in the stable. The whinnying horses clopped their hooves happily as he walked by the pens. "Yeah, I know," he said to them, "I know you've missed me. Big babies." The horses shook their manes and whinnied with delight as Ard made his way to the back of the stable, scratching each of their jaws as he passed. Even with all the anticipation of seeing Emagora again, he still found himself spending quality time with them. After he"d greeted almost all of the horses, he came upon a brilliant red stallion at the end of the stable. The massive equine stomped its hooves and snorted angrily as he approached. None of the villagers dared get close to the stallion, much less attempt to break him, but Ard knew him well and had developed an understanding relationship with the beast. "Hello, Hook," he said to the stallion who responded with a huge nod of his head. "How are we feeling today, sweet boy?"

Hook replied with an unimpressed grunt. Hook was the name Ard gave him due to the white marking lining his nose that resembled a fishhook.

"That good, huh?" Ard asked. "You angry with me for being gone so long?"

The horse grumbled impatiently.

"Well," he continued, "I don't know what could possibly make it better." He reached into his pocket and pulled out the blueberries. "I don't suppose these delicious, garden-fresh blueberries would do the trick?" Hook's staunch demeanor faded instantly, and the horse danced over to him with glee, eating the blueberries right from his hand—a sight that few in Pipton would ever believe.

"That's a good man," he said while stroking Hook's neck. "There's my big softy." He wiped his now slobbery hand on his coat tail and began scraping out the stables. One by one, the horses all allowed him right into their pens and munched on fresh hay as he scooped out their "little gifts". No matter what anyone said or thought of him, he was never unhappy to tend the horses. Most stableboys would jump at the chance to be something more, like a knight in Queen Leonora's Verian Army or a blacksmith in Hammerholm, but he was perfectly content with where he was. That was before he met Emagora.

He couldn't describe it. The feeling. The magnetism. As he

brushed one of the horses' tails, he found himself imagining the hair was hers. He imagined flower petals dangling in the strands, entwined in their auburn snare. He imagined her silky voice calling to him, saying his name over and over again. He couldn't explain why, and if he was honest, he didn't want to, but he felt connected to her. Connected in a way that made his heart beat faster and his palms sweat. He had to see her again. He had to.

After he finished his chores at the inn and his strength had returned, he prepared for his second delve into the Bardenwood. He sped toward the door, stopping only to fix his hair in the foyer mirror, something he'd never cared about doing before. In the rush, he obliviously bumped right into Gran who was bringing in some fresh squash from her garden. She fell to the ground spilling the squash all across the porch floor. Ard stumbled but caught himself easily.

"Oh, Gran! I'm so sorry!" he apologized.

Wincing and rubbing her hip, Gran rose from the ground with an aggravated look stained on her face. "Boy," she spat, "what in the Lords has gotten into you?" She bent over starting to pick up the squash. Ard stooped down to help her but she swatted his hands away. "Never you mind them squash!" she said angrily. "I've 'ad just about enough!"

"Gran," Ard sighed. "I'm sorry. I didn't see you, honest."

"T'ain't that! You've been actin' strange, Ard," she went on. "Where in the Ferals are you even off to?"

"Nowhere, Gran," he argued. "Just into town. I've done all my chores. I just don't want to be cooped up."

"You're sick, Arden," she protested. "You 'ought to be in bed! The 'ealer said—"

"I don't care what the healer said," he interrupted her. "I'm fine, Gran! I feel fine. Fantastic, really."

"I don't care how you feel," she said firmly. "You're not goin' into town. You're stayin' 'ere, in bed, restin' as much as you can. And that's that."

Ard gaped his mouth in protest. "Gran. I'm—"

She cut him off with a viciously pointed figure. "If you say 'I'm fine' again, so 'elp me, Lords, I'll 'ave you strapped to the bed for a fortnight! Now back inside. C'mon, right now." She grabbed his arm and started tugging him back through the doorway.

Ard wrenched his arm back and said, "No, Gran."

She paused, then grabbed at his coat and started pulling again, harder this time.

"I said NO, Gran!" he shouted, slapping her hands away.

"Ard," she breathed.

"No!" he shouted. "I don't have to do what you say, Gran. I'm not yours. And when I say I'm not staying here, I mean it. I'm not a boy anymore and you can't just order me around."

"In all your years, Arden," she murmured, "you've never acted this way. Not to me. What's wrong, pup? Can't I 'elp?"

"I'm *fine*," he repeated icily. He could feel the anger welling up inside of him. She had no idea what he was going through. How could she possibly know? She probably didn't even care for all he knew. He felt as if she just wanted to keep him at Sore Swallow his whole life. She treated him as if he would never be anything greater. Just like the rest of the town. Nothing but a village stableboy. The anger continued. "Just go back inside, Gran," he said dismissively, waving his hand. He stepped off the porch without saying another word.

Tears started welling up in her eyes. "Not even gonna say g'bye, then?" she called. He kept walking sternly into town, ignoring her.

"Yeah?" she called again, wiping her watery eyes. "Well go on then. Leave! 'Ave y'self a good time. And if this is how you want to act to me then don't even bother comin' 'ome!" His back remained away from her as he continued marching down the road.

After he stomped out of sight of the inn, he ducked into an alleyway to head back toward the Bardenwood. He needed to see Emagora again. He was starting to feel as if she were the only one who really understood him, especially with the way Gran was acting. With all that had happened to him, he was beginning to feel like his life in Pipton was slowly slipping away. He felt as if he were given a new purpose. A new meaning. Before, he'd never thought twice about whether or not the stories of the Bardenwood were true. Now, he knew exactly what the Bardenwood was.

A *forest.*

The trees didn't uproot themselves nor scoop up travelers into their branches. Witches certainly did not steal children, at least witches like Emagora didn't. They weren't hideous or evil. He was sure some witches were dangerous, but even some people in Pipton were dangerous. He was beginning to feel like everything he'd known his whole life was a lie. Now he was filled with wanderlust and a thirst for knowledge he'd never known before. What other secrets lie in between the gray trees of the Bardenwood? Were there fairies and dragons? Gnomes, elves, and goblins? What were the other people in the Settled Lands like? He suddenly realized he didn't even know what his kingdom's capital or even his own queen looked like. Much less the kings, queens, and people of the other kingdoms. He began to feel very small in the world. Things he never thought of before were all of a sudden flooding every part of his mind. This was why he yearned so badly to speak again with Emagora. She was his only connection to the world around him and the hidden world he'd unwittingly been thrust into. He had to see her again.

Sneaking quietly through the fields and past the dozens of tree stumps, he found himself staring once again into the shaded understory of the Bardenwood. The trees stood tall and unwavering this morning in the still air. The sun was out in full and its rays rippled down through the leaves in spots on the ground. He looked back toward Sore Swallow and saw a gray line of smoke rising from the chimney. "I'll be back, Gran," he said to himself. Once more, he crossed over the tree line and plunged into the forest.

Once he'd gotten far enough in, he looked around near the spot where the toadstool path was first revealed to him. Sure enough, a pearly toadstool sprouted right in front of his eyes. He smiled. He began following the path through the forest until it brought him to Emagora's tree wall. Before he could even knock on the giant tree door, it crackled open for him. He stepped excitedly inside, letting the tree close up behind him. Her garden looked much different this time. The sunlight revealed the whole haven to be an intense green. The lush moss was still coated in a crystal dew and the lanterns hung unlit throughout the branches. Instead of fireflies, butterflies of every color glided in and out of the shrubs and fruit trees, shimmering in the warm sun. The glimmer of her spring rippled off of lavish ferns and flowering shrubs as if they were dancing just for him.

"Emagora?" he announced. "It's me, Ard."

No answer.

He repeated, "Emagora? I'm back."

A rustling sound came from the giant apple tree above him. He looked up to see what it was, but there was only darkness. The thickness of the leaves made it hard to see with the contrast of the bright sunlight. With a gleaming flash, two white eyes glinted in the darkness, looking directly at him. A little unnerving, but he was sure it was her. He grabbed hold of the branches and climbed up toward her. His eyes adjusted and he was able to see her now. She was sitting on a thick branch with her arms wrapped around her legs and her chin resting on her knees. Her hair fell like a curtain over her back and hung down from off of the branch. When Ard reached her spot, she smiled at him, staring intensely with her hazy eyes. "Good morning, Arden Ford of Pipton," she said with a smile.

"Morning," he replied. "What are you doing up here?"

"I like to climb, of course!" she answered. "It makes me feel... important."

"Important?" he asked. "How so?"

"Everyone always looked down on me all my life," she said

with a sigh. "Sometimes it's nice to look down upon everything else."

Ard nodded his head in understanding. "I know how you feel," he said. He thought of his spot above the blacksmith's forge and smiled.

With a flip of her hair, she snapped back to her usual excited self. "Would you like to climb down?"

"Sure," he agreed.

Emagora bit her lip in excitement. "Race you!" she challenged. In a blur, she hopped down from branch to branch, speeding toward the ground like a crazed squirrel. Ard, feeling his energy surge through him again, instinctively followed by leaping directly to the garden floor. Thirty feet down and without stopping once, he landed lightly on the ground. Emagora swung down from the last branch a few moments after him, thinking she had won. Her face turned from a smile to a pouting frown when she saw him leaning against the trunk of the tree, boasting.

"Well," she said, "I guess your feet feel *much* lighter on the ground."

Ard laughed. "They do, actually. And I can do a lot more than that."

Emagora raised her eyebrows, impressed. "You're full of surprises, Arden Ford of Pipton," she said clapping her hands.

"Am I? I hadn't noticed." He tossed her an apple he'd snatched on the way down and she stumbled to catch it. "For you," he said through a flirty grin.

"My, my, stableboy," she said with blushing cheeks. "An apple for me? You know, here in the Bardenwood, an apple as a gift is considered a proposal. A *marriage* proposal."

The smooth smile on his face disappeared. "Oh, erm. I-I didn't...I had no idea," he stuttered.

Emagora nodded and stepped closer to him, placing a delicate hand on his chest. With the softest of bites to her lip, she slipped her fingers between the strings of his laced collar and grazed his bare skin. "Mhm, yes. Everyone knows of the

Appled Oath. And if I take a bite it means I accept, and we'll be mated for all eternity. You and I. One life. One soul. Never again drawn to another."

Ard's heart nearly beat out of his chest. The blood rushed to his face and flushed his cheeks to a candied red. His whole head felt like it was going to explode. He watched as Emagora opened her mouth to take a bite. Just before her teeth sunk into the apple's red flesh, her lips formed into a kittenish, "Got you."

"What?" Ard managed. "Wait, you were joking?"

"Of course, you silly thing," she laughed. "Though would it be so bad if I wasn't?"

"My Gran taught me to keep my mouth shut when asked questions like that," Ard said with his hands up.

"Smart woman," Emagora smiled. "Must be a redhead."

Ard laughed and rubbed the back of his head. He hoped Gran wasn't still upset with him. Maybe it was best that he get back home as soon as he could, but not without some answers. "Emagora," he said, straightening himself, "I have questions. Do you know what's happening to me?"

Emagora's face softened. "I might," she said unsure. He stood still, waiting for her to elaborate. She began to pace. "Ard, there is so much you don't know. So much you don't know about the Bardenwood, about witches, about this world."

"What world?" he asked.

"The one most humans are unaware of. The world hidden inside this forest. My world," Emagora said placing her hands over her heart. She could see Ard was not understanding. She took a deep breath then said, "A world of magic."

Ard suddenly looked nervous. "Magic?" he asked.

She nodded slowly.

"Magic doesn't exist," he said. "It's all tricks and schemes. Sleight of hand and such."

"Come now, stableboy, you mustn't be dense. The toadstool path?" she reminded him. "Or what about how I brought you here? Do you think I could have entered your dreams or whispered to you across fields if magic didn't exist?"

He remembered the first time he saw Emagora floating among the trees. The fact that she'd appeared in such a way inside his head unnerved him. She was powerful, no doubt. He was lucky to be on her good side. At least so far. "Fair enough," he relented. Still, his head raced with questions. "You told me I was special. Is that why you brought me here?"

She nodded her head again.

"Why? Why am I special?"

Emagora took a deep breath. He could tell she was trying to choose her words carefully. "Because right now," she said, "you may be the only one who can save the Bardenwood."

"Save the Bardenwood?" he repeated cluelessly. An unexpected heavy weight settled on his chest.

"Yes, yes!" she said happily. He could see her getting ready to bound off into her zippy chatter.

"Hold on," he struggled, holding both of his hands up. He didn't want her fluttery personality to overwhelm him. "How about this? You tell me everything you know from start to finish, and if I have a question I'll stop you. Okay?"

"Alright," she agreed, smiling.

"Now, start from the beginning."

6

A World Within Woods

"**M**agic," Emagora explained, "is as old as the dirt on the ground, the rocks on the mountain, and the stones in the stream. It's nature, you see? Just like the wind, the rain, the plants, and the animals. You can grow it, harvest it, and mold it to be practically anything you want. It's a part of your world and mine. Humans, however, only see magic as dangerous. Most humans anyway. They think it to be malicious and evil, but I like to see it as fire. Dangerous, yes. Harmful, absolutely. But look at all the good fire does! It keeps us warm, it lights up the darkness, it cooks our food, boils our water, but if you let it out of your control, fire can destroy everything and anything in its path."

Ard pondered this. "But," he said, "humans can control fire. We can even create it."

"I suppose that's the difference," Emagora said. "Humans can't use magic because it consumes them. Your hearts are just not strong enough. The witches who aren't born with magic like me were once average humans just like the people in your village. They let magic gain control, and like a wildfire it consumed them. Now they're slaves to it. Infested with it. All those horrible stories you hear about evil witches are true. There are few witches like me. In fact, I've never even met another bornwitch, but I know that humans aren't meant to harness magic. It's too powerful for them to command. Humans know this too. That's why witches have been hunted down and killed for decades, even if they were only suspected of using magic. It's why parents forbid their children from entering the forest. It's why you were so afraid of me when I told you what I was. Why I can never leave my garden."

Ard blushed, feeling slightly foolish. Entranced with her words, he asked, "So magic has been around all this time? Real magic?"

"Not exactly," she explained. "For a while now, magic has been...gone."

"Gone? What do you mean 'gone'?"

Emagora nodded her head, continuing, "Yes. Of sorts. It's why the Bardenwood looks the way it does. Lifeless, dead, cold like stone. Magic is a part of nature and when it's gone, everything else goes with it. Soon your fields and crops will turn gray, just like the Bardenwood. No crops, no food, no people. Everything is connected, you see?"

Confused, Ard asked, "But, what does all of that have to do with me?"

Emagora's eyes wandered up and down his body. Biting a fingernail, she said, "I think you may be...a Thorn."

Ard was stumped. "A Thorn? Like a bramble of thorns? What does that mean?"

Emagora sighed at having to explain more details. "Magic," she went on, "has a lord, just as you humans have your lords high in the sky and deep below. Our lord has been gone for a long time. And without him, magic has begun to vanish."

"Who is this *lord*?" Ard asked, trying to keep up. "Where has he run off to?"

"He is called the Child King," Emagora said. "He may appear as just a small boy but he has existed for far longer than you or

I. He is known in our world as the Bringer of Magic. Thorns are his born protectors, created by nature to shield him from any harm that should come his way. Similar to a rose's thorn you could say. They're born as simple humans, but upon reaching a certain age, they gain abilities like the ones you've experienced for example. Heightened senses, abnormal strength, agility—all signs of a Thorn."

Ard suddenly felt a sense of importance he'd never felt before. *A Thorn*, he thought to himself. *That's got quite a ring.* "This Child King," he said, focusing, "you said he's gone. Gone where?"

Emagora pointed at the giant dead oak tree in the center of her garden, where Ard and she met face to face for the first time. He stared at it, perplexed. Tossing a strand of hair over her shoulder, she went on, "Years ago, once the kingdoms realized the Child King existed, they joined together against him. In their misguided fear of magic, they imprisoned him beneath this oak tree, burying him deep beneath the ground. With our lord gone, many magical creatures became scarcer and scarcer. Fairies retreated into their hollows, the nymphs and dryads hardened into pines and boulders, even the giants disappeared without a trace. With the Child King gone, the balance of nature tipped and all these lands will soon become lifeless. Even my garden won't survive for much longer. My grasp on magic fades a little with each passing day. This is what the kingdoms did not realize."

Ard was thoroughly intrigued. He looked at the sinister-looking oak tree, bent and mangled like a wilted flower. Its boughs loomed over the mossy floor of Emagora's garden with a baleful shadow. The soil beneath it looked unforgivingly like a pool of quicksand, yet even with the oak's malicious appearance, he had no fear of it. "Why would the kingdoms imprison the Child King?" he asked. "What harm was he doing?"

"Magic is a powerful thing, Ard. To humans, it's a terribly scary thing. Anything unknown is scary to most people. It is the way of life, I'm afraid. The Child King is good. Kind. He is the embodiment of magic and nature. He is an ancient spirit made of gentleness and growth who cares for all magical and non-magical creatures. But, as I said, humans fear magic and its power. The kingdoms saw the Child King as a threat. A risk they couldn't let come to fruition. So, when they discovered they couldn't kill him, they locked him away, imprisoned with a curse they devised themselves. A curse that only one of his protectors can break. So, they hunted down the last of the Thorns and killed them all so there was no way for the Child King to return and erased him and our world of magic from all memory."

With an acute shiver, Ard felt his whole body tense. Chills ran up and down his limbs and back, pulsating through him like tiny bolts of lightning. His face changed from eager interest to silent pause as he settled all of his muscles to understand what the sensations were trying to tell him. He put an ear up into the air and closed his eyes, listening intently.

"What is it, Ard?" Emagora asked softly, as he stiffened like stone.

"Shhh!" he hushed, pushing his hands toward the ground. He could begin to hear sounds. Whispers. Like soft waves on a beach or wind blowing through trees. *Is that the wind?* he thought. *No.* He had grown to know what sound the wind made through the forest. The whispers started getting louder. All of a sudden, he was stricken with an intense odor. Just like rosemary in Gran's hair, it filled his nose and steeped down into his lungs, soaking out through his skin. He coughed at the smell. One he definitely couldn't mistake.

Smoke.

"Ard?" Emagora asked again, this time with a hint of panic. "What's wrong?"

Ignoring her, he flung himself up the tree, climbing nimbly up the branches like a ladder. From the canopy, he couldn't see the forest floor at all. Emagora and her garden were completely hidden by the treetops of the Bardenwood. As he burst through the top and scanned the horizon, his throat plunged into his stomach. Toward Pipton, a tower of billowing black smoke poured into the blue sky. As his mouth gaped open, the whispers he heard before came rippling to him. He closed his eyes trying to listen. Focusing harder, his blood ran cold as he heard it.

Screams.

Without the trees to block them out, the whispers he'd been hearing were screams. Men, women, and children. Horrified, he climbed back down the tree as fast as his body let him. He dropped to the ground halfway down landing with a soft thud. Emagora met him with her hands clasped together and a look of worry painted across her face.

"Ard," she breathed, "what's going on?"

Ard grabbed his coat, shooting his arms through the sleeves. "Something's happening in Pipton. There's a fire. I heard screaming."

Emagora's face went white. "What?"

He had no time to explain further. "I have to leave. Gran could be in trouble. I have to go!"

"Wait!" she cried, clutching his coat sleeve. "It could be dangerous! You could be hurt, Ard."

He gently clasped his hands around hers. Their warmth felt good against his cold, nervous fingers. "I have to do something, Emagora," he said.

Emagora looked softly at him with her foggy eyes. "Be careful, Arden Ford," she said, letting go of his sleeve. "You know not what awaits."

He nodded then dashed out the tree trunk door listening to it crack shut behind him. He bolted through the forest ignoring the toadstool path, letting the scent of smoke guide him back to Pipton. His whole body was trembling with chills. His breath raced as the cold air iced over the inside of his lungs. The scent of smoke was getting stronger as his heart pounded against his ribcage. With all the adrenaline, he didn't even notice the branches scratch his face or the brambles tear his pants and coat—nor did he notice the screams had stopped.

7

The Innkeeper and The Cobbler

C hest heaving from running, he could finally see the edge of the Bardenwood. He could see Pipton was hellishly ablaze. The brilliant orange light of the fire towered so high he couldn't even see the sky. The black smoke had begun seeping through the gray trees of the forest edge making the ground look like a swirling abyss. His sprint slowed into a choppy jog as he coughed from the smoke, barely able to keep going. Through the trees, he could see the shape of a man running toward him and the edge of the Bardenwood. The man looked familiar to him. As he got closer, he could see he was panicked and bleeding from a wound near his eye, like he'd been hit with something. Ard recognized him as Gell Busby's father, Normyn, the blacksmith whose forge he always perched on. Still choking on smoke, he pushed harder to reach the panicking blacksmith.

"Normyn!" he coughed. "Mr. Busby! Are you al—" Ard's mouth hung open. The blacksmith stopped running and stumbled heavily to his knees. As he fell forward onto the ground, Ard could see a crossbow bolt protruding from his back painted with running stains of crimson blood. He cupped his hand over his mouth in horror. He went to move out of the forest toward Normyn but froze instinctively. He looked past where the blacksmith had fallen and that's when he saw them.

A group of men approached whooping and yelling loudly, cheering for the shot that killed Normyn. They were rugged men with long, dirty hair, peeling sunburned skin, and tattooed scars across their faces that formed intricate markings unique to each face they were etched onto. They were dressed in an array of red-stained leather and melted down metal hammered into armor. They carried large scimitars that curved upwards and were stained with dried blood. Their chest plates bore a fiery red emblem that depicted a screaming girl tied to a burning pyre, an emblem Ard knew well from stories.

These were King Kolbran's riders, the Ashen Horde. He was certain. One of the riders who held a crossbow, leaped happily over to Normyn boasting about his kill shot. He held up his body and danced with it like a giant rag doll. The other riders wheezed with laughter as he dared to plant a kiss on the blacksmith's cold cheek. When the rider was content with his horrible mockery, he tossed Mr. Busby back into the dirt where he fell with a hard thump, splattering blood among the grass. The rider grabbed hold of Normyn's leg and started dragging his body back to Pipton. Ard, hidden behind one of the trees trying hard not to cough, felt his stomach begin to churn. It was all so horrible. He felt as if he were going to be sick. As soon as the riders were out of sight, he let out his cough he'd been holding in, clutching his chest as it choked him. The smoke was growing thick. He had to move. Creeping out of the woods, he ducked low in the tall grass of the field and began making his way back into Pipton unable to take his eyes off of the trail of Normyn Busby's blood.

His heart had not stopped at all. He could feel it beating wildly against his chest. He needed to get to Sore Swallow. From this distance, he couldn't see anything past the smoke, but he knew which direction to go. The closer he got to the inn, the better he was able to see that it was on fire too. He raced to it making sure no other riders saw him. When he reached the door of the inn, he was trembling with fear. His senses had all been dulled by the smell of smoke and the roar of the fire, which he could see was consuming every building in town. Bursting through the front door of the inn, he looked around desperately for any sign of Gran. He flew upstairs and kicked down the door in every room, clambering over embers falling from the ceiling.

No sign of her.

He started to speed downstairs when his foot snapped through one of the steps and he tumbled down hard, slamming his chest on the wooden floor of the foyer. The fire was growing fiercer. He gagged on the smoke as he struggled to get his breath back from the fall. He had to find Gran fast. With a slight stumble, he stood up to continue his search.

"Gran?" he called softly, unsure if the riders could hear him. "Gran, are you here?" The kitchen, the rooms, the loft, Gran was nowhere to be found. He ran outside and into the stable which was still intact. He could hear the voices of more riders further in town echoing through the smoke, laughing and shouting like a pack of wild dogs. He had to find Gran before they did. Knowing her, she probably found a good hiding spot and was waiting with a weapon for anyone that came her way. He hoped. He prayed. *Please*.

In the stable, all the horses were in a frightened frenzy, whinnying and kicking the doors of their stalls. Still coughing up smoke, Ard unhooked all the latches and they bolted out of the stable heading toward the fields in between Sore Swallow and the Bardenwood. As he made his way to the back of the stable, he realized that Hook was missing. The latch on his pen door was left unlocked. He had no time to look for him, but he hoped the stallion was safe.

"Gran!" he called. "Gran, where are you?" She was nowhere inside. Frantic, he sprinted around the stable and toward the back door of the inn to check inside one last time. As he passed through Gran's garden, his heart stopped.

The murder of Normyn Busby was the first time Ard had experienced the gripping power of death. He remembered how his stomach crumpled itself into knots and the drop of his throat to his chest. He could remember his nose burning as he tried to choke back tears, but it was nothing compared to what he was experiencing now.

Gran's body was strewn out in the dirt of her garden. She was on her back lying between the vines of her squash plants, the same ones she'd been gathering when he left hours ago. As he came upon her lying there, his brain protected him by imagining her asleep, but the stab wound and blood-soaked ground gave away the truth. He approached her body, unable to catch his breath. Tears he had never cried welled in his eyes like lakes overflowing from a rainstorm. His face contorted and pressed together tightly, squeezing the teardrops from his eyes. They rolled down his cheeks and dropped off of his chin swirling in the dirt and blood. The world around him was so still, all he could hear was a shrill ringing in his ears. He fell to his knees, dizzy with shock.

"Gran?" he whimpered over the ringing. "Gran, it's me, Ard. Your pup." Her eyes were shut, and her mouth hung open slightly. "Gran?" he said, one more time, feigning a smile. "Gran, there's a fire. We have to go now. It's not safe."

Cold...quiet.

Sickeningly quiet.

He frantically cradled her into his arms, shaking her back and forth. "Gran! Gran, it's me! It's Ard! Wake up, Gran. Ungh... oh no, not you. I'm sorry, Gran! Gran, listen to me! I'm sorry. What can I do? Gran! Why didn't you run?" The tears blinded him as he choked on his words. "Gran, you can't leave. Please don't leave me! I'M SORRY GRAN!" His voice was shrill and his face and throat hurt through every word.

Voices of men drew closer. More riders were coming. Praying

they hadn't heard him, Ard silenced his crying, swallowing the tears so hard that his ears popped, ringing like cannon fire. Head reeling and still whimpering, he began pulling Gran's body toward the blueberry shrubs in her garden to hide from the riders. He could hear them clear as day now. They were rounding the corner. Panicking, he flung himself into the bushes leaving Gran where she was. He softened his breathing by clasping his hands over his mouth, praying that the riders didn't find him. Their leathery boots thudded toward her body. Through the bushes, he could see her face. It looked as if she were sleeping. Even with the life drained from her cheeks, she looked like she could smile at any moment. Rosemary sprigs still clung to the graying strands of her ginger hair. He wished he could smell them just once more, but the billowing smoke denied him the kindness.

Without a word from the men, Gran's body was dragged across the ground out of her garden and out of Ard's sight. The footsteps of the riders were drowned out by the sound of the crackling fire as they disappeared back into town. Approaching a state of shock, he emerged slowly from the shrubs, trembling with every step. Barely able to stand, he rounded the corner of the inn and could see Gran's feet being dragged into the street at the end of the alley. Swallowing down more tears, he tiptoed to the corner and peeked around.

In the street, a group of riders had villagers lined up on their knees. Three riders stood guard over them while others were busy dragging bodies to a large heap in the center of the square. Bodies...

Bodies.

Ard's mouth hung open as he glanced through the pile and noticed the tiny shape of Dail Fletcher who had given him a cookie at the gathering. His face was pale white and was coated in streaks of blood. Ard turned away in horror when he couldn't tell if it was Dail's blood or the blood of the other villagers piled on top of him. The tears refused to stop. His whole face was wet and hot as the heat of the flames swept down the street. This couldn't be happening. Pipton was just a simple, woodcutting village. This couldn't be happening. *Not here. Not my home.*

Just as he was about to give up hope, he saw a familiar pair of eyes meeting his in the line of captive villagers. Mr. Brinkley, hands behind his head and knees in the dirt, let out a silent sigh of relief as he noticed him peeking around the corner. Ard put a shaking finger to his lips, signaling the cobbler to act like he'd never seen him, and Mr. Brinkley returned back to his captive state. Ard dried his face. He had to do something. Mr. Brinkley was all he had left.

Mr. Brinkley was all he had left.

He climbed onto the roof where he could get a better view of where all the riders were. There were only three guarding the captive villagers. The men were monstrously large, and he knew he barely stood a chance fighting one, much less three of them. He had to find a way to distract them and give the villagers the chance to run. Ard knew this village better than all three of the brutes even while it was ablaze. A plan quickly grew in his head. He took a deep breath and hopped back down into the alley. Peeking around the corner, he could see Mr. Brinkley still keeping his composure. Two riders were sitting on the ground, picking their teeth with knives while the other stood watch over the villagers. Ard took a deep breath, exhaled, and focused his energy into his legs. They surged with strength and he bolted out of the alley and down the street barreling toward the riders.

The brutes were so unaware, Ard was practically on top of them before they even noticed him. At full speed, he charged into the standing rider, ramming him to the ground. Without hesitating, he sped down an alley hearing one of them yell, "After him!" He looked back and just as he'd hoped, the riders had sent one of them to catch him. As he raced through the alley, he could hear the rider growling fiercely. The building to his right was blazing and the flames were so close that he could feel his skin burn. Keeping close to the wall on the left, he kept running. When he reached the end of the alley, he darted left around the building and entered it through a back door, heading back the way the rider was coming. He leaped over a counter and waited at another door which led back into the alley.

He made it just in time. The rider that was chasing him was barreling down the passage. Ard opened the alley door and backed up. Charging forward, he crashed all of his weight feet first into the rider, sending him careening through the opposite wall and into the fire. The rider instantly released screams of pain as the fire enveloped him in a burning sheathe of smoke and light. Ard got up, ran out the back door, and climbed up onto the roof to make his way toward the street again. Peeking over the side, he could see a second rider sprinting down the alleyway to aid the one on fire as his screams cut through the air like a knife. His plan was working.

Dashing to the street side of the building and peering over, Ard could see the last rider forcing the villagers to stay where they were, kicking them and yelling. Their faces were scared but hopeful, darting to and fro looking for any chance to bolt. As the rider made his way toward Ard's side of the street, Ard planted his feet then leaped over the side aiming straight for him. His boots landed square in the middle of the rider's back, sending his body flying into the dirt. Ard rolled forward, letting the gravel take the brunt of his fall. The rider, who was slowly recovering from the attack, started scrambling to his feet.

Ard didn't have time to waste.

Reaching down, he grabbed hold of a large rock, grasping it firmly in his hand. He could see the rider bare his yellowing teeth in anger. His face, decorated with the labyrinthine markings all the riders shared, was one Ard knew he'd never forget. Animal bones hung from the rider's clothes, clinking as he stood. Ard charged at him and swung the rock with all his might letting it collide with the brute's skull. A gruesome crack rung out through the streets and the rider hit the ground again, still conscious, but barely able to form words or keep his eyes open.

Ard lost all control and plunged the rock into his head, striking over and over again. It was all an immense blur. He barely knew what was happening, even as the rider's blood splattered against his shirt. All he kept thinking about was Gran. Thinking about her body lying cold on the ground. The only thing he saw in that moment of fury was her body being dragged across the dirt to the burn pile. His mind was lost for a moment. One second, he was charging at the rider, the next he was staring at a dead man's body on the ground while clutching a blood-drenched rock. Horrified, he let the stone fall among the gravel. Turning to the villagers, whose faces were riddled with fearful gratitude, he let out a chest heaving, "Run!"

They wasted no time. Scattering like roaches, they all disappeared between the buildings and the roar of the fire. In the frenzy, Ard caught the terrified eyes of Madsyn Wickwyle. Her golden hair was dried with mud and her face was bruised. Her petticoats were ripped and tattered and her mouth hung open with busted lips. It looked as if she were dragged across the ground and beaten. A terrible feeling twisted in his gut as he saw the terror in her eyes. For the first time, Ard and Madsyn had something in common. Fear. He wanted to say something. Anything. He could tell she felt the same, but neither of them could find the words. In a flash, she disappeared into the chaos.

Mr. Brinkley, weak from a head wound, hobbled over to Ard letting him wrap his arm around his shoulders for support. "Come on, Brink!" he demanded. "We have to go. Right now!" Mr. Brinkley was breathing hard but did his best to move quickly. They had to move before the other riders returned. With nowhere else to go, they ran for the edge of the Bardenwood. Ard prayed to the Lords Above that the riders wouldn't follow them inside. The sky had grown dark from the towering smoke which billowed high above the trees now. Mr. Brinkley was slowing down as they crossed the field but Ard knew every second counted. In the open like this, they were sitting ducks and would be run down just like Normyn Busby. "Brink, we can't stop!" he urged. "No, no, we can't stop! Keep going! Come on, Brinkley!"

The old cobbler was coughing and wildly out of breath. As he bent over, hands on his knees, he sputtered, "I can't, lad! I can't. I 'ave to rest." Mr. Brinkley fell flat on his knees. To his horror, Ard heard the sound of hooves clobbering the ground. Looking back toward Pipton, he could see a group of riders on horseback hurtling through the field toward them. He looked to Mr. Brinkley, eyes filled with fear and tears, but the cobbler just stared back.

"Go," he breathed, putting his hand to Ard's cheek.

Ard froze, unable to verbalize a single word.

"Go, now!" he repeated, more firmly this time.

"N-no," Ard stammered, beginning to shake. "Not you too. I-I can't! Brink, I can't! I can't!"

"Lords 'ave you, boy! GO!" Mr. Brinkley growled. "Do as I say!"

Ard could hear the hoofbeats getting louder. He was unable to move, riddled with hysterical panic. Mr. Brinkley stood up and grabbed hold of his collar. Throwing him in the direction of the forest, he barked, "I said go! If you don't run, then Flora and I will 'ave died for naught! You run, Arden Ford, and don't look back. Don't you dare look back, dear boy. Run!"

Hot, stinging tears washed down his face as he stared at the old cobbler, he who had been his only friend in Pipton. The only person other than Gran who cared about him. Mr. Brinkley had watched him grow up from a small boy to the young man he was today. He was face to face with a horrible choice. He couldn't save Gran, but here he stood possibly able to save Mr. Brinkley. Possibly able to save one life that mattered. Possibly able to die defending that one life. But, Mr. Brinkley was right. Ard had to live if he ever wanted to avenge Gran and Sore Swallow. If he wanted justice he would have to live to see it. But, beneath it all, he was *scared*. He needed to run because he was scared. The thundering sound of the horses was nearly deafening. He could hear the riders whooping and whistling. There was no time.

Ard looked into the withered blue eyes of the old cobbler one last time. A blue spent from years of squinting behind finger-smudged spectacles. A blue spent from years of laughter. Years of smiles. A blue he knew he'd never see the like of again. He looked for as long as he dared before turning and darting into the forest, trying hard not to imagine what the riders would do to his best friend. He quickly made it to the tree line and plunged into the Bardenwood. As his legs burned from running, his heart sank into his stomach. Was he making the right choice? A few yards in, he thought about looking back but forced himself not to. He couldn't. He couldn't look. Over the sound of the fire and crunch of the leaves beneath his feet, he heard Mr. Brinkley's voice ring out, "Don't stop, Arden! Don't you stop runnin', boy! Go! Go! Run, Arden! Don't—"

Mr. Brinkley's last words echoed through the trees, burning into Ard's memory like the fire that blazed behind him.

He ran as long as he could. His clothes were stained with sweat and smoke. He gagged at the smell. He'd run far enough into the forest to get fresh air, but his nerves pressed his lungs to his ribs, making it hard to breathe. His smoke-blackened face contorted so much it hurt him, but he didn't care about the pain. All he could focus on was death. All he could focus on were their faces. Gran, Mr. Brinkley, Normyn Busby, Dail Fletcher. Everyone. Every time he closed his eyes he saw them. Even the faces of the villagers piled on top of one another haunted him. He clenched the dirt and soil into his hands, letting his sadness burn to anger. His teeth ground together as his whole body erupted into a fit of rage, screaming and thrashing. His fists pounded the ground so hard the leaves around him launched into the air. He'd lost everything. His home, his family, his best friend. He'd even lost his innocence murdering the rider with nothing but a stone in his hand.

He wished he'd done more to the rider. Made it worse for him than just blows to the head. He wished he'd killed all of the riders.

He imagined them burning in their own flames until they were nothing but ash and dust. How could his world go from exciting to nightmarish in a matter of hours? He tried desperately to understand. The tears fell again as he coughed and heaved from misery. He was starting to realize that he was completely alone. The Bardenwood sat insidiously still all around him, cold and unapologetic. The light of the sun brought him no peace as it tried desperately to kiss his face through the leaves. The forest he had come to know began to terrify him again, just like when he was a child. He knew there was only one place left for him to go.

Ard knew the way to Emagora's garden by heart now. His face was streaked with smokey tear stains as he walked through the woods drained of all emotion. He had cried every tear his body would allow. He wandered through the forest like a ghost, dazed and in shock. He felt like a shell. All he wanted to do was fall asleep and never wake up, forget everything that happened even for a few minutes. He just wanted to be away from his own thoughts.

When he got to her garden, Emagora was waiting for him wedged between the tree trunk door. She looked like she'd been waiting there for hours. Her foggy eyes reflected in the twilight of the coming evening. As he approached, she leaped over to him and wrapped her arms around his neck without a word. He could smell her hair. It smelled like the wild shrubs that grew in her garden mixed with rain and wet soil. As he clutched her cloak, he could feel the tree bark and fibers graze across his skin in tiny vibrations. Suddenly, the vibrations turned to fierce trembles as the forest began spinning around him in a wild vortex of gray. He recoiled from Emagora's embrace and shut his eyes, trying to steady himself. "Ard," he heard her say, "you're going to be alright." Her voice sounded distant and muffled over the ringing that plagued his ears. Grinding his teeth, he put his hands to his head, trying anything to make the fit stop, but his world came crashing to a halt as he let his body fall into Emagora's arms, knocking them both to the ground.

8

The Blackstone Ritual

Ard awoke staring into the flames of candles. Blinking blindly, he could make out that he was still in Emagora's garden. His shirt was clean and drying in a nearby branch and the smoke had been wiped from his cheeks. He could feel his head resting on a soft bed of grass that grew so thick it felt like a pillow. His bare back grazed against fuzzy moss that his body had pressed a spot in. As he shuffled in his spot, his senses began coming back to him. He could hear bumblebees and butterflies fluttering from flower to flower, preparing intensely for the winter season. Emagora was sitting next to a tree with her head tucked into her knees across from him. Her hair furled into a pool around her feet. He let out an achy groan and her head shot up, her misty eyes meeting his with excited relief. "Ard!" she yelped, crawling over to him. "Oh, Ard! Are you all alright? Are you hurt?" Her hands rested on his bare chest and the middle of his back as she tried to sit him up slowly.

He shook his head sullenly, realizing that everything that happened wasn't a horrible nightmare like he'd hoped. "I'm alright," he groaned. "How long was I out?"

"Just the night," she said softly, brushing his hair out of his face. Silence sat between both of them. The rustling of the leaves and insects was all that could be heard. She struggled to find words, but she knew some had to be spoken. Nervously, she asked, "Ard? What happened?"

He looked down, trying hard not to visualize anything too vividly. He didn't want to cry in front of her. He didn't want to seem weak, but he could still smell the smoke in his clothes. In his hair. In his skin. He could still see Gran being dragged away. He could still feel the heat of the flames. Struggling to keep himself together, he said, "Ashen Horde. They burned the whole village down and killed everyone they could." He paused, closing his eyes tightly. He choked back the tears hard then continued. "They...they killed my grandmother."

Emagora put a hand to her mouth as tears glazed over her white eyes.

"They killed her," he repeated. "In her garden. She was gathering squash. Probably for dinner...probably for me. They killed Mr. Brinkley too. My best friend. Right outside the forest... and I...ran. I left him."

"Oh, Ard," she breathed, putting a hand over her mouth. "Please don't blame yourself."

"I should've been there," he snarled. "I should've been there to help her. I should've stayed there to help Brink. But...I ran... like a coward.

She stroked his face with her hand. He let its warmth send tingles through his body. "Ard," she whispered, "you're anything but. You must know that it isn't your fault."

"I..." he tried as his eyes grew misty. "I didn't even get to tell her I was sorry. When I left, I was awful to her. She was worried about me and the only thing I was concerned with was myself. These woods. This world. Now I've lost her...I've lost her." He bit his lip, still trying to withhold the tears. He drew a shaky breath.

Emagora's hand moved to his back and she scratched it

lightly. He could feel her tiny nails move in sweet circles across his bare skin, lifting goosebumps with every trace. It felt so nice. Gran would always do that when he was...sad. Sadness.

He couldn't be sad. There was no room for sadness anymore. Everything inside him morphed into anger. Anger for Gran, anger for Mr. Brinkley, anger for Pipton. His emotions were out of control. He wanted revenge. He wanted to get back at the riders for taking away the only people he loved. He stood abruptly, staring down at Emagora who remained on the mossy ground. She looked frightened of him, shrinking into herself, but he didn't care. "This Child King," he asked sternly. "Can he kill Kolbran?"

She remained still. He could see her breathing start to quicken.

He repeated, "Emagora. Can the Child King kill Kolbran?"

"Ard, I don't know," she admitted. She grew uneasy and started shuffling slowly away from him.

Ignoring her nervousness, he stepped toward her as his rage grew. "If I set him free, will he help me avenge the people I loved? Will he destroy the Ashen Horde? Will he kill King Kolbran? Can he do it?"

"I said I don't know," she repeated boldly. "Ard, I just don't. The Child King is kind and cares for all living beings. Even non-magical ones. Even evil ones. It's not my place to speak for him."

"The Ashen Horde," he growled, "aren't beings. They're vermin. They're filth! And Kolbran is nothing but a coward. Spineless wretch! He can burn. The whole of Ashar can burn too for all I care! They can all burn."

"I'm sorry, Ard," she squeaked. "I don't know what he'll do. Maybe he'll help you, maybe he won't, but I can't tell you which."

"But," he pointed out, "you *can* tell me how to bring him back."

"Maybe," she corrected cautiously.

"I'm a Thorn, Emagora," he said. "You said so yourself, didn't you? You said I was special. You told me I could release him."

Emagora was now backed against a tree, eyes wide and focused on him as he grew more and more intense. "I don't even know if you *are* a Thorn, Ard," she relented. "Many creatures can do what you do, not just Thorns. For the ritual to work, it has to be performed by a Thorn. No other."

"There's a ritual? So you *do* know!" he exclaimed, taking aggressive steps toward her. "What ritual?"

"Ard...calm down. You're scaring me," she breathed. "Please."

"Emagora!" he snapped. "What ritual?"

In an auburn blur, she scurried behind the tree in fear.

He sighed. "Emagora?" he called toward the tree. "I'm...I'm so sorry." Her face peeked from behind the trunk. "I didn't mean to be so harsh. I'm just...it's all just so hard." He rubbed the back of his neck and fought with his emotions, walking away from her and the tree. He wanted to cry, he wanted to yell, he wanted to run away, he wanted to fight. Everything was so disorienting. Tears started welling up in his eyes again, stinging so much he struggled to keep them open.

"It's alright, you know," Emagora said, stepping out from behind the tree. "I know how you feel. I once lost everything too. Everyone. There's nothing we could have done. Sometimes things can't be changed and that's just the way it is, but there is always hope. In every dark forest, there is green. Sometimes we just have to wait for the sun to show it to us." Ard looked at her with tearful eyes as she continued softly, "I'm sorry for your grandmother, Ard. I'm sorry about your home. Truly, I am." She took hold of his hand. Her fingers felt warm against the empty cold that claimed his. "I don't know if you can release the Child King, and I don't know if he'll even give you what you want if you do, but I know you feel as if you have to try. I'll tell you what you must do."

Ard looked into her foggy white eyes. This close, he could see her pupils floating like dark discs under a frozen lake. She brushed her hair behind her ears and for a moment he forgot the terrible things that happened to him. Just one moment. Letting himself calm down, he sighed, "I'll never be able to thank you enough."

She gave his hand a gentle squeeze. "You'll never have to, stableboy."

"I'm sorry I scared you."

"Stop apologizing. You've gone through a great deal. We all lose our way sometimes. Just remember to follow the toadstools."

His heart fluttered, but he knew he had to stay focused. "So," he said, "what do I have to do?"

Emagora sat back and focused on him, making sure he understood her. "It will not be an easy task."

"I'm ready. I'll do whatever it takes."

"Alright then," she said, plainly as possible. "You'll need blackstone."

Before she was able to continue, he let out a scoffing laugh. "Blackstone? The rarest gem in all of the Settled Lands? Yeah, alright."

"I thought you said you'd do whatever it took," she chuckled.

"Within reason of course! I mean, blackstone? You must be joking."

"I'm afraid not, Arden Ford of Pipton," she replied, trying to remain serious.

"How am I going to get my hands on blackstone, Emagora?" he asked frustratingly. "The most I've got are a few metals from Pipton."

"You wanted to know what it took to free the Child King and I'm telling you," she said plainly. "Do you want these answers or not?"

He took a breath in and let it out slowly. "Alright. Go on, then."

"As I said," she continued, "you'll need pure blackstone. Once you have that, you'll need to bury it at the base of the dead oak there." She pointed at the blackened tree that stood silently in the center of her garden. "Once you've done that, the ritual calls for the blackstone spot to be soiled with the blood of a willing

Thorn."

Ard went stiff with unease. "Blood? How much blood?"

"I don't know," she confessed. "All I know is that the ritual calls for it. It could be one drop, it could be an entire jar. Magic and curses aren't exactly perfect practices."

"Well, that's reassuring."

She stifled a laugh. "Ard, you don't have to do this, you know. You could find a new home somewhere. Anywhere you wanted!"

"I have no home, Emagora," he said with a tightened jaw, pulling his shirt off of the branch. "My home and the people I love were taken from me. Besides, you said yourself without the Child King the rest of the Settled Lands will wither and die. If I can bring this lord of yours back, maybe there's something he can do for me in return. If I don't do something, the Ashen Horde will move on to other villages, maybe even cities. They'll spare no one. Men, women, children, it doesn't matter to them and Kolbran is just the same. We were told by our queen that this wasn't happening, and we were foolish enough to believe it. Even she might not know the truth. I have to do something. I have to stop this."

"If you go then you must be careful," she warned. "The leaders in the kingdoms know Thorns are needed to free the Child King. That's why they had them all hunted down and killed after they imprisoned him. If you actually are a Thorn and anyone finds out, you're as good as dead."

He gulped but nodded his head affirmatively. He pulled his shirt over his shoulders.

Emagora went on, "I wish there was more I could do. If I don't stay here, then there'll be no one to tend my garden. I don't think being in the company of a witch makes you any safer either."

Ard knew she was right but attempted to make her feel better. "You've done plenty," he said, smiling. "I don't know what would've happened to me if you weren't here. Now you've given me hope, something I didn't think was possible after yesterday.

I'm happy to have met you. So, if being in the company of witches means feeling this way, then being in the company of witches is just fine with me."

Emagora glowed with happiness and her cheeks blushed red. After a moment, her smile faded slowly. "When will you leave?"

"There's no time to waste," he said. "Every second counts and the Riders won't stop. Not to mention they're on horseback. I have to get moving."

Twirling her finger in the grass, she asked, "Where will you go?"

"Well," he said, "I figured Mossa Castille would be my best bet. Kolbran's bound to have riders scattered eastward, and I doubt blackstone will be anywhere near there anyway. I'll need to head west to the city and find a jeweler or a miner. Something. I don't know. I figured the richest city in the Settled Lands would be a good place to start though." He reached up into a tree and picked a few apples from its branches. "Can I have these?"

"Yes, of course," she answered inexpressibly.

Ard knelt down to where she was sitting and lifted her chin to his, looking into her eyes intently. "I'll be back as soon as I can. I promise," he swore to her. She nodded and forced a half-hearted smile. "Take care of the garden and don't come out for anyone," he continued. "I don't know what I'll do if something happens to you too."

Emagora laughed lightly. "Oh, Arden. You hardly know me."

"But," he replied, edging closer to her, "you're all I've got now. I can't lose you. I *won't* lose you."

Her eyes glazed with forming tears, and she threw her arms around his neck. "Thank you, Arden Ford, of Pipton," she sniffed.

"What for?"

"For being the only friend I've ever had," she said, wiping a single tear from her cheek. Ard began to feel like he shouldn't leave. He'd never thought that he was probably the only person who had ever been kind to her since she discovered what she was.

Emagora survived here in the woods all alone probably since she was a little girl, and now, he was about to leave her. Even though he didn't know when he'd return, he felt connected to her somehow. Like they shared something. He started to question what his true feelings for her were. He had never known what love was or what it felt like to be protective over someone. He'd never had to be protective of Gran. No one dared to antagonize her. The only person he'd ever had to protect or worry about was himself.

Even though they hadn't known each other very long, he couldn't help the way he felt.

"Take care of yourself, Emagora," he said as their embrace ended.

She wiped her eyes on her dress sleeve and perked up to her usual cheerful self. Smiling with wide eyes, she said, "You'll need more food than a few apples." Before he could reply, she exploded into dozens of leaves and flower petals that floated to the ground, vanishing.

Ard's mouth hung open in shock. "Emagora?" he called frantically. Her gleaming eyes peeked from around the trunk of a tree several feet away. He could see her smiling.

"Come on, stableboy," she urged him. "You've got quite a journey ahead of you."

9

The Stripling and the Stableboy

Never in his life did Ard think he would have to sneak into his own village. Hidden in the treeline, he could see Pipton was still smoldering. The blaze had done its worst, leaving the whole village a decimated, broken shadow of its former self. The smells were almost too great for him to bear. The air was thick and pungent with a hot mixture of ash, smoke, and charred brick. He'd been waiting for nightfall. With his new night vision, there was no better way to get in and out without being seen. His ears were tuned to the center of town all afternoon listening to the sound of riders' laughter go from back-slapping revelry to drunken snorting. He heard wine casks uncork and thick mead slosh in skull goblets. They were celebrating.

Celebrating, he thought with a clenched jaw. He knew what they were laughing at. What they were cheering for. Death. He knew staying focused was important, but every time he looked up at the battered silhouette of Sore Swallow, a wave of grief made his breath shake. There wasn't a single part of him that wanted to venture back into Pipton, but he knew to make it to Mossa Castille he'd need as many supplies as he could carry.

Darkness fell a lot faster with the help of the remaining

smoke. Checking once more for any guards, Ard moved across the field ducking low in the tall grass. The closer he got to town, the more damage he could see. Ash littered the streets and settled like morbid snow on the charred skeletons of the shops and homes. Luckily his home was on the edge of town. From the sound of it, the riders were all in the town square. He could see the faint orange glow of their victory fire down the street. He took a shaky breath trying not to think about what he knew fueled the flames. Quiet as he could, he crept inside the remains of Sore Swallow. The stone chimney still stood, but it was charred with streaks of flame-shaped black. The blueprint his great-great-grandfather drew that hung above the fireplace was gone. Probably burned to ash. The only part left of the foyer was the floor, which wasn't saying much. The beams from the ceiling had fallen and cracked it into mounds of wooden wreckage. Somehow, a part of the stairs survived, but not enough to reach what was left of the second floor. The ceiling of the lobby was nothing but a gaping hole from where the inn must have caved in on itself, so getting to his room in the loft was impossible. His clothes wouldn't have survived anyway. Sifting through the wreckage he was able to find an old, itchy blanket. It was covered in soot, but if he tied the corners he'd have a bag and a source of warmth for when the night set in. He balled it up and tucked it under his arm.

The kitchen was a ruin, but he was able to find two of Gran's cooking knives. A bit dull, but anything he could use as a weapon or tool was useful enough. He stuck them in his pant pockets and moved on, trying hard not to dwell on memories of Gran and his childhood home. He sifted through what he could, but everything inside the inn was either useless or too difficult to unlodge. He made his way to Gran's garden which luckily sat just outside the reach of the blaze. He pulled a few carrots and potatoes from the ground and dusted the dirt off of them. Not exceptionally appetizing now, but he knew if he got hungry enough on the road he'd be grateful for them. Hopefully.

He rounded the inn and peeked out the warped door frame of the front door down the street. A group of riders was gathered in a circle by their fire watching two of them wrestle about in a sweaty tussle. He was looking to see if his path to the next building was clear, but all he could focus on were the flames. Flames fueled by his fellow villagers. Fueled by his best friend and grandmother. As they flickered wildly against the darkness, the world around him muted to a terrible ringing in his head. He couldn't stay here a moment longer. He couldn't look anymore. He didn't care what else the other ruined buildings had to offer. He just wanted to leave. He wrapped his supplies in the blanket, slung it over his shoulder and made his way out of the village, hoping nothing in Mossa Castille reminded him of this twisted version of his home.

⤙⤙⥤⥤

The road was painfully hard on Ard's feet. After a few days of travel, his boots had been worn so much that his toes could feel the cold air seep through the peeling cracks in the sole. Gran had been nagging him to get new ones and Mr. Brinkley was finally about to make him some. He tried hard to avoid the thoughts, but every step he took and every day that passed, something always reminded him of Pipton.

With each passing thought, his head raced with images of Gran's body being dragged to a burn pile or Mr. Brinkley alone in the field, shouting for Ard to run as he was mowed down. Every time he thought of them, his nose started to sting as he tried to fight bursting into tears, but every moment they crossed his mind, so did the thought of revenge. So did the thought of burning Kolbran with his own flames. Ard's billowing anger pushed him forward on his mission. Kept him driven. Kept him focused.

Alone on the road, he traveled on with a near lifeless gait. His emotions were so exhausted he hadn't even uttered a word since leaving Emagora's garden. He began to wonder if he'd ever speak again. Night after night, he sat alone with his campfires, hidden from the road behind hills and trees, thinking of the faces of the riders. Thinking of his vengeance. The only emotion that flowed through him now was anguish. The fury he held inside of him kept him alive and kept him focused.

This morning, he awoke to the sound of shouting. At first, the sound came as a faint echo, but as he listened more closely, letting his new senses regain from a rough night's sleep, he could hear them more clearly.

"Help!" the voice called. "Hello? Somebody!"

Blinking his eyes to adjust to the overcast sky, he grabbed his blanket, stomped out and buried his fire, then rushed off to where the voice was coming from. The voice's cries lead him a mile up the road and a few yards into a small patch of thin woods. The trees stood still in the crisp, windless morning. With the sun hidden behind the darkening clouds, everything seemed coated in a gloomy, silver tint. The shouting was close now. Ard crept through the saplings and crouched behind a shrub. Peeking through its leaves, he saw the source of all the racket. Laughing at himself, he stood from behind the bushes and looked upon a boy hopelessly stuck in a hunter's trapping pit.

The boy was small, probably the same size Ard was at his age. He had sandy blonde hair and brown freckles scattered across his dirty cheeks. His tattered coat was torn in a few places and his shoes and pants were coated in mud from trying to climb up the walls of the pit. When he looked upward noticing Ard, his eyes went wide with fear as he cried, "Please don't eat me, sir! Honest, I got no meat on me! I'm too gangly, I am!"

Ard laughed for the first time in what seemed like ages. "Eat you?" he snickered. "I'm not going to eat you, boy. This is a hunter's trap and I don't suspect he'll be happy to find he's caught a scrawny stripling instead of a nice, fat doe."

The boy went on. "W-well," he stuttered. "I've got a few metals on me but you can have 'em all! On my life, I swear it.

Just please get me out!"

Ard scanned around the pit for any sort of vine or long branch he could use to hoist the boy out. "How did you manage to get in this pickle, boy?"

"I fell in, sir," the boy replied. "I was just walking about you see, and—,"

"I'm no sir," Ard interrupted.

"Sorry, s—I mean sorry," the boy corrected.

"Waste of a good trap if you ask me," Ard laughed.

"Y-yes, sir," the boy chuckled, turning a bashful red. "I suppose it is."

Ard grabbed a long branch and lowered it into the pit. "Grab on," he directed. "I'll pull you out."

"Thank you, sir!" the boy exclaimed. Reaching his small, dirty hands upward, he clutched the branch and started to walk his feet up the moistened walls of the pit. Ard pulled up on the branch and lifted him out with ease. "Oh!" he gasped with relief. "You're strong. Thank you muchly! I'm sure glad you came along." The boy reached into his pockets to pull out the coins he'd mentioned earlier.

Ard held up a hand. "Keep your metals, kid. You really ought to be more careful." The boy dusted himself off with an embarrassed look on his face. He couldn't have been more than thirteen years old. At his tallest, he barely reached Ard's chest. He was dirty as could be, but where was Ard's room to talk? He couldn't even remember the last time he had a wash. The poor boy looked like he hadn't eaten in days. Ard looked him up and down then curiously asked, "You've got a name I'm sure?"

The boy cleared his throat then straightened himself, ready to give a proper greeting. Chin up, he recited, "Kinn, sir. Kinn Sturly of Tailton." His voice was wheezy as if he'd cried too much as a baby. "It is a...erm...privilege and an honor to make your acquaintance." He put his hand out to Ard's.

"Arden Ford of Pipton," he said with a firm shake. "Tailton, yeah? That's just north of my village back east. What's a guppy like you doing this far from home?"

Kinn looked down and muttered, "Well...I don't got a home no more, sir."

Ard's stomach sank. "What happened?" he asked, fearing the answer.

"Ashen Horde," he said, still looking down. "They came out of nowhere in the middle of the night, they did. Most people they got right in their own beds, some they trapped inside with fire. I barely made it out, sir."

Ard's brain surged with memories he had been trying hard to suppress. It was just as he thought. What happened to his village was happening to others. The riders were taking over all the Clustertowns just as he feared. And with a stronghold like the Cluster at Kolbran's disposal, who knew what his next move would be? He had to keep moving. The more time he spent dawdling, the more lives Kolbran and his army destroyed.

"I'm sorry for your loss, kid," he said, without compassion. "If you head back down this road then head north you should arrive in Cottington. Find you some lodging. Good luck." He began walking out of the woods and back toward the road, eager to press on.

"Wait, sir!" Kinn protested. "Can I come with you, sir? Could I?"

"No. You'll slow me down."

"Honest, I won't!" he pressed further. "Please, sir, I won't be no trouble. No trouble at all!"

Ard turned to the boy and grimaced, "The only thing I know you're good for is getting caught in traps and I can't afford any more delays. You'd better get a move on. It's at least three and a half days to Cottington." He continued marching toward the road.

"I'll do whatever you want," Kinn pleaded. "I'll catch and make food, build your fires, anything!"

Ard rolled his eyes, exasperated. "Mossa Castille is a few more days away and I have to get there as soon as possible. The last thing I need is some danger prone tot tagging along behind me who's probably never even been out of his own village." He tried one last time to leave.

Kinn's footsteps crashed through the underbrush close behind him. "You're going to Mossa Castille? I've been there! I know the way, sir!"

Ard didn't believe him. "You've been to Mossa Castille?" he mocked, still walking.

"Yes, sir!" he squeaked. "Loads of times! My father owned a salmon fishery back home. We would deliver catches there all the time, sir. I could help you, really I could!"

Ard paused. Having someone who knew the ins and outs of Mossa Castille could be useful, especially if he were having to possibly steal the blackstone which he deviously hoped would be the case. Ignoring the thought that some human interaction might actually please him, he turned to Kinn who was stumbling through the woods to keep up. "Hm," Ard said, stroking his chin. "I could use a servant boy."

Kinn smiled then stood tall like a knight with his hands clapped firmly at his sides. "Arden Ford of Pipton," he recited, "I, Kinn Sturly of Tailton, do hereby pledge to you my service for saving my life. Should I fail to keep up with you or endanger your mission, you may relieve yourself of my service however and whenever you may see fit."

Ard mocked Kinn's formality, "And I, Arden Ford of Pipton, do hereby accept the terms of your faithful service, Kinn Sturly of Tailton. Now, hurry up. I haven't got time to waste."

"Right!" Kinn exclaimed. "Erm...sir?"

"I told you," Ard corrected. "I'm no sir."

"Right, sorry." His cheeks turned red. "I was just wondering..."

"Yes?"

"Well," he said, "you wouldn't happen to have anything to... erm...eat, would you? Before we go?"

Ard suddenly realized his own rations were running low. All he had left were two carrots and half of a potato after foolishly going through all of Emagora's fruit too quickly. Taking a good look at Kinn, he could see why he would be starving. He was scrawny as could be and covered from head to toe in mud and dirt. Ard was no better off, but at least he was grown. Kinn was just a kid. He'd been all alone probably for much longer than himself and he didn't have anything but the shirt on his back and ratty shoes on his feet. He didn't even have anything to keep warm with for when the cold night set in. Ard reached into his bag and relinquished one of the carrots and the rest of the potato. Kinn gobbled them up gratefully before they even got back to the road.

"So," Ard said, pretending not to enjoy finally socializing with someone, "you're from Tailton, are you? That's a fishing village. And you, the son of a fisherman. How good are you at fishing?"

Swallowing the last bit of potato, Kinn grinned, "How good are you at finding water?"

Ard laughed and felt warm inside for the first time since leaving Pipton. Here was this boy, no older than thirteen, days away from home after experiencing the most traumatizing event he'd probably ever faced, hungry, exhausted, and yet still he smiled. Still, he was strong. Ard would never let him know, but Kinn comforted him. If he was able to hold it together after losing his home and his family, then Ard certainly could. "Right then," he said, tossing his bag at him. "Make yourself useful."

Kinn struggled with the bag after almost dropping it but replied happily, "Yes sir, Mr. Ford!" Ard turned and smiled to himself. The journey to Mossa Castille may prove to be more interesting than he thought. Kinn situated himself with the bag then asked, "What you going to Mossa Castille for, sir?"

"Blackstone," he answered, walking ahead. "You'd double in usefulness if you knew where I could get some."

"Blackstone? I didn't even think such a gem was real."

"Nope," Ard said, "real as ever. Just very rare. So, you don't know then?"

"Sorry," Kinn apologized. "Haven't a clue, Mr. Ford."

"Just 'Ard' is fine."

Kinn fumbled over his words. "Sorry, sir...I mean, Arden. Ard." He swung his head, tossing his sandy blonde bangs out of his face as he struggled with the bag.

"So," Ard continued, trying to talk over the crunch of the gravel beneath their feet, "how long ago did you escape Tailton?"

"Nearly a week if I'm right," he replied plainly.

Ard couldn't believe how nonchalant Kinn was about it. "What have you been living off of, mate?"

"Berries mostly," Kinn answered. "Never learned to hunt. I can fish though! Boy, can I fish! Just haven't come across any live water yet."

Ard was shocked. "You've been surviving off of berries for a week?"

"*Nearly* a week," Kinn corrected. "There's loads of blackberry bushes along the road. Rather tart this time of year, but I'm not complaining."

Ard tried to imagine what it had been like for him these past few days. How was this kid not in worse shape? How was he even talking at all? How had he not been stricken emotionally? Where were his scars, his waking nightmares, where was his fear? A child's world, he concluded. As they continued traveling, he looked at Kinn with silent awe. Finally situated with the bag, Kinn asked innocently from behind, "What you need blackstone for, s—Ard?"

Ard knew he couldn't tell him the reason. It was too dangerous for anyone else to know and he remembered what Emagora told him. *If you actually are a Thorn and anyone finds out, you're as good as dead.* He didn't have the luxury of trusting anyone. "None of your concern," he grumbled. "As soon as we reach Mossa Castille, you're free to go."

"Yes, sir, Mr. Ard, sir" Kinn replied nicely. "As you wish!" Ard knew it wouldn't be the last time he "freed" Kinn from his contract, but he didn't let it bother him. For now he had a guide to Mossa Castille and someone carrying his bag. He could complain later.

"Do you miss home?" Kinn asked with soft enthusiasm.

Ard swallowed. "Every minute of every day."

"I miss my dad," Kinn reminisced. "I think about him all the time."

Ard replied with a single nod as if he didn't want to continue the conversation, but Kinn continued on obliviously. "Did the Ashen Riders get Pipton too?" he asked. "Was your family killed or did they make it out?"

Ard's nose burned and he was painfully made aware that the wound was still fresh. The only people he'd ever loved were murdered, the village he'd lived in his whole life was probably ash by now, and anyone he'd ever known was either dead or as far away from the Cluster as possible. How was he supposed to just get over that? How was he supposed to ignore everything around him that reminded him of Gran and Sore Swallow? Ard knew Kinn meant no harm in being so obnoxious. He was just a kid. Rather than explode with emotion, Ard turned to him. "No. My family didn't survive. And you really ought to be a bit less blunt when talking about these things."

Kinn's face softened with embarrassment. "Sorry, sir. I meant no harm, honest." Ard turned back around and continued walking, confident Kinn would continue on with more innocently unsavory comments. "Well, it's not much farther to Mossa Castille. Only about a day or—"

Ard stopped and put a hand up to silence him, but he kept on chatting and crunching the gravel loudly. He snatched him by the shoulder as he passed by cluelessly and hissed, "Wait!" He put his head into the air and closed his eyes.

After a sufficiently awkward pause, Kinn whispered, "What is it?" Ard ignored him, opened his eyes, and walked off of the road into the trees. Kinn struggled to follow, fumbling with the bag. "Ard," he repeated louder, "what is it?"

"Water. Come on, keep up."

Kinn struggled with the bag, trying desperately to move branches out of his path. "How do you know?"

"I...smelled it." The phrase sounded strange even to himself. Kinn sniffed the air, confused. "I don't smell anything."

"Nevermind," he dismissed. *The smell of water?* he thought to himself. He'd never imagined it before, but he could smell it all the same. It smelled like when rain first touches the ground mixed with an earthy perfume from the decay of soaked leaves on a bank. He didn't know how, but as he pulled aside one last branch, he discovered his senses were right. In the center of a clearing sat a shaded pond surrounded by tall reeds. A light fog rose from its edges, sifting through the dead leaves and fallen twigs littered on the water's surface. The deafening sound of crickets chirping and frogs hollering rung out around the clearing.

Kinn clambered out of the trees and a smile spread across his face. "Oh!" he gasped. "Yes! No more sucking dew off of leaves. What are you? Some kind of human bloodhound or something?" Ard laughed as Kinn dropped the bag to the ground and danced over to the water excitedly. He crouched down at the bank and cupped his hands into the pond, slurping it up gratefully.

All of a sudden, a voice rang out across the water, "Help! Can you help me?" Through the mist, Kinn was able to make out the hazy figure of a boy stranded on a tiny island in the center of the pond. He was waving his arms wildly trying to grab attention. "Hello, there!" the boy called. "I need help!" Kinn stood slowly and backed away from the water, careful not to take his eyes off of the island. "Help!" the boy repeated identically. "Can you help me? Hello, there! I need help!" As Kinn continued backing away, he bumped into Ard who was making his way toward the bank.

"What's wrong with you?" Ard said with a light push.

"Ard," he whispered. His face was white with fear but Ard ignored it.

"What?" he asked, putting his arms outward. "Are you just going to leave him? What if I had just left you in that trap pit back there?" He walked closer to the pond.

"Sir, wait! Don't!" As Ard turned to retort, his foot sunk into the ground underneath the murky water. The clatter of crickets and frogs silenced to an eerie halt and a loud splash came from the center of the pond. He whipped around, eyes wide. The boy on the island was gone.

10

A Dangerous Deal

Ard knew he had a knack for getting into trouble, but something seemed different this time. He felt in danger. He frantically scanned the pond, trying to see where the boy went. Seconds passed and the ripples from the splash were slowly lapping against the bank. He tried to pull his foot out but it wouldn't budge. It didn't feel like a normal foot-in-the-mud situation. He had a sinking feeling that something was holding him there. Making sure not to put his other foot near the water, he desperately tried to pull backward out of the muck but the hold refused to give. He was stuck.

Kinn rushed to the bank. "Come on!" he shouted. "Pull your foot out!"

"I'm trying!" Ard yelled back frantically. "It's stuck tight! Get a stick or something! Maybe we can pry it out." Kinn nodded then dashed off into the trees.

Ard reached down and tried wiggling his foot out, but all it did was hurt his ankle. Suddenly, a voice grated across the water like a knife against a whetstone. *"Frozen with fear or stuck, my dear? You made a mistake by coming here,"* the voice hissed. Ard looked up from his foot and witnessed the most bone-chilling sight he'd ever seen.

Near the island where the boy vanished, floating weightlessly in the water, were two glowing yellow eyes staring straight at him. Horrified, he watched as the figure rose up slowly above the water revealing the eyes to be attached to something far more sinister. He had heard stories of kelpies before—shapeshifting spirits with a hunger for human flesh—but he'd always secretly hoped they were just that. Stories. Stories to keep children from playing near the water's edge or trusting strangers, but as the creature swam closer, he knew exactly what he was looking at— and it was no fairy tale.

Its head was shaped like a horse's that hadn't eaten in months and its black, leathery skin stretched across spindly bones. Its spine stuck out from its back, stretching its hide so tightly in places that pieces of white bone had torn through the skin. It had pointed, horse-like ears that sat above its head and fell to either side like broken pond reeds. Its slimy, algae-ridden mane swayed side to side in the water with each stroke of its crocodilian tail whose tip was splayed with long strands of white horsehair. Spiny, fish-like fins sprouted from its hips and sides, coated in a clotted slime. Paddling with sinewy, webbed front legs, the creature inched closer and closer with each passing second, never breaking its hungry gaze.

Ard, now practically paralyzed, felt a hand grab his shoulder. Kinn had returned with a large stick. "Here! Try this!" he said hurriedly. Snatching it out of his hands, Ard thrust it down into the mud near his foot, pushing the stick in different directions to try and loosen the hold. Nothing. Not even a wiggle. Trying to pull the branch out again, it snapped into pieces in his hand. "It's not working!" he yelled helplessly.

The voice of the kelpie hissed again as it inched closer and closer through the murky water, slicing through the mist and leaves. *First one morsel, now sit two. There's room in my pond for both of you.* The voice was tinged with wheezy clicking sounds followed by raspy, separated whinnies that echoed around the pond with an otherworldly resonance. At this distance, Ard could see the terrible maw of the creature which was blotched with stains of blood. Muddy red saliva clung to its pointed, jutted teeth as it spoke again, *"I wonder, I wonder, how does it taste? Chewing too fast might be a waste."*

Kinn pointed at Ard's foot, jumping up and down. "Your laces!" he yelled. "Your laces! Untie your laces, Ard!"

With croaking clicks and huffs, the kelpie mimicked Kinn's voice identically, *"'Your laces! Your laces!' Nowhere to go. If you struggle, I'll eat you slow."* The beast licked its yellowing teeth hungrily with its long, wicked tongue.

Ard shot his hands into the water, fiddling with his bootstraps. He was terrified beyond belief, more frightened than he'd ever been in his life. He wanted to scream, but he couldn't get the sound out of his lungs. The kelpie was only a few feet away now. Pretty soon it would be dragging him down into the depths to drown, then chewing on his bones like a rabid dog. Thankfully he'd never been one to tie his boots too tightly. Once the bootstraps were loose enough, he wrenched his foot out and scrambled out of the water onto the bank just as the kelpie was preparing to lunge at him. The creature reared its menacing head, neighing and spitting in anger. All it had to do was cross the bank and take him, but it just threw itself about furiously.

"What's happening?" Ard choked out.

"Kelpies can't leave their ponds!" Kinn exclaimed. "Get away from the bank, sir!"

Letting out a guttural shriek, the kelpie thrashed and spun violently while Kinn helped Ard to his feet. Shaking, he looked at Kinn with immense relief. "Thanks, Kinn," he said, breathing heavily.

Kinn nodded with a scared smile. "Let's get out of here," he said, tugging at his sleeve. "I don't like being this close to it." They looked back at the kelpie who was floating eye level in the water now. The shape of its gaunt body sat like a specter beneath the shallows near the bank and its gleaming yellow eyes glared at them hatefully. Ard nodded, then grabbed his bag and set out for the road.

Just as they were about to head back through the trees, the kelpie's voice screamed with ear-splitting urgency, *"Come back! Come baaaack! My bones are weak. I know what it is that which you seeeeeek!"*

Ard turned around and saw the creature wading in the spot where his foot was stuck moments ago. It was dangerously close to the water's edge, but it was sure not to cross it. The creature's yellow eyes had gone from menacing to desperate and its long tail flicked from side to side, sending rippling waves through the reeds, beckoning them to stay. "What did you say?" Ard whispered back, dropping the bag to the ground.

"Ard!" Kinn warned. "No, don't listen to it! It's a trick!"

The kelpie nickered on. *"Blackstone, blackstone, coveted jewel. Come close to the water, it's nice and cool."* It drew slow breaths, salivating as it waited on his response.

Ard looked at Kinn, shocked that the kelpie knew what he was searching for. Nervously and sure not to get too close, he took a step toward the creature. "How did you know I was searching for blackstone?" he asked, raising an eyebrow.

"Ard, don't!"

"Shh!" he commanded. Turning back to the kelpie who now swayed side to side with anticipation, he asked another question, "You know where I can find some. Don't you, creature?"

The kelpie rolled its lips back over its teeth into a gnarly grin. *"Deal, deal,"* it hissed, *"I'll make thee a deal. I'll take one lick to be my meal."*

Fast to respond, he repeated, "You tell me where I can find blackstone and you can take one lick, yes?"

The kelpie nodded hungrily, still swaying from side to side. Its tail rose from the water, letting the algae that coated its body splash back into the pond like the drumming fingers of someone growing impatient. Ard looked back at Kinn who was shaking his head with a terrified look stained on his face. "Don't!" he whispered harshly. "One lick and he'll peel your skin from the bone!" Ard ignored him and turned back to the creature.

"*Yes, yessss,*" the creature agreed. "*A deal's a deal, you'll find the gem in Mossa Castille.*"

Ard took a few more steps closer to the kelpie. "You'll have to do better than that," he demanded. With the kelpie unable to harm him, his fear of it had slightly dissipated. He was planning to beat the beast at its own game.

"*You ask too much,*" it growled. "*Come just a bit closer. Else our deal will quickly be over.*"

Ard took more cautious steps toward the bank. He could see the kelpie now with nightmarish detail. Its eyes were sunken into their sockets and the muscles around its jaw pulsed with anticipation. Its cheeks ruffled like gills with every breath it took, and its dark hide dripped with a muddy green slime. With its piercing glare still unbroken, the kelpie chomped its teeth repeatedly against each other making a ghastly clacking sound. Careful to keep his composure, he huffed, "Well? Let's have it."

The kelpie was growing impatient. It groaned, "*The Hound Queen's contest. The winner shall see some shining blackstone for his to be.*"

Ard paused. He didn't know how he could win one of Leonora's contests, but it was as good of a lead as he was getting from the creature. He'd figure out the contest later, but now he knew his journey to Mossa Castille was the right decision. "Very well, kelpie," he relented. "A deal's a deal. Come take your lick." The creature grinned with excitement and moved forward then stopped abruptly when it reached the water's edge. It stretched its neck as far as it could across the bank, but Ard was perfectly out of reach. It stretched again, but he couldn't be touched. Its grotesque smile shifted into an anguished snarl as it tried desperately to reach him, unable to leave its watery prison. "Come on," Ard egged triumphantly. "*Take* your lick. That was the deal, wasn't it? You didn't say I had to deliver it to you. Or did you? Maybe I'm not remembering correctly."

Straining hopelessly, the creature thrashed over its misuse of words. *"CURSE YOU!"* it roared, clawing at the bank. *"Trickster! You won't get away!"*

Ard leaned forward and stared right into the creature's anguished neon eyes and finished its rhyme coldly, "But from this pond, you'll never stray." The creature released a horrid scream that turned Ard and Kinn's blood to frost. Whipping around defeatedly, it lashed its tail splashing water all over the bank, then dove back beneath the murky surface. As the ripples settled, the crickets and frogs resumed their deafening chorus.

Kinn looked at Ard, mouth still gaping. "You're a right gambler, you are, sir!" he cheered. "I never thought I'd see a kelpie in my life, much less witness a man outsmart one. You could've been easy meat!"

Ard sighed with relief, still shaking from the encounter with the monster. "Well if it weren't for you, I probably would've been," he admitted. "I'm sorry I didn't listen to you, Kinn."

"S'all right," Kinn said, shrugging. "Rarely anyone believes a kid small like me. Besides, I imagine plenty of folks believe that kelpies aren't real. Boy, were they wrong!"

Ard laughed lightly, "I was one of those 'folks' once upon a time. Guess I'm a believer now."

Kinn dusted off Ard's coat for him as he passed, flicking the dirt and grass blades to the ground. "You think there are more fairy tale creatures out here, s—Ard?"

"Well," Ard observed, "I can't imagine we can call them 'fairy tale creatures' anymore. That kelpie seemed pretty real to me don't you think?"

"Realer than I'd hoped," Kinn shuddered. Pointing down at Ard's feet, he continued, "Sir! I mean, Ard. Your boot!"

Picking up his bag from where he'd dropped it, Ard replied, "Would you like to go and ask the kelpie to give it back? Or shall I?"

Kinn looked back at the misty pond, which sat dark and looming in the shaded clearing. Turning on his heels he sped back to the road calling, "We'll get you a new pair in Mossa Castille, we will."

11

The Floral City

Later that day, when Ard finally gave into Kinn's nagging about his bare foot catching frostbite and falling off, the two made camp out of sight of the road for the evening. Earlier that afternoon, Ard found a small creek free of any menacing beasts or other unexpected dangers. There, Kinn used his knife to sharpen a small branch into a spear and managed to catch a decent haul of seven small bream. They cooked the fish on a less than spectacularly constructed spit made of twigs over a small fire that Ard built. As the two munched on the crispy filets and spat out the stray scales and tiny bones, they held conversation, a totally unavoidable circumstance while traveling with a curious thirteen-year-old.

"It's a lovely city, Mossa Castille. Really it is. There's nothing like it, truly. There're gardens and plants everywhere you look. There're all sorts of things to buy and so many things to see. There's fancy carriages, fancy food, and fancy taverns that my dad never let me go into. Oh! And just wait until you see Silber Bay! It's just enormous. My dad says, well used to say, that it's chock-full of nasty pirates. Even the beaches are said to be littered with gold and buried treasure. I'd love to find some treasure one day, wouldn't you?"

"You ever seen Queen Leonora?"

"Well, I've never been to Mossa Castille, so...no," Ard said flatly.

"Oh," Kinn repeated. "That makes sense. Well, I hear she's got a terrible temper. But she's awfully pretty! I mean there's really no one like her, just gorgeous. And she's got this horrible, nasty dog that follows her around. Big, beastly thing. It's huge! Might as well be a horse. Wherever she goes, there it is. Just awful looking. It's got this gigantic head, and sharp, sharp teeth." Kinn bared his teeth and formed his fingers into fangs.

Ard nodded again and said, "I suppose that's why they call her the Hound Queen."

He raised his eyebrows. "You ought not say that in Mossa Castille," he scolded. "She does *not* like that name. That's the name people who don't like her use. You'd probably be executed on the spot if you said something like that where someone could hear you."

"Say something like what?" Ard joked. "Like *Hound Queen*?"

Kinn gasped.

"Oh," he joked on. "Should I not say *Hound Queen*?"

Kinn clapped his hands over his mouth stifling a smile.

"Is *Hound Queen* a bad word?" he feigned.

"Stop saying *Hound Queen*!" Kinn commanded with a nervous giggle.

Ard raised his voice, "What's wrong with *Hound Queen*?"

Kinn, chuckling, yelled louder, "Because *Hound Queen* is not a nice thing to say!"

Ard took another bite of his fish and smiled. "You can talk about anything you want out here, Kinn. No one's going to arrest you and chop off your head for talking about something."

Kinn swallowed his bite of fish. "Really?"

Ard nodded. "Say what you want. I won't arrest you."

Kinn looked down and his smile melted. "Can I...talk about my dad?"

Ard looked at him as he slumped over in his spot by the fire. Kinn *was* hurting. He knew he couldn't have been that strong. The poor boy probably hadn't had a chance to confide in another human since it all happened. At least Ard had Emagora afterward. Kinn presumably had no one. Ard may have very well been the first face he'd seen since escaping Tailton. He put a hand on his shoulder and answered, "Sure, mate."

Kinn looked into the fire as golden teardrops formed in his eyes. "He was my best friend."

"What was he like?"

"He was big," he said, choking back tears. "Bigger than me and you put together, he was. Arms like tree branches and shoulders like rocks. He could pick me up and toss me right in the air. No problem."

"He was a fisherman, yeah?"

"The best in Tailton," he boasted. "Any salmon you've ever eaten probably was caught by my dad. We lived in a big shack right on the Witchfoot. Each season Dad would stretch nets across a gap in the river and pull in hundreds of salmon a day. We'd filet them, salt them, package them, and deliver them. We did it all."

"Must be in the blood," Ard said, holding up his fish. "You really know how to catch."

Kinn looked up from the fire. His tears had dried and he was smiling again. "I hope I'm as good as he was one day."

"I'd say you're well on your way," Ard said, taking another bite.

"What about your dad?"

By now, Ard was used to him being so candid and didn't get so easily offended at his questions. "I never knew him," he answered.

"Well," Kinn said, "what would you think he was like?"

"Probably scum," he scoffed. "I've never really thought about it. Never wanted to. I don't even want to know his name to be honest. The only thing I know is that my grandmother's son dropped me off on her doorstep and never came back. All of Pipton pitied my Gran for having to bring up her unwanted grandson. He shamed her. So wherever he is now makes no difference to me. He could be drunk in a far off pub for all I care."

"That's rough," Kinn said. "And your mom?"

"Don't know," he admitted. "Gran never knew her."

"Well, what about her? Your grandmother. Was she nice to you?"

"She was the best."

"What did she do?" Kinn asked, tossing his stick of fish bones to the ground.

"She ran an inn," he said. "The only inn Pipton ever knew. Sore Swallow Inn. My great-great-grandfather built it along with most of Pipton. I was the stableboy there ever since I was tall enough to reach the tie posts."

"Seems like hard work," Kinn smirked

"Not really. It was our work. It's what we did, just like you and your dad."

Kinn nodded then looked down sadly. "Well, I'm sorry about your grandmother, Ard."

"And I'm sorry about your dad."

Kinn smiled then stuck another bream filet on his stick. "What do you think they were doing here anyway?" he asked.

"Who? The Ashen Horde? No idea. There were always rumors of it happening but no one ever believed them. The Burnt King rising up again and all."

"Where did the Ashen Horde even come from? Why are they so ornery?"

"Did your father never tell you that one? That'd surprise me," Ard joked.

Kinn shook his head. He situated himself comfortably and began blowing on his cooked fish to cool it off. Ard could tell he was eager to hear more.

"Well," he began, "I suppose I have time for a quick bedtime story. I don't know the whole bit, but Gran used to tell it to me all of the time. Before you and I were born, while the Settled Lands were still young, King Kolbran was named ruler of the eastern kingdom of Ashar."

"I've heard of Ashar!" Kinn jumped. "There's no grass there! Or snow. Just hills of sand as far as the eye can see."

"Yes," Ard continued. "But it wasn't always that way. You ever heard of the Cleft?"

"No, sir," Kinn answered.

"Long ago, a terrible earthquake happened across the western border of Ashar that formed the Cleft, a giant cliff impossible to cross or climb that cracked its way miles across the land. Since that day, the Sunlands were never the same. Its rivers ran dry and rains barely fell turning the once fruitful land into a barren desert. Trade became impossible because no one dared to venture across the Sunlands. And with the city of Ashar being the last oasis left, people flooded its gates. That's when things got difficult for Kolbran. His subjects were starving, his city overpopulated. These tough years under the scorching sun turned him resentful. He had the largest of the Settled Lands as his own but had nothing to show for it. Playing on the anger and frustrations of his people, he formed the Ashen Horde and waged war on the other kingdoms."

"But they beat him right?"

"Well, are you under the rule of a vicious tyrant?" Ard asked him.

He shook his head bashfully.

"No, you're not," he laughed. "Kolbran and his horde were beaten back into the Sunlands and never seen again, until now anyway. During one of the battles, Kolbran was badly burned by fire. That's why they call him the Burnt King. They say his skin melted into his armor and now he's part metal."

"That must have hurt terribly," Kinn said through a bite of fish.

Ard laughed, "I can't imagine it feeling good."

"So you think he's come back?" he asked. "To take over the Settled Lands."

"I do," Ard said. "They want what we have, Kinn. Just as you said, nothing grows there. Kolbran and his men will kill anyone in their path to take the Lushlands. They murdered a boy younger than you back in Pipton."

His eyes widened and he stopped chewing. "How could they be so evil? My dad always said that all people were good deep down no matter how bad they were on the outside."

"People are good, Kinn, but the world isn't. We're not born with evil in our hearts, we soak it up as we grow. That's what Gran taught me. People like you and I need to do all that we can to be good. 'Farm the kindly,' Gran always told me. Fight the good fights. It's the only thing we can do."

Kinn nodded understandingly. A brief silence sat between them as they stared into the crackling fire. Tiny sparks flickered upward into the chilly night air, dancing in and out of the low-hanging branches. After it got too quiet, Kinn perked up the courage and asked, "Ard? Can I ask you something?"

"You just did," he replied sarcastically, leaning back on his bag.

Ignoring him, he pressed, "What do you need blackstone so bad for?"

Ard pursed his lips, weighing whether or not he should tell Kinn his reasons for being in Mossa Castille. Trusting only himself, he said, "Maybe I'll tell you another time. It's late. You should get some rest."

"But," Kinn protested, "I'm not even tired!"

"Well," Ard groaned, stretching his arms widely, "I am. Goodnight, Kinn."

"Goodnight," Kinn pouted. Ard, hearing his shuffling, took off his coat and tossed it to him. Before Kinn could say a word, he rolled over to get some sleep. Burying his face into the garment, he whispered under the crackling of the fire, "Thank you, sir."

Ard's senses allowed him to overhear. Even though being

called "sir" annoyed him, Kinn's small, grateful whisper drew a slow smile out of him. He always enjoyed being an only child. No one to look after but himself, no having to share what was his, all the attention on him. Despite all those things, he thought briefly about what it would have been like if he grew up with a sibling. If he ever had, he would have hoped it to feel like Kinn whispering a thank you under his breath.

⤜❧⤏

That night, Ard dreamed he was back in Pipton, right at the spot in the field between Sore Swallow and the Bardenwood. Right where he saw her for the first time.

"Emagora!" he called out.

The witch's tiny figure pranced from out of the woods cheerfully and embraced him around the neck. Laughing, she said in her silky voice, "Hello, Arden Ford of Pipton."

He crossed his arms. "You entered my dream again," he said, playing offended.

"Now wait just a moment, stableboy," she said, placing her hands on her tiny hips. "How do you know you aren't just dreaming this on your own?"

"Because I can feel the difference," he retorted. "You and your witchy tricks can't fool me."

"I'm so glad!" she chuckled. "How's the journey going? Are you safe?"

"For now," he said. "I stumbled upon a kelpie this morning that nearly tore the flesh from my bones, but other than that—"

Emagora interrupted excitedly, "A kelpie? How incredible! What did it look like?"

"Really nice actually," he said with restrained sarcasm. "Yeah, he really looked like he was doing well for himself. Lost a bit of weight, new tunic, freshly shined boots, the whole bit. Great smile too."

She giggled again. "Sorry, Ard. It's just that they're so rare! Even I've never seen one. Magical creatures have grown even more afraid of humans since the Child King has gone. Oh, how I miss the little faerie darlings. Even goblins made good company when the occasion called for it. You hardly ever see any of us around and the humans who do are locked away for being lunatics. I doubt you'll ever see a kelpie again."

"Well I should hope so," he laughed. "I doubt even the Lords Below would enjoy afternoon tea with one."

"I wouldn't mind it," she said coyly. "I find rare, magical creatures to be interesting conversationalists."

"Of course you would," he laughed. "It wasn't a totally fruitless situation though. According to the kelpie, Queen Leonora is holding a contest and the winner gets a bit of blackstone as a prize."

"Hm," she pondered. "I wouldn't be too sure about that. Kelpies aren't known to be very trustworthy spirits."

"Well," he explained, "it said the contest is in Mossa Castille. I was heading there anyway. So if it was lying, I'll just find another way to get some."

Emagora shrugged. "Just be careful, Ard," she warned. "Kelpies aren't the only thing you should be worried about. Don't trust a single soul. You never know what they could be planning. And if you really are a Thorn, you're one of the most wanted creatures in the Settled Lands. So, be cautious."

Ard nodded. "I will."

Brushing her hair behind her ears, she said, "Well, I should be going. My spell only works for a short time. I just wanted to make sure you were alright."

"I appreciate it," he thanked her. "I wish you were here to keep me company."

"Oh," she said fanning her hand, "I wouldn't do well on the road. You can't watch things grow when you're moving all the time, now can you?"

"I suppose not," he said. "Well, feel free to enter my dreams anytime."

Emagora laughed then leaped back through the trees into

the Bardenwood. He went to chase after her, but the piercing light of the sun shining through the leaves tore him from the dream.

Ard awoke and blinked his eyes to the sharp morning sun. Its rays felt warm against his chilled skin—it was the first time he remembered the sun shining since his birthday. He closed his eyes gratefully and took a deep breath. The sun made him think of Gran. He imagined her soft, wrinkly hands brushing his hair out of his face like she would do some mornings. The moment began to turn sad, so he pushed the thoughts from his mind. Rolling over, he stretched his legs with a long squeeze. Kinn was still fast asleep with his mouth hanging wide open. The fire had smoldered out in the night and only a small line of gray smoke remained, slithering into the air. He stood up, stretching his back with an audible grunt. His body was still getting used to sleeping on the ground. With no cushions or bedding, he was beginning to realize how unappreciative he was of his bed. He picked up his bag and walked over to Kinn. Kicking him in the shoulder, he croaked in a crackled morning voice, "Kinn. Time to move."

Kinn grumbled and stretched his arms toward the sky, eyes still shut. "Yes, sir. Right away, Mr. Ford," he groaned. Rolling back over, he started snoozing again.

Ard rolled his eyes, kicking him once more. "Ahem," he coughed. "Kinn."

He shot up. "Sorry, sir!" he said, dusting his pants off. His sandy blonde hair was sticking up all over the place. "Ready when you are, sir."

Ard stomped out the embers, letting the smoke filter into the sky. The two walked out of the thin woods and back out onto the road. After a few steps, Ard's vision strangely started to blur. He squinted and blinked voraciously trying hard to focus. It was happening again. His senses were going haywire.

He was able to smell the weeds growing through the gravel in the road. The pungent smell stained his nose and swept through his face and head, dizzying him. The sound of birds chirping rung deafeningly in his ears as he twitched and coughed uncontrollably. Something was wrong.

Kinn looked at him with alarm. "Ard? What's wrong?" He placed a hand on his back. Ard's body recoiled spastically from his touch and he toppled to the ground, scattering dust and gravel into his face. The taste of dirt exploded in his mouth, seeping into his cheeks and gums. The taste fell all the way down his throat and into his stomach. Combined with the wild spinning of the world around him, the taste nauseated him. He could hear Kinn yelling his name but his frail, squeaky voice was drowned out by the sounds of the birds and the footsteps of insects in the trees. His eyes blurred, making it difficult to see. Just like in Pipton and the Bardenwood, Ard slipped back into the dark of unconsciousness.

Ard hated the disorientation he felt after waking up from a fit. As he came to, his whole body started to shake violently. *No*, he thought. *Not again.* His nausea kicked back in as he imagined his senses overloading for a fourth time. As his body shook from side to side, he realized it wasn't his senses. He was moving. His eyes blinked open and he found himself staring at the gravel road watching the pebbles pass by. He was lying on his stomach on the back of a cart. He could hear the clopping of hooves on the road ahead of him. Rubbing his temples, he pushed himself up. All around him on the back of the cart sat large brown barrels. There was an older man driving the cart and he could see the small sandy-haired head of Kinn sitting right next to him, chatting his ear off. He groaned lightly and Kinn whipped around.

"Ard, sir!" he smiled. "You're awake!" He clambered over the barrels and squatted next to him, rubbing his back.

"How long was I out?"

"Just a day and night," he replied. "How are you feeling?"

"Splendid," Ard grunted, blinking from the sun. "Where are we?"

"Right outside of Mossa Castille!" Kinn said, standing back up. "Take a look for yourself!"

Ard stood up next to him and looked to the road ahead. Unable to believe his eyes, he looked for the first time upon the shining capital of his kingdom, a place he'd only ever imagined in stories. Glistening in the late afternoon sun, the legendary Floral City stood statuesque in all its glory. The city levels started on the shore of Silber Bay then climbed up a large, greened cliff where Queen Leonora's dazzling castle towered above the thundering cobalt waves. Ard could smell the salt in the air from the bay. It was just as he imagined. Clean and crisp with a subtle hint of spice from the sand on the shore.

"Welcome to Mossa Castille, lads," announced the old cart driver.

"Ard, this is Mr. Eldin," Kinn introduced cordially. "He's a potato farmer. He came upon us a few minutes after you fainted. He let us tag along with him to the Floral City."

Ard looked at Mr. Eldin and nodded his head, "Thank you for the lift, sir." Stretching one arm upward, he grabbed his bag and gave Kinn a look. "We can make it from here on foot."

The potato farmer waved his hand welcomingly. "No problem, young sir, no problem at all. Glad to see you're feeling better. Master Kinn tells me you're in search of some blackstone, eh?" Ard shot Kinn a glare to which he looked away from guiltily. Mr. Eldin continued, "Well, I doubt you'd win, but Queen Leonora is hosting a contest tomorrow in the Grandpit. It's normally some type of race or brawl. The city's been buzzing about it for weeks now. Sure to be one incredible showdown. The winner takes home a chest of blackstone coins probably from the queen's very own vault. Worth a king's ransom I'd wager."

The kelpie was right. Ard had to get into this contest. For

now, though, he was thinking of all the ways to make Kinn pay for blabbing. "Appreciate the tip," he said flatly, hopping down onto the gravel road. "Kinn, come on."

Kinn gave Mr. Eldin's hand a firm shake as the cart slowed to a stop. "Thank you for your service, Sir Eldin of Mossa Castille. We won't forget it."

The potato farmer smiled with a polite laugh. "I'm no sir, lad," he corrected. "Farewell, and may the Lords Above grant fortune to you both!" He tipped his hat and Kinn hopped down onto the gravel. The noise of the cart rumbled away as Ard glared at him menacingly. "I'm sorry, Ard," he said. "I thought maybe he could help."

"Kinn," he scolded, "I'm trusting you. From now on, my business in Mossa Castille is my business. In fact, you won't have to worry about it for much longer anyway. Once we reach the city, you can point me in the direction of a cobbler so I can get a new pair of boots and then you can be on your way."

Kinn protested, "Actually, I was thinking maybe I could stick with you for a while. I promise I won't be a blabbermouth no more. I'll show you I'm worth having by your side." Rolling his eyes, Ard marched toward the city, limping over rocks with his sore, bare foot. Kinn grabbed the bag out of his hands and threw it over his shoulder. Smiling, he said, "I'll take that as a yes."

"The contest isn't until tomorrow, my queen. More competitors will sign up then. Most knights and warriors wait until the last moment to announce their participation. It ensures the element of surprise."

Queen Leonora paced in front of her throne impatiently. As her anticipation for the contest grew, so did her anger. Sir Ellys stood before his queen trying to calm her. "Twelve?" she sighed. "Twelve champions? Is that the best we could do? I've planned this contest for months. I've spread word as far as Flitsten Isle and Pyce. Now here, on the eve of my great spectacle, stand a mere twelve contestants?"

"As I've said, Your Majesty," Ellys repeated, "most contestants will make a grand scene entering tomorrow before the contest. You know this. You'll have plenty of competitors."

Leonora passed in front of her throne for the hundredth time running her fingers through the fur of her hound whose head hung over the dais sleepily. "Twelve," she scoffed. "Thirty. A hundred. It matters not. How many of them do you suppose will be Thorns, Randyn?"

Sir Ellys tightened his expression. "I am unsure, Your Grace," he relented.

"Exactly," she said, holding her hands out exasperatedly. "I have no way of knowing if my plan will work. As you've said, a Thorn would certainly never make a spectacle of themselves. How many more of them could there possibly be? And even so, how many of them know of the curse?"

"Your plan will work, my queen," Ellys said firmly. "With blackstone as the prize, any Thorn that knows of the curse is sure to be present. They won't be able to resist the temptation."

Leonora rolled her eyes as she grew more and more irritated. "How can I be sure they'll enter?" she retorted "This contest comes at a grand price, you well know."

"A price that will be repaid in full when your plan succeeds. The Thorns will enter, Your Grace," Ellys said. "And if not, I'll have guards positioned at every entrance. We'll make certain that anything suspicious is reported directly to you." Leonora slumped down into her throne and let her forehead rest on her thumb and forefinger. The hound perked up, sensing her aggravation as Sir Ellys stepped forward onto the dais. "I'll assemble the guards and inform them of their positions," he said. "Is there anything else you require of me, Your Majesty?"

Unchanged in her irritated position, Leonora waved her hand. "No, Randyn. Thank you," she said flatly. "You are free to leave."

With a polite bow and throw of his cloak, Sir Ellys strode out of the throne room.

Mossa Castille was more spectacular than Ard could have ever imagined. The gravel road soon turned to polished cobblestone. The walls of people's homes were painted with dazzling murals rich with history and climbing vines clung to every brick and tile. Ard and Kinn passed by what seemed to be infinite markets whose display tables were littered with intricate, colorful jewelry, food, clothing, anything one could possibly imagine. Ard thought to himself, *Who would be stupid enough to have jewelry displayed right out here in the open?* But, as he looked around, he could see that theft and robbery weren't a problem here in the Floral City. All the citizens were adorned in incredibly expensive clothing. Most of them looked like they were accustomed to a level of opulence that simply did not exist in the Cluster. No one had the need to pilfer or steal because they could afford whatever they wanted. Ard gawked at them as they passed. Their wardrobe alone was enough to estrange him.

Everyone seemed too busy in this city. People passed by without taking any notice of him or Kinn at all, yelling at each other, chatting with merchants, laughing wildly from pub windows. He began to think of all the opportunities for pranks the city presented. Victims everywhere he looked, ripe for the merrymaking. Kinn seemed right at home as he strolled through the city. Perhaps he had truly been here before. He seemed to know where he was going. Ard secretly wished he knew his way around a large city. As he let him lead the way to the square to find him a pair of boots, the two melted into the crowd like regular Castillians.

"There it is!" Kinn exclaimed. "Best shoes in the kingdom. Or so says the sign." Kinn pointed to a large shop that read *Floral City Footwear - 'Best shoes in the kingdom'.* Ard felt a lump in his throat when he saw the cobbler in the market square. It made him think of Brinkley Feet back in Pipton. Why did he never get those new boots made? Mr. Brinkley would have given them to him no questions asked. Ard began to wonder about fate. He began to wonder if he had just gone to get the new boots, maybe the Ashen Horde would have never ransacked Pipton. Maybe Mr. Brinkley would still be alive. Maybe Gran would still be alive. He forced the memories back into the depths of his mind, attempting to focus on why he was in Mossa Castille in the first place. He would avenge Mr. Brinkley. He would avenge Gran and Sore Swallow. For now, however, he needed to buy boots.

"Wait," he said to Kinn who was happily skipping to the shop. "I have nothing. I can't buy any boots without metals."

"Did the kelpie take your boot *and* twist your knickers?" Kinn joked. "Hold on a moment, will ya?" Without another word, he ran over to the shop and walked right in before Ard could stop him. After a few minutes and after most of Ard's fingernails were worn to the nub, he emerged with two brand new boots dangling from his arm followed by a smiling man in a leather apron. Ard watched as the man shook Kinn's tiny hand while both of them laughed. He waved goodbye and jogged back over to Ard, presenting him with the boots. They were perfectly sized and were the finest pair of boots he had ever seen.

"No way you paid for these," he said skeptically. "What did you do, Kinn?"

"Well," he boasted, "you remember Mr. Eldin, yeah? The potato farmer? Well, I told him about your boot problem and he turns out to be a very good friend of Mr. Feltry, the owner of Floral City Footwear, who, by the way, owed Mr. Eldin a favor which is now paid off in full. With interest." Kinn put his arms out and smiled, beckoning for his due credit.

"Alright," Ard relented. "Props to you then. Thanks, Kinn."

Kinn straightened his shirt sleeves proudly. "Am I worthy of staying in your company now, Sir Arden Ford of Pipton?" he asked coyly.

Ard laughed then narrowed his eyes saying, "Find me a new shirt and a safe place to stay and we'll see."

12

The Grandpit Champion

Kinn's usefulness in Mossa Castille had so far proven its worth; however, their stay in the Floral City had resorted to secretly climbing into the dusty attic of a haberdashery. It was a bit cramped and the boys had to stay quiet most of the time, but it was dry, safe, and free. Ard and Kinn were even able to find new clothes in a box marked *Undesirables* that had found their way into the attic for storage. Ard couldn't get past the number of undesirables that the people of Mossa Castille apparently didn't want. Anyone in Pipton would've gladly worn every garment in this box. He found himself a decent long-sleeved tunic, some dark pants that were so long he had to tuck them into his boots, and a nice gray jerkin to keep warm. Kinn fancied an oversized brown duster that dragged behind him as he walked and a red undershirt to match his boots which were still crusted with dried mud. The clothes weren't much, but the two were happy to be in something fresher than the clothes they'd been wearing for the past week.

The next day, after sleeping soundly in a pile of coats, Ard and Kinn were up early to find food. The streets were already being filled with the scents of fresh-baked pastries, meats, and other flavorful dishes. Without any money, Ard was forced to do a bit of pickpocketing, something he swore he'd never do when he was in Pipton, at least not thoroughly. He found pickpocketing to be a fun sport and a hilarious way to get people to pay more attention, but he always returned what he pilfered. He was a lot of things back in Pipton, but never a thief.

He picked a fitting target, a man who spit on an old woman begging for money. Creeping up behind him while Kinn asked for directions as a distraction, Ard reached into the man's purse and dug out a few metals. He made sure to take only what he and Kinn needed, but it seemed unfitting that some of the metals should not see their way into the hands of the beggar woman. Ard dropped a few pieces into her cup and put a finger to his lips, pointing at the man who shamed her. The woman began laughing as they disappeared back into the crowd before anyone noticed. After finally deciding on one of the dozens of kitchens throughout the city, the boys were able to enjoy a decent breakfast of apple pastries and hot sausages with a few metals left to spare.

Queen Leonora's contest was being held at noon in her immense arena known as the Grandpit. Castillians, as well as citizens from other kingdoms, traveled from far and wide to witness her opulent events. People in carriages and on foot were excitedly clambering to arrive and get the best seats. The boys were nearly trampled as they made their way slowly through the market and to the arena for Ard to enter. He had barely slept the night before. He had absolutely no idea how he was going to win this contest, especially considering he'd never been in a fight in his life. He'd narrowly escaped many, but other than fighting off the riders in Pipton, hand-to-hand combat was something completely unknown to him. Racing he may be good at so long as it was a foot race. He had no idea how to operate any type of chariot. The only thing he could do with a chariot was clean up after the horses. The contestants entering were sure to outmatch him in size and experience. He would have to rely on his quick-thinking to win and take home the blackstone reward—and of course his new Thorn abilities.

So far, he had kept his nerves under control. That was until the other competitors started arriving. He and Kinn gaped at mountainous men from all over the Settled Lands as they strode through the streets of Mossa Castille adorned in animal furs,, and plenty of battle scars to boot. Some competitors entered on horseback followed by a chorus of cheers from people waiting in line. Kinn looked at Ard with a concerned frown. "Mr. Ard, sir," he said, "I don't think this is the smartest of ideas. No offense to your smarts."

Gulping, he responded, "Yeah, well stealing blackstone from Queen Leonora herself isn't exactly the best idea either. I'm decent at pickpocketing, but not too experienced with dodging royal security. Got another plan?"

Kinn shook his head helplessly. "Maybe we can look for some elsewhere," he suggested. "I'm sure someone's bound to know where to get some!"

"I don't have that kind of time," Ard said. "The Ashen Horde are probably on their way here right this moment. They must've already reached Cottington and Hammerholm by now."

Kinn looked down helplessly.

Ard let out a heavy sigh. "Well, I guess I should head in." The boys looked to the competitor's entrance which was guarded by two of the queen's green-clad soldiers. "If I make it, meet me back at the haberdashery."

"And if you don't?"

Ard struggled with his words. "If I...don't make it, then it was a pleasure knowing you, Kinn Sturly of Tailton." He stuck his hand out for him to shake.

Kinn's hand was clammy with nervousness. Ard could feel his tiny body holding back from quivering. "Good luck, Sir Arden Ford of Pipton," he said encouragingly. "Lords know you'll need it."

Ard turned toward the competitor's entrance and slowly

approached the two guards. The onlookers took no notice of him as they tried desperately to catch a glimpse of any famous warriors who might be entering. The guards stopped him as he tried to pass.

"The spectator entrances are on the east and west side, Tiny," one of the guards said grumpily.

"Thanks for the tip, green bean," Ard snarked, continuing to walk through.

The guard grabbed his arm stopping him again. "Competitors only," he grunted.

The other guard put a hand on the soldier's back calmly. "All are allowed to enter, soldier," he said. "Queen's orders. Besides, it might be a good bit of fun to watch this shrimp get bloodied up."

Ard simply rolled his eyes. It wasn't the first time he'd been picked on for his size and it surely wasn't his last. "That's neat," he said. "I didn't know the queen's guards doubled as jesters."

"Watch your tongue, boy," one of them warned.

"Oh dear," Ard taunted, "it seems I've hurt the poor fool's feelings. Keep at it, mate! I'm sure you'll get funnier eventually."

The guard moved out of the way and shot him a nasty look. "Be on your way, pest. Can't wait to see you lose."

Ard had grown accustomed to people picking on him. He wasn't about to let two numbskull guards get under his skin. "Gentlemen," he said suavely as he walked past them, head held high. His confidence didn't last long. The entrance led through a cold, dark corridor that opened into a torch-lit room where all the contestants were relinquishing their weapons and armor. These men didn't even need armor the way their muscles looked. Sinewy and covered in burly hair from chin to ankles, the brawlers towered above him, surely outweighing him by the dozens, maybe hundreds. As he walked past them, he was met by laughs and jeers. Some of the men chomped their teeth at him while others ignored him entirely. He wiped beads of sweat off his brow from the nerves as he approached one of the guards.

As Ard was patted down rather thoroughly, he could feel his face turn red.

"Any weapons?" the guard asked sternly.

He shook his head.

The guard pointed to a bench where the other contestants were sitting. "Remove your shirt and any armor then wait there for further instruction," he directed.

Nodding anxiously, Ard took off his jerkin and tunic and crumbled them into a ball. He had never been embarrassed about his body until now. Although he was lean, his teenage muscles paled in comparison to the other shirtless competitors whose bodies were hard and cracked like boulders. They all took turns pointing and laughing at him as he awkwardly walked to his spot at the end of the bench. After their laughter stopped, he let out a quivering sigh.

"What are you doing here, boy?" said a man sitting next to him.

"Same reason as you," Ard said flatly. "I need that blackstone."

"Ah," the man said. "And I suppose you have a plan to take all thirty-seven of us out to get it?"

"I'll take my chances," he retorted.

The man chuckled. He was much larger than Ard but somehow he didn't feel threatened by him like the other contestants. His braided, black, and gray peppered hair was tied back in a ponytail and his beard grew thick and wiry around his chin and lips. He was aged but seemed incredibly strong. Even though he boasted multiple scars on his face and limbs, he bore a kind face with laugh lines crinkled near his dark, angular eyes. He reminded Ard of Mr. Brinkley somehow. Smiling, the man said, "Well, you are braver than most to be here, young one. I honor you for that."

Ard relinquished a small smile. "Thanks. Arden Ford of Pipton," he said, reaching his hand over.

"Junda," the man said with a firm shake. "Junda Ru Yen of Vargyn."

"Oh," Ard said, surprised. "You're Vargynian?"

"And why should I not be?" the man asked.

"Forgive me. I just didn't know Vargynians spoke Gylish."

The man laughed. "And what else should we speak? I am sure it would surprise you to know we read and write as well."

Ard's face warmed with foolishness. "Sorry. I guess I can be a bit dense sometimes. I meant no offense, honest."

The man smiled and shook his head. "One is not dense for learning, only for refusing to. All is forgiven young one."

Ard nodded. "So, if you're Vargynian, what are you doing here? I thought there was no violence allowed in Vargyn. I didn't think there'd be any warriors up there."

"And here I was imagining there were none in a Clustertown like Pipton," he retorted.

"Fair enough," Ard laughed.

"There are warriors all across this land, young one," he said plainly. "One in us all. We need only find something to fight for."

"Is that why you're here?" he asked. "Are you fighting for something?"

"Not all of us are here by choice, young one."

Ard was confused. He had seen contestants arriving to enter and they didn't seem to be forced at all. In fact, some of them seemed frighteningly delighted to be entering. Even he volunteered on his own accord. "Are you saying you're here against your will?"

"Did you think I was here for some meaningless black gemstone?" Junda reproached. "No, young one. Prisoners of the queen often face this fate. Better this than execution. At least here you can fight for what is left of you. Senseless acts of violence such as this tournament only darken the world. This is nothing but a tasteless show of power meant to pleasure the worst parts of people's minds. Only fools like yourself would enter an event like this willingly." He chuckled with disdain.

"I'm no fool," Ard said defensively. "You have no idea who I am or of the reason I entered."

"Yes," he relented. "You are right, young one. I do not know why you need this blackstone. Your reasons are your own and I wish you luck. But, I do not need to know why you are here. The only thing I need to know is whether or not you are going to kill me."

"Kill you?" Ard asked, confused. "What do you mean?"

Out of nowhere, a door slammed and a tall man adorned in silver strode into the room. The contestants perked up as his boots clopped to the center of the room, armor clinking. Hands clasped tightly behind his back, the man spoke in an assertive voice. "Good afternoon, champions. My name is Sir Randyn Ellys, captain of the queen's guard, high commander of the Verian Army, and arbitrator of today's tournament."

He was frightening, but not the kind of frightening that the contestants were. Sir Ellys sported no scars, wasn't exceptionally large and didn't growl or grimace when he spoke. Although, something about him made Ard more nervous than he was when he walked into the competitor's entrance. His eyes were dark like a snake's and his lips curled inward when he spoke as if they were concealing fangs or malicious secrets. An impressive golden-hilted rapier swung from his hip as he paced across the room. No doubt, this man was dangerous.

His voice sliced through the soft roar of an excited crowd in the arena as he said, "I am here to instruct you on the rules of today's contest. This match will not be a one on one event. Today, all thirty-eight of you will enter the arena at the same time. You will be granted no armor, helmets or otherwise. You will enter the arena precisely as you are now. Weapon caches will be stationed randomly throughout the arena and you may use any you so choose. The match begins as soon as the doors are open and the match will be over when only one of you is left standing. The surviving and winning champion shall receive a handsome amount of blackstone as their prize, but it shall not be easily attained. Today, anything goes. Today is life or death. Today, you fight in the presence of Queen Leonora, Ruler and

Protector of the Lushlands. May the Lords Above grant you strength, may the Lords Below guide your blows, and may Galexia Herself light a star in your name should you fall. Good luck, champions." With a soft bow and throw of his cloak, Sir Ellys marched out the door, shortly letting in the cheering of the crowd.

Ard's face went white. *Life or death?* He knew the contest would be hard, painful even, but he didn't think it would cost him his life. He had to escape. Even with his weird new abilities, he didn't stand a chance against these brutes. His heart was beating so strongly he thought it might be visible to the other contestants. He leaned over onto his knees to hide it. Junda put a hand on his back with a light slap. "Worry not, young one," Junda said reassuringly. "Perhaps I will kill you last...if you make it that far."

Ard was not in the mood for a laugh. Before he could get up and run out, the guards began herding the contestants into cells stationed around the arena. He was separated from Junda and placed in a cell with bars on three sides and a door on the other facing the arena. The cheering was practically deafening now. It reverberated off the cell walls and hummed in the metal bars. There was no turning back now. His chest heaved. He wanted to cry but his body wouldn't let him. All of his muscles were on full alert while his brain raced with thoughts of strategy. Would he go for the weapons first? He was definitely faster than the other contestants. Or so he hoped. What weapon would he use? A sword would be too heavy. He wasn't skilled enough with a bow and even if he was, he wouldn't have time to use it before the others got to him. Maybe a knife of some sort. He could handle a knife. What if there wasn't a knife? What would he use then? What if there are only swords? Or spears? His mind was going to explode. He needed to focus.

Suddenly, he heard the deep beating of drums rumble from the other side of the door. *Boom, b-boom. Boom, b-boom.* The drums echoed through the arena and rattled the walls of the cell as the crowd roared with excitement. The drums began to speed up, and the faster they went, the louder the crowd got. Just when Ard's heart was syncing to the speed of the drums, a bellowing horn rang out and the door to his cell started to raise open slowly, letting the high noon sun pour inside. He saw his advantage. The other contestants were large and would have to wait a few seconds before their doors were opened. This was his chance. He slid under the door and scrambled into the arena— an arena that may become his tomb.

❦

"How stands the hour, Sir Ellys?" asked Queen Leonora as she positioned herself beneath the shade of her viewing booth.

"Approaching noon, Your Grace," Sir Ellys responded.

Leonora breathed a thoughtful sigh. "And how many champions will be performing today?"

"Thirty-eight, Your Grace."

Leonora leaned back into her seat hidden beneath her sunshade. The head of her ghoulish hound rested heavily on her collar. Its body wrapped around her shoulders as it laid on a raised platform behind her chair, camouflaging into the dark. "Do we suspect any of them?" Leonora asked impatiently.

"It's difficult to tell, my queen," Sir Ellys replied. "If any of the competitors indeed are Thorns, it will be made clear in combat."

Leonora looked to Ellys and curiously asked, "When was the last time you saw a Thorn, Randyn?"

"Years, my queen," he responded reminiscently. "Many years. Most difficult hunts I've ever undertaken."

"Yes," Leonora said coldly. "I could see why. Thorns... incredible creatures, I'd imagine. Resilient. Resourceful. Clever, clever things. Promise me something, Randyn."

"Anything, Your Grace."

"Promise me that this will work."

"I swear it, my queen," Ellys pledged as drums began beating throughout the arena. "If they know of the curse, they will be here today. Whether entered in your contest or hidden among the rabble, they will come. If any of them are left in the Verdamaïn, I will see them captured."

Leonora paused and stroked the panting muzzle of her hound. The drums began beating faster and faster as the crowd rustled in their seats. "Put the guards on high alert," she ordered. "I want men stationed at every exit and corridor."

"Yes, Your Highness," Ellys said with a small bow. As he turned to leave, a horn blasted out over the stadium rumbling every seat. The doors of the arena started to slowly raise and the first contestant bolted out toward the center of the field where numerous weapons were positioned ready for use. It was just a boy. A boy who would surely meet his end quickly.

Leonora changed her mind and motioned for Ellys to stand and watch with her as she said, "Join me?"

He was right. As his eyes adjusted to the sunlight, Ard could see that he was the only one in the arena so far. The crowd rolled with laughter as he bolted toward the center of the field. Ignoring them, he sped toward the first cluster of weapon racks. Spears, swords, axes, and knives of all kinds were right in his grasp. He knew he had to think quickly; he could see all of the weapons in his grasp, but the more indecisive he was, the more time he lost. He grabbed a small dagger and slid it into his belt loop, then grabbed a long spear that was lightweight but sharper than most of the other choices. As soon as he held the spear in his grip, the crowd cheered loudly. Scanning the immense audience, he could see the stiff frame of Sir Ellys perched in a decadent booth alongside Queen Leonora who was hidden by the shade of a green awning. Her fabled hound was nowhere to be seen.

Applause erupted from the audience as Ard looked to see the other contestants hurtling toward him from all sides. He was trapped. He was finally realizing that he was not going to make it out of this arena alive. He tried searching for Junda but before he could think, one of the champions had reached him. The man tackled him into the dirt sending his spear flying. Ard hit the ground so hard it knocked the breath from his lungs. As he coughed to get it back, choking on the dust of the arena floor, the champion wrapped one hand around his neck and started to strangle him. He picked Ard off of the ground with ease and held him high in the air for the crowd to see. Ard could hear them all cheer louder as the champion smiled triumphantly. Tears welled up in his eyes, blinding him as he gasped for air. He clawed desperately for the knife in his belt loop but couldn't get his hands to work properly. His limbs were tingling as they began to numb. This was it. He was going to be strangled to death in front of hundreds of cheering men, women, and children. Suddenly, he could breathe again and he fell to the ground. The contestant who was strangling him crumbled like a besieged castle beside him with an arrow embedded into his temple. Ard watched as his eyes dilated almost immediately, frozen wide open.

Barely able to get his breath back and running on pure adrenaline, Ard leaped up trying to get a good look at his surroundings. There were already bodies on the ground. As he scanned the stone-walled arena, he could see another champion charging right for him like a raging bull. Before he had the chance to prepare himself for another scuffle, an arrow sliced right through the tip of his ear and went straight into the head of the charging contestant who thudded to the ground lifelessly. Ard cried out in pain and put a hand to his ear. He could feel the hot blood drip through his fingers. Spinning around, he could see where the arrow came from. Another champion was loading a third bolt into a crossbow and was aiming it straight for Ard's head. He looked around for something to hide behind but there was nothing but other contestants grappling with each other. Before the archer could loose the arrow, a spear sunk into his back and the crossbow snapped out of his hands rocketing the bolt into the leg of another champion.

As the archer fell to the ground, Ard could see the thrower of the spear was Junda. The old Vargynian nodded to him with a small grin. Out of nowhere, another competitor tackled Junda from the side. Ard knew he had to help him, but as he sped to Junda's rescue he was blocked by two more champions armed with battle axes and sets of sharpened yellow teeth. Suddenly, his muscles felt that familiar surge of energy. His legs burned with strength as he began running faster, aiming straight for the two brutes.

Faster.

Faster.

Faster.

Baring his teeth angrily, Ard could feel his rage boiling over. Suddenly unafraid, he felt his face relax and eyes widen as his strength grew. This was the boy who had lost it all. This was the boy whose home and family were stripped from him without warning. For the first time, Ard felt like he was something greater. The stableboy was gone. This was the Thorn.

Ard timed it perfectly. The first champion swung too early and his battle-ax thudded to the ground, leaving him completely open to an attack. Using all of his momentum, Ard rebounded off of the ax handle and sent one of his knees crashing into the man's jaw, knocking him to the ground. The second warrior, now snarling with rage, swung his ax wildly trying to land a blow, but with zero success. Ard ducked in and out of reach each time with ease as if he knew exactly where the ax would swing. With each miss, he landed bone-shattering punches to the attacker's ribs and face. Ard had never hit so hard in his life. He knew his knuckles would be badly bruised later, maybe even broken, but he didn't care. With a final, sailing uppercut, Ard knocked the man out, scattering shards of his sharpened teeth into the dirt. The crowd roared, but too soon. The other warrior Ard had forgotten about broke a wooden stave against his back, knocking him into the dirt. He tried to stand back up, but the pain kept him down. He felt like his back was broken. The sting shot all the way through to his fingertips like lightning. The warrior picked Ard up and turned his face to his.

A perfect window.

With a devastating headbutt to the brute's jaw, he was instantly free. As the man spit blood from his mouth, Ard raised his elbow and crashed it into the top of his skull, driving him into the ground with a thud. Head reeling, he continued to run toward Junda who was still grappling with his attacker. Ard leaped over the bodies of more competitors who had met their end. So many had already fallen. Blood melted into the dirt and congealed into a pasty mud. Ard's reflexes threw him to the ground onto his stomach. He watched as a throwing ax was hurled above his head narrowly missing his back. The crowd cheered loudly at his finesse as the ax sailed through the air into the side of Junda's attacker. Blood was everywhere he looked. He whirled around to see another throwing ax heading straight for his face. He leaned backward out of the way just in time.

What looked to be the final contestant now bounded at him angrily and weaponless, face soaked in blood. As the crowd cheered wildly, he sped off toward the man leaping over more dead contestants. Ard was about to unleash all the fury he'd stored for the destruction of his home on this unknowing stranger trying to kill him.

Even though he was unarmed, letting him get too close would be a mistake. A few feet from the charging lout, Ard reached down and grabbed a handful of dirt then tossed it into the man's eyes. Blinded, slowed, and now open to attack, he leaped onto the warrior-like a cat and pinned him to the ground. But this champion wasn't going down so easily. He flipped Ard over his head and onto the ground behind him. Ard rolled, readying himself for another attack when he saw what happened to Junda.

The old Vargynian was propped up on his knees balancing gruesomely on a throwing ax buried in his chest. The same throwing ax Ard had dodged moments ago. The same throwing ax this champion had meant for him. With clenched teeth, he glared at the final contestant who was now getting up and recovering from the dirt being thrown in his eyes. Ard had no space to build up speed now and would have to fight him toe to toe. Still, he wasn't afraid. The bloodied warrior lunged, trying desperately to land a solid hit on Ard, but his reflexes were too fast. He would dodge and counter before the man was ever able to deal a decent blow. Ard drew his knife from his belt loop, cutting the brute whenever he missed. Ducking low, he cut him behind the knees, forcing him to the ground. The warrior was defeated and he knew it. Kneeling, out of breath, and growling, he spit blood onto the field as Ard moved in closer. Breathing hard, the final gladiator grunted, "Go on, boy! Finish me off."

The crowd chanted maniacally, "*Kill him, kill him, kill him!*"

"Do it," he spat through bloody teeth. "It's what the people want. I would've done the same to you."

Ard brandished the knife he held in his hand. "Maybe I'm not like any of you," he said over the chorus of the audience. He could feel the sweat drying in the dirt on his skin as the crowd continued chanting. The sun blazed against his shoulders but he ignored it. The blood from his ear had flowed down his neck and onto his chest, slowly making its way down the length of his stomach.

"Well," the brute growled, "maybe you're like that dusty Vargynian over there." He gestured toward Junda, the old warrior who had saved Ard's life after only knowing him for a few minutes. His body had crumpled onto the ax and leaned against it as blood dripped onto the ground. Coughing up sand and dirt, the barbarian laughed on, "Too weak to stand. Although, he seems to be propped up nice and comfy now."

Before Ard could think, he leaned back and kicked the man in the chest with all of his might sending his body soaring ten yards into one of the weapon caches. Impaled on the multitude of razor-sharp weapons, the man's mouth gaped open. Ard watched as his last breath passed across his drying lips. The crowd exploded with ear-splitting applause. Ard turned to view the royal booth and saw Sir Ellys leaning in toward Leonora's chair hidden beneath the shade while the applause rippled across the entire arena in tremendous waves. He had won. He couldn't believe it, but he had made it out alive. However, there was only one thing he could wrap his mind around. One thing he couldn't shake. It reverberated within him, drowning out the cheering.

He had killed someone...and it felt good.

Ard stood heaving as the crowd's applause rumbled endlessly. He was feeling dizzy and faint, but he fought with himself to not pass out again. Still panting, he squatted down and hung his head between his knees as the crowd roared. After a few seconds, he heard footsteps walking toward him. Looking up, he saw three green-clad guards approaching. One grabbed hold of his arm, gently hoisting him up. He raised his arm high in the air by his wrist and the crowd erupted once more with deafening praise. He could feel the world spin as he stood up, desperately trying to stay conscious. The guards escorted him across the field and up to Leonora's booth.

When they reached her canopy, Sir Ellys met them and placed his hand firmly on Ard's shoulder. "Congratulations, champion," he said with a cold smile. "You've won."

Ard, who was still out of breath, managed, "Thank you, sir."

"Champion," Sir Ellys continued in his nocuous tone, "I present to you, Her Grand Majesty Queen Leonora Veleno, Ruler and Protector of the Lushlands, Chief Magistrate of the Steppes of Veria, Grand Sentinel of Silber Bay, and orchestrator of today's competition."

Ard looked to the center of the booth where Leonora was seated. Still hidden beneath the shade, all that showed of her were the ripples of a dress that flowed onto the floor. The sun was so bright, he couldn't see her face from the contrast. The gown moved slowly, then out of the dark strode one of the most beautiful creatures he had ever laid eyes on. Wrapped in an emerald sheen gown speckled with tiny white jewels, Leonora approached him with intense poise. Through the thin material, he could see parts of his queen that he'd never seen on any woman before. Her raven hair rippled to her curvaceous hips like the currents in a river. Her delicate hands were decorated with silver rings and bracelets while her face was painted beautifully with glittering makeup. He wondered if her powders were made of jewels crushed into dust. The smell of her jasmine perfume infatuated him as he tried hopelessly to focus on her face. This was the first time he was seeing his queen and he already felt like he'd do anything she asked of him. Leonora spoke with a voice that was warm like the sun. "The Lords Above have certainly smiled upon you this day, Champion," she said with a raised eyebrow and curvaceous smile.

Ard, trying hard not to fumble with his words, gave a polite bow. "Thank you, my queen."

Leonora smiled and her painted eyes crinkled happily. "How polite you are, Champion. What is your name and where do you come from?"

Ard's heart still raced as he replied, "Arden Ford of Pipton, Your Majesty. In the Cluster." He shied away from explaining what happened in Pipton. He remembered Leonora's order that Lord Herman read at the last gathering. Maybe she didn't know about the Ashen Horde, but Ard wasn't sure he could trust her yet. Even if she truly believed Kolbran wasn't rising against the west again he didn't want to upset her. Surely someone who had earned the name *Hound Queen* and a widespread fear of saying it was someone he did not want to test. He was here for the blackstone and he needed to focus on that mission.

"Ah," Leonora said, "our dear lumber supplier. How are things in the eastern reaches of my Verdamaïn?"

"Fine, Your Majesty" he lied. "Bit boring really."

Leonora chuckled softly, "I could imagine so. Well, thus far you've certainly made yourself quite known here in the

Floral City." She gestured toward the crowd of people who still applauded while filing out of the arena.

Ard scanned the immense audience and replied, "Yes, I suppose I have."

With an unsettling shuffle, a large shadow moved from behind Leonora's seat. Into the sun poured the most terrifying beast Ard had ever seen. Even the kelpie didn't make his blood run so cold. Leonora's legendary hound stared into his eyes, deciding whether he was friend or foe. The creature was the size of a large horse and towered above even the tallest human. It had wiry, cavern black fur and from the tips of its massive paws sprouted long claws that clacked eerily against the ground. Its eyes were a crystalline blue like the color of a frozen lake and its ghostly gaze made Ard's body tremble. As it slowly approached Leonora, it bared its vicious teeth at him.

"Now, now, my treasure," she said to the dog. "Calm." Leonora looked back at Ard and laughed apologetically, "The poor dear rarely meets a friendly face. Do not be afraid. No harm shall come to you unless I command it."

Ard laughed nervously, "Please don't command it, Your Majesty."

Leonora chuckled, "You amuse me, Champion."

He nodded graciously, careful to never take his eyes off of the hound.

"Well," she continued, "I suppose a feast is in order."

"Feast, Your Majesty?"

"Of course!" she beamed. "How else to present a winning champion with his award?"

"Oh," he said bashfully, "of course, Your Majesty."

She smiled again. The way her mouth moved was bewitching. Her lips, which were stained a forest green, curled with an enchanting delicacy. Ard felt his heart race every time she spoke. "Sir Ellys," she called, "have my champion cleaned and properly clothed. I'll have my servants prepare a proper dinner." She looked at Ard. "Tonight, we feast in your honor, Arden Ford of Pipton."

As Ard moved to follow Sir Ellys, he realized he'd almost forgotten. "Your Majesty?" he said. "May I ask you a question?"

"Yes, Champion. Anything," she replied, scratching the chin of her hound.

"Might I bring a friend?"

13

Dinner With A Queen

Ard had little trouble staying focused on his business in Mossa Castille, but the treatment he and Kinn were receiving in Queen Leonora's castle proved more difficult to stay his course. After the contest and reuniting with Kinn, who had somehow sweet-talked his way into the arena, the boys were escorted by carriage to Leonora's castle outlooking Silber Bay. Doors were opened for them everywhere they went. Both the boys received their own private quarters where they were able to enjoy a hot bath and fresh clothes made from the finest seamstresses in the Floral City. He was finally able to wash the oily grease from his hair and the dirt from his limbs which had accumulated so much that he felt encrusted with stone. The scents of the soaps and oils flowed into his nose and seeped through his entire body, relaxing him to the point of immobility. Kinn was given a juniper tunic and silver belt, while Ard was dressed in a handsome white shirt with gold trim and a fresh pair of pants that were dyed a pastel seafoam green. The whole outfit paired nicely with his new boots which had undergone a decent shining after the chaos of the contest. Although he was still slightly in shock from seeing men die around him for sport, he couldn't deny the enchantment of Leonora's superb hospitality. He felt as if he could stay in the castle forever.

Once the boys were freshly cleaned and clothed, they were escorted by Sir Ellys to a feast Leonora had planned for Ard, the Grandpit Champion. There were guards everywhere. Shiny, metal soldiers with stern faces were stationed staunchly at every door, hallway, and entrance of the entire castle. The men stationed ground level gripped ornate brass spears that towered above their heads and the ones on the castle walls and turrets were armed with deadly crossbows coated in silver. Ard couldn't believe how many there were. Their armor gleamed in the sun, polished to perfection. Even the soldiers of Mossa Castille were glamorous. Throughout the castle, flowers and hedges lined the outdoor passages while vibrant hummingbirds zoomed in and out of the leaves. His eyes darted around trying to focus on one of them, but all he could see were green and purple blurs. From the walls to the stained stone floor, everything was kept beautifully clean. There were even places in the floor so polished that Ard could see his reflection shining up at him through the resin. Just as Kinn had said, Leonora and her city were beauty personified.

As they were guided through the immense palace, Ard felt butterflies fluttering in his stomach. Seeing Leonora again was something he was more than eagerly looking forward to.

The guards brought the them through two giant, wooden doors into a banquet hall. A grand, flaming chandelier hung from the center of the ceiling illuminating ornate murals splashed colorfully against the walls. Ard was instantly greeted by droves of different people dressed in fine clothes similar to his own. They shook his hand congratulating him as wine rocked back and forth in their goblets sending the ripe aroma blasting into his nostrils. He could smell the wine in the air, on their breath, and even in their clothes. The scent was strong, but not overwhelming. The guards brought them to the far end of the hall where Leonora sat at the center of a grand table with her monstrous hound sitting statuesque beside her. The queen and the giant dog stood with a regality so intense it made Kinn reluctant to approach. This was the first time he was laying eyes on the fearsome Hound of The Floral City. People often spoke of its terrifying stature throughout the kingdom but Kinn was certainly unprepared for what the beast would look like up close. Its icy blue eyes stared with a steadfast relentlessness as the two approached. A new face meant new danger to the highly trained animal and its chilling gaze held.

As the boys and the guards approached, Leonora stood with a delicate smile. She was dressed in a dazzling turquoise gown with subtle lace revealing her shoulders and arms. She wore shimmering silver earrings and a diamond necklace that gleamed orange in the light of the chandelier flames. The dress curved at her waist then flowed across the floor as if she were melting into it. Her hair, which normally fell fluidly to her hips, was tied in a stylishly loose braid that hung over her shoulder. Her eyes were dusted with more of her glittering powder and her lips were painted a venomous, dark blue. Leonora was absolutely breathtaking. It was no wonder why everyone in the kingdom talked so much about her looks.

"Welcome, champion," she said, gesturing toward the table.

Both boys responded by taking a polite knee.

Leonora continued silkily, "Rise. Tonight, we feast in your honor. Please, have a seat." Leonora gestured to the seats on either side of her. Soft applause sounded throughout the banquet hall as the boys made their way to their seats. The guards who had escorted them fell back into their positions across the banquet hall and Sir Ellys positioned himself behind the queen just out of earshot. Poor Kinn was seated directly below the panting maw of Leonora's hound. *Maybe that will keep him quiet*, Ard thought. As the boys sat down, the clapping stopped and the guests made their way to their seats. With a wave of her jewelry embellished hand, Leonora summoned servants who carried dozens of trays of food into the hall.

As the servants brought the food around, Ard filled his plate with as much as he could. Diced chicken and seasoned potatoes, pheasant pies, rye bread and cheese, rice saffron, peacock fritters, shrimp skewers...he couldn't get enough. Even with his new heightened taste buds, this was the best food he had ever eaten. As the boys gorged themselves, Leonora sipped from a crystal goblet filled with dark red wine. Ard wondered if it might be blood in her cup the way people talked of her. Shaking the silly thought from his mind, he continued eating.

"So," she indulged, "Champion, I trust you've enjoyed your stay so far in the castle?"

Ard swallowed his food politely. "Yes, Your Majesty," he said.

"Excellent," she smiled. "Winners of my tournaments are treated like royalty here in Mossa Castille. I do hope your service has been of the finest quality."

Kinn interrupted from the other side of Leonora, "Oh yes, Your Grace! I feel like a lordly man, I tell you."

Leonora laughed. "Do you? I'm happy to hear it. I'm afraid we haven't had the pleasure of formally meeting yet, my lord."

Kinn turned red with embarrassment. "Apologies, Your Highness. How rude of me," he said. He stood from his chair formally like when Ard rescued him. "Kinn Sturly of Tailton, Your Majesty, at your loyal service," he wheezed.

Leonora clapped her hands with delight. "My," she said, "you flatter me with your manners, Kinn Sturly of Tailton. It is a pleasure to meet you." She put her hand out courtly to Kinn and he pressed a smooth kiss at the top of her knuckles. He may have been a pain, but Ard couldn't deny that for a kid his age he had a fair bit of spunk. Even he didn't have the guts to kiss the hand of a queen. As Kinn sat back down in his chair, Leonora continued, "How are things in the Village of Tailton, Sir Kinn."

Before Kinn could answer, Ard pretended to cough violently.

Leonora turned to him, alarmed, "Are you alright, champion?"

"Fine," Ard acted, still coughing. "I'm alright. Thank you,

Your Majesty."

When Leonora turned back to Kinn, Ard met eyes with him and lightly shook his head, praying that he didn't continue blabbing. If Kinn said what happened to Tailton, Ard would be caught in a lie. He didn't particularly care to find out what happened to those who lied to Leonora.

"Things are...good," Kinn replied, thankfully catching on. "Spectacular, really!"

"I'm happy to hear it," Leonora smiled, taking another sultry sip of wine. Ard let out a silent sigh of relief as the queen turned back to him. "That was quite a show you put on today, Champion," she gushed. "It's quite rare to see such strength in one so young as yourself."

"Thank you, Your Majesty," Ard replied, trying not to boast.

After another sip of wine, Leonora asked, "Come now, child. You needn't be modest. Where might I ask does a boy from Pipton learn to fight with such grace? And without barely a scratch." Her eyes glanced at his ear.

Ard hadn't even noticed that the cut from his ear had perfectly healed. That surely must have raised her suspicion. Thankfully, he had grown accustomed to lying. "A blacksmith I worked for in Pipton, Your Majesty," he said without hesitation.

Leonora seemed surprised. "A blacksmith?" she asked. "Hm, he must have been quite the instructor. I must recruit him to train some of my soldiers. Is he the one who informed you of my contest?"

He took another bite of food to give himself time to come up with a response. "Yes, Your Majesty."

"Your journey from Pipton must have been quite long, Champion," Leonora continued. "A little over a week, is that right?"

"Yes, Your Majesty. Just about."

"And you traveled all this way just to compete in my Grandpit?" she asked. "How delightful."

Ard couldn't tell if she was genuinely interested in his story or interrogating him. Her ivy eyes seemed kind, but something about her was making his hair stand on end. She sipped wine like a colorful viper curled in a pathway. He took another bite of food to try and avoid conversation.

Leonora straightened her braid and continued, "I must say we've never had a Clustish challenger, much less a Clustish champion. You shall have quite a story to tell when you return home, child. That is if you're returning home. You're more than welcome to stay here in Mossa Castille if it pleases you. With blackstone as your prize, there will be few things unavailable to you here."

"How much is blackstone worth exactly, Your Majesty?" he asked.

"More than silver, more than gold, more than sapphires and rubies, more than the finest diamonds we can mine. It is the rarest of all gemstones and its worth, practically limitless."

"Really?" he said in disbelief. He suddenly wondered if keeping the blackstone for himself was the better idea. He could build a new life, possibly one with Emagora. What would that be like? He'd never thought about it before. Even Emagora herself said he could find a new home somewhere. *Anywhere you wanted,* he remembered her saying. The idea was enticing. Just he and Emagora living together in the forest. He tried remembering the smell of the flowers in her hair, but the only smell he could remember was that of rosemary. *No,* he thought. What life could be built properly with the Ashen Horde running free? He quickly dismissed the idea as he thought of Gran, Mr. Brinkley, and Sore Swallow. Who would avenge them if he just hid himself in the Bardenwood away from the world? Besides, without the Child King, his home in Emagora's garden would never last. The thought of her beautiful green haven decaying to gray made his heart feel uncomfortably heavy.

"Certainly," Leonora said after another sip of wine, snapping Ard out of his daydream. "Very few people in the kingdom possess blackstone where most will never see it in their—"

"Honestly," Kinn interrupted again, "I didn't even believe it existed until now...Your Majesty."

Leonora smiled and scratched the chest of her hound which towered above Kinn. A low growl rumbled from its throat and he nervously returned to eating, silent as a mouse. Ard laughed to himself as Leonora continued, "One blackstone coin is enough to grant you most anything here in the Verdamaïn, even elsewhere I'm sure."

Ard smiled knowingly. *Elsewhere*, he thought. Elsewhere like Emagora's garden where hopefully the blackstone would grant him vengeance. "I hope so, Your Grace," he said. "I hope so."

"Well," she asked with yet another sip of wine, "whatever will you use your prize for, Champion? What business back in Pipton brought you to compete?"

Ard was growing nervous now. He wondered if he should tell the truth. As beautiful as she was, he was finding it harder and harder to trust her intentions. He struggled with a lie as he watched her indigo lips caress the rim of her wine goblet. Suddenly, the thought of the wine being blood didn't seem so farfetched. "My grandmother...erm...owns an inn in Pipton. I plan to fix it up, Your Majesty," he lied.

"Well," Leonora breathed, "I must see the finished product. It shall undeniably be the finest inn Pipton has ever seen."

"I can only hope, Your Majesty," he said, faking a smile. Sore Swallow *was* the best inn Pipton had ever seen. The only one. No amount of rebuilding could change that. He thought of all the things the old inn had been through. It had survived every summer storm, every snowy winter, even a few kitchen fires he'd accidentally started as a boy. All of this made him think of Gran. The food in front of him was decadent and wonderful, without question, but it could never compare to any of her cooking. None of it had her touch. None of it had her love. None of it smelled like rosemary.

Smiling back at him, Leonora asked, "Have you had enough

to eat, Champion?"

"Mm," he mumbled after one final bite, "yes, thank you."

"Excellent," she beamed. Standing slowly, she silenced the room without a word. As everyone settled in their seats, their queen projected, "My fellow Castillians. I wish to thank you all for attending tonight. Our champion has fought bravely today, more valiantly than we've seen in a very long time. Tonight, we thank him for his strength. We praise him for his courage, for not all of us possess the boldness to compete in such a brutal venture, and certainly not at an age so young. The Lords Above have smiled on him this day, and we all bore witness to it. For that, we thank him."

The guests repeated, "For that, we thank him."

Sir Ellys approached with a small chest that shone gold in the light of the chandelier, handing it to Leonora. Kinn's eyes went wide as he gaped at the chest. Ard could tell he wanted to burst with words but the panting maw of the hound behind him kept him silent. Guards positioned him at the front of the table facing Leonora as she continued, "Arden Ford of Pipton, I hereby present you with your prize. Fifty pieces of blackstone coin from the heart of the Verdamaïn as promised for your success. May the Lords Above grant you many blessings."

The room echoed with applause and whistling cheers. Leonora opened the chest and revealed the blackstone coins to Ard. They were dazzling beyond compare. Imprinted with the Mossa Castille insignia, a doe encircled by two scythes, their sable shine sparkled in the flames of the chandelier like hot embers smoldering beneath a fire. He thanked his queen with a short bow. As she handed the chest to him, Leonora held the prize just out of reach. Leaning in close to him, looking right into his eyes, she added under the applause, "And may they grant you safety." Leonora squinted her eyes into a clever smile then relinquished the chest, clapping softly along with the crowd.

14

A Welcome Overstayed

With another forced smile, Ard returned to his seat at the table as the applause softened. Something about what Leonora said made him terribly uncomfortable. The smile she gave him wasn't the one he liked. It wasn't the one that made his heart flutter and cheeks flush like when he met her after the tournament. No—that smile meant something else. Something about it seemed malicious. Her words seeped into his mind like a poison, tarnishing the beautiful image of the queen he'd become infatuated with.

And may They grant you safety...

The phrase repeated in his head like an echo as he battled with whether or not to trust her. The strange faces of the noble people attending the banquet smiled at him, but no grin seemed truthful anymore. He suddenly felt that it was time for him and Kinn to go. Everything in Leonora's castle had suddenly become unwelcoming and unsafe. The smiles of the partygoers, the taste of the food, even the feel of the clothes against his skin. It all felt like the first time he set foot into the Bardenwood, or the first time he laid eyes on Emagora or hearing the splash of the water in the kelpie's pond. He'd learned to listen to these sensory urges and this time they were screaming—*leave.*

Ard looked at Kinn who seemed to be feeling the same way. In reality, he was probably just ready to get away from the enormous beast that hovered over him. They had to figure out how to leave the party unnoticed. The longer they stayed here, the closer Kolbran got to overtaking the other Clustertowns. He couldn't let that happen. He'd received what he was searching for. The blackstone was his and now it was time to head back to Emagora's garden. He wished she was here with him. He wondered if she had ever been to a big city. She probably wouldn't like it. Then again, if she would enjoy any city it might be Mossa Castille. There were flowers and shrubs everywhere after all. Plants were a part of the lifestyle and architecture here.

While he was busy daydreaming about Emagora, the doors of the banquet hall burst open. Three guards carried in a man who was yelling in hysterics.

"The queen!" he sputtered. "Please! You don't understand. I must speak with Queen Leonora!"

Ard knew that voice. As the man was brought closer, he could see an unmistakable red beard. Lord Herald Herman was thrown at the feet of Leonora. The hound bounded from the other side of the table to defend its mistress. It snarled menacingly at Herman, but Leonora calmed it with a soft touch of her hand. Sir Ellys now approached the throne, stepping in front of Leonora as well. "What is the meaning of this?" he boomed. "How dare you interrupt a royal celebration?"

"Please, sir!" Herman exclaimed, dusting himself off. "I am Lord Herald Herman of Pipton and I bring news for the queen. You must let me speak!"

Leonora stepped from behind Ellys and her hound, silencing everyone in the room. "My lord," she said calmly. "Please, explain yourself."

"Your Majesty," Herman said, kneeling and out of breath, "Pipton has been attacked!"

Short gasps echoed throughout the hall. With everyone's

attention on Lord Herman, Ard knew this was he and Kinn's only chance to escape. If Lord Herman recognized him, Leonora would know he lied about Pipton. Who knew what she would do to him then? With a look, he signaled for Kinn to follow him out. Kinn looked confused but followed anyway. While Lord Herman's hysterics held the gaze of everyone in the room, the boys quietly made their way through a back door behind the table and left the banquet hall with the chest full of blackstone. They dashed through the halls, slowing down when walking past guards so as not to raise suspicion. Finally, Ard's skills at sneaking around were being put to decent use. He brought Kinn to his quarters first. As Kinn hurried inside, he grabbed his shoulders before he could close the door. "Kinn, I need you to pack your things. And be quick about it!" Kinn took a breath to protest, but he shut the door in his face and made his way down the hall to his own quarters. They were leaving Mossa Castille. Tonight.

"Attacked?" Leonora asked, clasping her hands together. "By whom, my lord?"

"The Ashen Horde!" he cried. "The brutes were bearing the Crimson Pyre!"

More gasps from the nobles, but Leonora remained still. Turning her chin up strongly, she asked, "How many, my lord?"

Lord Herman thought hard. "I'm unsure, Your Majesty," he admitted. "They struck so suddenly. We had no warning. There must have been a hundred or so of them at least, maybe more. Very few of us made it out. Myself included. I sent those I could to Hammerholm for safety. That was ten days ago, Your Majesty. They've no doubt reached Cottington by now. The Cluster will be overrun within the month."

Leonora tightened her jaw and said, "Thank you, my lord. My sincerest apologies for what you've lost." She turned to her advisor. "Sir Ellys," she commanded, "send a squadron of your finest men to the Cluster at first light tomorrow. Settle this. If there is anything your men are unable to resolve, you will report to me. Is that understood?"

"It shall be done, Your Grace," Sir Ellys responded. Throwing his cloak, he marched out of the hall to ready his men.

Leonora turned to the crowd of people in the hall whose faces were painted with fear. "My dear people," she announced, "it appears that I may have made a mistake. We can no longer sit idly by while these rumors of Ashar go unchecked. I have men prepared to investigate the matter further, but until then, rest assured that we are safe within these walls. Kolbran shall not enter our Floral City. He shall not have our towers, nor our jewels, nor any of our pleasures. The Verdamaïn was promised to us and us alone by Galexia Herself. Please return to your homes and worry not. Mossa Castille is in no danger. May the Lords Above shine on your paths home. Thank you."

The people clapped and began filing out of the banquet hall. Whispers fizzled throughout the crowd and their faces looked worried, confused about what was to come. Their shuffling steps echoed off of the painted walls and rung the crystals of the chandelier. They trusted their queen, but the recent rumors of the Ashen Horde moving on the west were becoming too real of a notion. Word would spread very quickly of Kolbran's march on the Lushlands. Leonora turned back to Lord Herman. "My lord," she said flatly, "you may stay here in Mossa Castille for the time being. Gather yourself and my guards will escort you to a room. If anything else comes to your attention about this matter you will report to me directly. Is that clear?"

Lord Herman bowed low. "I swear it, Your Majesty," he promised. Leonora waved her hand and bid the guards to show him out. Finally turning back to the table with a whip of her ebony hair, Leonora realized the champion and his talkative friend had vanished. She scanned the banquet hall but couldn't see them through the mass of nobles. Inhaling slowly, she marched toward her seat at the table and sat down, vexed so much her teeth ground together tightly behind her blue lips. "Guards!" she called angrily. More of her shining soldiers appeared before her almost immediately. "Find the champion and his friend. Bring them to me at once. Go."

The soldiers bowed in response and jogged out of the room, exiting through every door to better search for the boys. Leonora shut her emerald eyes coldly as her hound plodded up to the opposite side of the table across from her. With a soft snap of its jaws, it beckoned for her attention. Opening her eyes, she stretched out a hand and scratched the cheek of the dog lovingly. As the hound shut its eyes to enjoy the scratch, Leonora spoke to herself, "What now, my treasure?"

Ard burst into Kinn's room, locking the door tightly behind him. "Time to go."

"Almost done!" Kinn said as he shoved clothes into a pack. Ard rolled his eyes, listening closely for footsteps outside the door. "Where are we going?" Kinn asked.

"Away. Out of Mossa Castille," Ard responded.

"Why? What's wrong?"

"Can you just hurry up? Please?" He was growing frantic. Guards would be at their door at any moment.

Kinn shoved more items into his pack. "I just don't understand why you won't tell me why we have to go."

Ard walked over to him, helping him pack. "Can you just trust me? We need to go. There are guards looking for us. We don't have much time."

"Well," Kinn said, "we did disappear in the middle of a royal celebration. Maybe we should just go back, Ard. We could say we weren't feeling well from the food or something."

Ard retorted, "Do you think they'll be as happy to see us now knowing we're liars?"

"We didn't lie! Well—"

"Oh yes we did," Ard said. "Herman is sure to tell the queen when Pipton was attacked. We told her everything was fine and dandy in the Cluster. She probably thinks we're a couple of Kolbran's spies."

Kinn's eyes widened. "But," he whimpered, "we're not spies! Maybe we should've told her the truth. When the guards come for us, we can just tell them."

"Do you really think she'll believe us? Don't be stupid. We lied right to her face. You've heard the stories. She'll have us hanged in the square or worse, fed to that mongrel that follows her around."

"Mmph!" Kinn whined. "Then why did you make me lie?"

"Back in Pipton," Ard explained as he tied up his bag, "Leonora sent a decree that said anyone who spoke of the Ashen Horde would be punished. I wasn't taking any chances. I need this blackstone."

Kinn pleaded, "What do you even need it for, Ard? We've got all we've ever wanted now that you won that tournament! We could stay here in Mossa Castille and be treated as lordly as you like. I mean, take a look at that bathtub and tell me you still want to leave. Go on, I dare you!"

Suddenly, Ard froze. Before Kinn could ask what was wrong, he put a finger to his lips to silence him. Listening intently, he could hear multiple footsteps coming up the hallway to their room. "We have to go," Ard said, alarmed. "Now!" He moved toward the window of their room and peered out. A sheer drop to the street with no way to climb down and certainly no way to survive a jump. Maybe he could make it, but there was no way Kinn would live through a drop from this height. Before he could formulate another plan, the door of the room burst open.

Three guards stepped inside with triumphant grins stretched across their smug faces. "Enjoying the stay, boys?" the first one asked menacingly, stepping closer. "Can we get you anything? Fresh towels? More soap?"

Ard felt that familiar surge in his muscles and responded with, "No, I think we're alright, gentlemen. Looks like you'll be needing a new table though."

The guards looked at each other, confused, but before they could respond, all three of them were slammed with the full weight of a dining table Ard had effortlessly tossed across the room. Kinn stared at the unconscious guards on the ground and gaped at him. "How did you—"

"Grab your bag! Let's go!"

Kinn snatched his bag and followed Ard out of the room running as fast he could. Ard remembered the way to exit the castle but when they got to the door, it was guarded by another group of emerald guards. They hid around the corner of the hallway, careful not to peek too long. Ard counted twelve guards. There was no way he could take all of them at once, not even with his new strength. Kinn looked up at him and whispered, "Now what do we do? I don't suppose you have any more tables."

"Give me a minute," Ard said, ignoring his joke. He took a good look around and noticed that the only source of light was coming from a torch on the wall across from him. He knew if he could douse the torch after sneaking by the guards, he'd blind them and be able to grab Kinn and escape. He worried that he was giving him too many hints about being a Thorn, but there was no other way for them to leave safely. "Alright," he ordered, "I need you to stay right here, Kinn. Don't move and be quiet until I come to get you. Got it?"

"Wait!" Kinn whispered harshly. "Where are you going?"

"Shhh!" Ard hissed. "Just do what I told you!" He pulled a shirt out of his bag and silently rounded the corner heading for the torch. Careful to move slowly and quietly, he reached the torch and threw the shirt over it to snuff the flame. As the hall went dark, Ard could see the soldiers clear as day stumbling around trying to orient themselves. He went back to the hallway and saw Kinn looking around in the darkness. He looked scared to death. Ard knew he'd shout if he grabbed him too hard, so he slowly put his hand over Kinn's mouth and whispered, "It's me. Come on!"

Kinn clutched his bag close to his chest and whimpered, "Ard, I can't see!"

"Just follow me. I've got you, mate." He grabbed hold of Kinn's tiny, clammy hand and lead him toward the exit. While the guards shuffled along the walls trying to find a torch to light, the boys slipped right past and escaped into the night.

Once they were clear of any guards and Kinn was able to see again, he asked, "How did you do that?"

"Do what?"

"Don't play dumb. How did you sneak past those guards!"

"No time to explain," Ard said. "We need to leave the city. Do you think for one second that Leonora won't turn this capitol inside out looking for us? We are the number one threat to Mossa Castille as far as she's concerned. It won't be long now. Pretty soon she'll have the whole Verian Army searching for us."

Kinn's face went white. "I-I don't think I'd do so well in a cell," he stuttered.

"And I don't imagine you'd do so well with a rope around your neck either," Ard retorted. Kinn clutched his throat, imagining what it would feel like. "Exactly. We need horses. We need horses yesterday."

"There's a stable not far from here," Kinn said shakily.

"Well, come on then," Ard pressed. "No time to waste."

Kinn led the way to the stable down the street from the haberdashery they had secretly lodged in before Ard won the tournament. The stable was much larger and better constructed than Sore Swallow's. All the pens had large metal padlocks on them and the horses each had their own feed and water stations. Ard knew one of the blackstone coins would easily afford two horses for himself and Kinn. He reached into his bag, pulled out the chest of coins, and took one out, twirling the piece in his fingers. "I'm going to find the stablemaster," he said. "Stay out of sight and don't spook the horses," Kinn responded with a firm nod. Ard walked around the stable to the street side then stopped in his tracks. A smell drifted past his nose. At first, he couldn't gather what the scent was, then as he peered into the street, he knew exactly what he was smelling.

The street was filled with guards. He could smell them. They reeked of metal and leather with a hint of lemon they used to keep their armor sparkling. The soldiers were interrogating civilians and banging on doors searching for something. They were too far for him to focus on what they were saying, but he knew they were looking for him. Leonora would have her entire militia searching for them by morning. The guards were making their way down the street and would approach the stable in a matter of minutes. He ran back to Kinn who had plopped himself down against a haystack near the horse pens. "Don't tell me," he said plainly as he approached. "There are more guards and we have to go right now."

He shrugged, unable to deny it, and grabbed Kinn's arm dragging him to the pens. "Pick a horse," he demanded.

"Right. How are you going to get the beasts out?"

Ard approached one of the pens and grabbed the padlock. He knew he had gotten stronger, but he didn't know if he was strong enough to break the lock. With all of his might, he pulled down on the padlock and it snapped off with a metallic crack. Kinn's jaw hit the floor. "Well," he lied with a small laugh, "must be dummy locks to keep thieves away. You picked a horse yet?"

Kinn looked down shamefully.

"What's wrong?" Ard asked, saddling up his horse.

"I...I don't know how to ride," he admitted.

Ard knew he couldn't judge him. Most people in the Cluster weren't able to ride since having a horse was quite a luxury. Had he not been a stableboy his whole life, he might have never learned to ride either. His senses picked up the clinking of armor coming closer to the stable. They were running out of time to leave. Hurriedly, he ordered, "Give me your foot and climb on! We'll ride together."

He cupped his hand and boosted Kinn onto the horse who was grumbling with soft whinnies. He climbed on behind him and grabbed the reins. The soldiers were close now. There was no way they wouldn't see them leave the stable, but they had no choice. He spurred the horse and it galloped straight for the exit, but they were too late. A group of five guards barred the way and the horse skidded to a stop. The guards realized who the boys were and immediately moved to seize them. Ard's body surged again. With the momentum of the horse stopping, he swung his leg off of the saddle and kicked into the first guard, knocking him ten feet back into a tie post.

One.

Before he could turn to face the others, another of the soldiers grabbed him from behind and held him tightly. As another approached, Ard lifted both of his legs and kicked him in the breastplate, denting his armor and knocking the one who held him into a wall. Both men fell to the ground.

Three.

The last two guards drew their swords while Kinn cheered from atop the horse, "Yeah! Get 'em, Ard! Go for their legs!" Ard had already planned it. He sped toward the guards and slid low into the first, knocking him to the ground. Before the other could swing his sword, Ard whipped around and grabbed him by his armor collar and crashed his helmet into the face of the soldier he'd knocked down, causing them both to go limp.

Five.

The stable fell quiet again as Ard picked off one of the broadswords from the soldiers. Swords had always been peculiarly heavy things to him, but he was able to wield the blade with ease. He swung it in a few circles, chuckled, then sheathed it perfectly.

"You know something?" Kinn said. "You're actually starting to scare me."

Ard tied the sword around his waist and picked off the soldier's side dagger. "I'm starting to scare myself if I'm honest," he said as he tossed the dagger to Kinn.

"Um..." he hesitated.

"You'll need it," Ard said as he slid another side dagger into his own boot.

"I've never used one of these before," Kinn admitted.

"You ever used a filet knife? Back in Tailton?"

"Of course I did. Loads of times."

"Same concept," Ard pointed out. "We don't have a choice anymore, Kinn. We're going to have to defend ourselves. We can't be the good guys if we're dead."

Kinn looked at the dagger for a moment, brandishing it in the soft moonlight. With a determined nod, he slipped the dagger into its sheath and fastened the buckle around his waist. Even at its tightest, the belt was huge on him, sagging past his thigh, but Ard could already see him carrying himself differently. Rather than saying anything about it, he climbed onto the horse and they galloped out of the stable, leaving Mossa Castille as far behind as they could.

⤖⤖⤖

"We've searched everywhere, Your Grace," the soldier said. "There's no sign of the champion or his friend in the city."

Leonora narrowed her eyes and glared at the green guard. "Everywhere? Curious. If you have looked 'everywhere' in the city and were unable to find them...where do you suppose they might have gone?"

The soldier looked down in silence.

Leonora leaned down from her throne and continued, "The correct answer would be that they're not in the city. Have your men checked the outskirts and the docks?"

The soldier turned red with shame, "I'm...not sure, Your Grace."

Leonora took a deep breath and looked at the soldier menacingly. "Then, what are you waiting for, captain? Find. Out."

The soldier bowed quickly and walked out of the throne room followed by a grumble from Leonora's hound. Sighing, the queen scratched her giant dog until it settled. Turning to Sir Ellys who stood beside her throne, she said, "If they've left the city on foot they can't have gone very far."

"And if by boat, Your Grace?"

"There are no ships leaving the harbor this time of night," she pointed out. "Besides, the dock masters would have reported anything suspicious to the guards. No, they're heading back to the Cluster, whatever's left of it."

"Shall I send troops to retrieve them, my queen?"

"No," she said as she walked to a window. She looked out into the night, scanning her glorious city. Even at night Mossa Castille was breathtaking. Evening torches bounced their yellow lights off of the white brick and green walls of the buildings, casting long, flickering shadows onto the cobblestone streets. "No, Randyn, I think not."

"Your Grace?" he asked, confused.

"You saw what the boy did to those guards," Leonora said. "You saw him in the Grandpit. He's a Thorn. You know it as well as I do. This is not some mere convict runaway. That creature took my bait and now I'm left with nothing but imbecile guards and a barren hook."

"I'll assemble some men and go myself, my queen," Sir Ellys offered. "I've hunted Thorns for you before, I would be honored to do it again."

Leonora turned from the window without a reply and sauntered back to her throne where her loyal counterpart awaited her. She reached up to the giant canine and scratched its enormous chin with her gem encrusted nails. Its fur slid over them like a wire brush as her hands vanished beneath its thick coat. The beast's piercing blue eyes opened and shut in comfort as it leaned into Leonora's touch. Looking over her shoulder at Sir Ellys, she breathed, "Never send a man to do a hound's job."

15

Into the Bardenwood

The lights of Mossa Castille were now a distant glow. The clear night sky was speckled with stars and the moonlight lit their way. Their pace had slowed to a steady trot since leaving the city. Ard knew he'd hear the soldiers coming long before they caught sight of him and Kinn, so they decided to give the horse a break and take it slow.

"Do you think they're still looking for us?" Kinn asked.

"Without a doubt," Ard replied. "I imagine they'll send more guards to hunt us down soon."

"What will we do then? What if they catch us? I know I've said it before, but I really don't fancy being hanged."

"We'll be fine," Ard said. Although, he didn't really know. If they weren't captured and executed by Leonora's guards, they would be captured and killed by the Ashen Horde. Ard had no idea what came next, at least not for Kinn. What would he do? He had nowhere to go. He might be safe if he headed north to Hammerholm. Leonora's men wouldn't be looking for him there. It was Ard they wanted, and Hammerholm was also the only Clustertown with a militia. They'd stand the best chance at fending off the Ashen Horde and then he'd be safe. Maybe he could stay with Emagora in her garden if he weren't terrified of witches.

"Well," Kinn said, "I guess our best bet now is to head north to Hammerholm, right? Maybe they haven't been attacked yet?"

"Yes," Ard replied. "Yes, I suppose so." He thought of Pipton and the flames of his anguish began billowing again. The only place he wanted to go was exactly where he couldn't. He wanted his bed, he wanted his kitchen, he wanted his loft, and his window. He wanted his battered wardrobe, the creaky stairs, the leaky stable, and his trusty pitchfork. He wanted chores and pranks and gatherings and lumber. He wanted home.

"I wish we could go back home," Kinn sighed.

"Well we can't," Ard said angrily. "Kolbran took that from us."

"Where will we go if the Cluster is gone?" Kinn asked. "We can't go back to Mossa Castille."

Ard remained silent. He didn't know the answer. All he knew was that he had to get back to Emagora's garden. The uncertainty of his errand was suddenly starting to unnerve him. What if Emagora's ritual didn't work? He began to wonder if breaking the curse would claim his life. What if the Child King didn't help him? Maybe Emagora was right. He didn't have to do this. He could build himself a new life anywhere he wanted. Maybe he could convince her to go with him. As he wondered about a new life, the thought of Gran and Mr. Brinkley crept their way in between. Who would avenge them if not him? Would they have truly died for nothing if he just started over someplace else? Things were becoming complicated in a way that he had not anticipated. Freeing an imprisoned magical king with a blood ritual to avenge his family seemed a lot easier when he first set out from Pipton. As his mind raced with questions, a distant sound echoed through the night. "What was that?"

Kinn looked confused. "What was what?"

Ard slowed the horse to a stop and turned to look back down the road to Mossa Castille whose glow had faded into the darkness. Listening intently, the sound didn't come again. Letting himself relax, he turned back around to see Kinn staring curiously at him.

"What was it?" Kinn asked. "I didn't hear anything."

"Nothing," Ard said. "I thought I heard…"

Before he could finish his sentence, the sound came again. Their faces turned white as the sound sliced through the darkness and rippled over the hills. The horse whinnied and started stomping uncomfortably. The sound was unmistakable. Leonora's hound howled with blood-curdling triumph. It had picked up their scent.

Kinn stuttered, "W- was that…"

"Yes," Ard replied fearfully. "Leonora must've sent it after us."

"I th-think I would have preferred the entire Verian Army," Kinn stammered, snatching the reins from his hands. The horse began to gallop as he kicked it violently. "Yah! Yah, horse!"

"Stop!" Ard demanded, pulling the reins back from him.

"What?" Kinn protested. "You want to wait up for that thing? I'm sure he'd love to tag along with us."

"That monster," Ard spat, "is almost twice the size of this horse and has no riders weighing it down. Do you honestly think we can outrun it?"

"We can surely try!"

"I don't think so," Ard said flatly. The horse slowed to a stop as he leaped down onto the road and stared into the night. The insidious tree line of the Bardenwood stood staunchly in the still air across the hilly field near the road. Ard knew they had no choice. "Kinn," he commanded, "get off the horse."

Kinn clambered down reluctantly. "Why?" he whined. "We need to get out of here!"

"Take off your coat," Ard said.

"What?"

"*Take off your coat*," he repeated, stripping it off him.

"Hey! What are you doing?" he cried, struggling against him.

Ard tied the jacket to the saddle then took off his own. "We need to throw this thing off our scent."

"How?" Kinn said, wrapping his arms around himself to keep warm.

Ard tied his own jacket to the stirrups and left one sleeve to drag the ground. He threw Kinn's bag to him and threw his own over his shoulder. With a hard slap, he sent the horse careening down the road toward the Cluster.

Kinn's mouth gaped. "Are you crazy? How are we supposed to outrun the hound on foot?"

"That should throw the beast off long enough for us to find some water," Ard said. "We'll wash our scent off then he won't be able to find us."

"And just where are we supposed to find water?" Kinn asked. Ard ignored him, marching toward the Bardenwood without pause. As Kinn realized where he was heading, his eyes widened with fear. "You're completely off it, you are," he breathed. "You know, before I thought maybe you were crazy, but now I see that you're a full-blown loony!"

"Out here on the hills, we're sitting ducks," Ard pointed out. "The wind blows west and carries our scent right into the beast's nostrils. There's nothing out here to mask our smell, nowhere to hide. That thing will run us down even on a horse, and you know as well as I do that we don't stand a chance fighting it. This is our only choice."

Kinn stopped right in his tracks and dropped his bag to the ground. "No," he said defiantly.

Ard stopped and turned to look at him. "What do you mean, 'no'?"

"No," he repeated emphatically. "That's precisely what I mean."

"So, you want to stay out here in the open and let Leonora's hound pick its teeth with your rib cage? That's what you want?"

"Rather that than even think about stepping between them trees," he said, pointing at the Bardenwood. "I've heard the tales. I'm not walking an inch into them wretched woods until you tell me the real reason that dog is after us."

"What are you talking about, Kinn?"

"I may be small, but I'm not stupid you know. You won that blackstone fair and square. It's not like you stole it. Leonora wouldn't send her most precious *treasure* after some Clustish stableboy who left a dinner party early."

Ard smirked. "So, you're an expert on Queen Leonora's capture tactics now? Where do you find the time to know everything? I have to know."

Kinn pressed further, "What do you need that blackstone for, Ard?"

"I've told you," he said. "That's none of your—"

Kinn shoved him in the chest, cutting him off. Not enough to do any harm, but he was surprised at how strong he was for being so small. "What," he repeated through clenched teeth, "do you need that blackstone for? Tell me!"

"Why do you care so much anyway?" Ard groaned. "I didn't ask you to tag along."

"Yeah?" Kinn argued. "Well, maybe I should have just left you passed out on that road. Maybe then I wouldn't be running for my life right now."

"Maybe you wouldn't," he agreed sarcastically. "And maybe I should have left your rotten ass in that pit to starve. Maybe then I wouldn't be explaining myself to a pint-sized pest that knows everything while running for *my* life. Can we please go now?"

"No," he repeated flatly, crossing his arms. "Not until you tell me why I have to. If I'm going to travel with you as your stupid 'servant boy' then I deserve to know why."

Ard debated leaving him, but the thought of him being mauled by a vicious beast wasn't exactly a pleasant one. He sighed with a grunt. "Fine, you insufferable little imp! On my seventeenth birthday a few weeks ago, I was visited in my dreams by a witch who lives in a garden in the Bardenwood. She told me I was something called a Thorn and that I'm the only one who can free an ancient king from imprisonment with a magic ritual that requires my blood and a bit of blackstone so he can bring magic and life back into the Settled Lands, but in return, I'm going to have him destroy the Ashen Horde and King Kolbran for good so that I can avenge my family. This king just so happens to be buried in Emagora's garden, which is in the Bardenwood which is where we need to be right now if you want to live."

Kinn's face was blank. Suddenly, he burst into laughter, leaning over and slapping his knees. Ard stood there and let him laugh it out. As he cackled on wildly, Ard said, "Go ahead, get it all out."

"Oh man!" he giggled. "That's a good one. You're a right jokester you are, sir. Brilliant story, just brilliant."

"Yeah. I worked hard on it."

Kinn's laugh subsided as he realized he was completely serious. "You're not joking."

Ard shook his head with an obvious look on his face.

"Well," Kinn pondered, "what...how...wait, when..." Before he could begin questioning him further, he was interrupted by another bone-chilling howl from the hound. It was much closer this time, sending cold quakes darting down his spine. As soon as the howl stopped, Kinn picked up his bag and sprinted toward the Bardenwood, followed by Ard who was laughing quietly to himself.

When they reached the sinister line of gray trees, Kinn slowed down. Ard jogged ahead of him and passed under the canopy. "Are you sure the trees don't eat people?" Kinn called to him. "I've heard that's happened before. Yeah, I've definitely heard the trees eat people. People-eating trees. Yep, those look like the people-eating kind."

"Do I look like I'm getting eaten?" Ard asked with his arms out.

Kinn shook his head. He stepped toward the benevolent forest, staring upwards at the dark tips of the trees whose branches clawed desperately at the night sky to swallow up the stars. Ard waited patiently within the tree line. He remembered what it was like the first time he stepped into the Bardenwood. Crossing that line was probably the bravest he'd ever been. The fear of the forest ran hot through almost everyone in the Lushlands and taking that first step took every bit of courage he could muster. As Kinn inched closer, Ard reached out his hand. Kinn grabbed it and clutched at his shirt. His eyes shut tightly as his feet crunched against the leaves of the forest floor. Ard patted him on the back affectionately. "You alright, mate?" he asked.

"Mhm," Kinn muttered, opening one of his eyes. "I'm alright I think."

"Good," he said, pulling away, "because I don't think you'll be *as* alright when Leonora's dog catches up with us."

"Right," Kinn said, nodding. An awkward silence sat between them save for his nervous breathing. Ard looked at him with patience. He knew how hard it must be for him to be beneath these trees. He waited a bit longer until Kinn looked back at him and said, "Well, you first!"

❧❧❧

The Bardenwood grew much thicker here in the fertile ground near Mossa Castille. After all, the soils in the Lushlands were a major commodity. Merchants sold jars and barrels by the cartload in other kingdoms. People far and wide speak of Mossa Castille's soil, rich enough to grow any crop, any fruit, ant tree or plant. Ard and Kinn trudged through the underbrush, trying desperately to keep their feet out of brambles. The canopy made it dark, but Ard's new and improved vision led the way. After what seemed like miles, the scent of water floated into his nostrils. He knew they had to reach it as quickly as possible to wash off their scent. Their only hope was to confuse Leonora's hound because if it found them...he didn't want to imagine the result.

As Ard sniffed the air, Kinn asked, "What is it? Do you smell water? Or maybe a nice fish sandwich? That would be nice, wouldn't it?"

Ignoring his joke, Ard responded with a firm nod. He wanted to stay focused. The Bardenwood may have hidden kind hearts like Emagora's from the world, but he shuddered to think what other creatures lurked within its depths, especially in the middle of the night. Between each step, he listened intently for any sign of danger. His sense of hearing was starting to become more controlled. He could hear sounds like the flapping of a moth's wings, the quaking whine of tree trunks supporting the weight of their branches, he could even hear the sound of Kinn's heartbeat thumping wildly behind his ribcage, although most anyone could if it wasn't for his incessantly chattering teeth. The night was cold, but he was able to stay focused enough to ignore it. He wondered if maybe being a Thorn gave him some power over the elements. What if Thorns were capable of more than just strength and seeing in the dark? He began to imagine what it would be like if he were able to control nature itself. He pictured himself molding a thunderstorm from the air or hoisting boulders from the earth. The thought of it all excited him. He never felt truly capable before discovering who he was. What he was. As he marched through the woods, he did so with a growing appreciation of himself.

The thickness of the trees slowly started to wane. The boys were able to pass through more comfortably now. The water was close. Ard could smell it. He could hear its current passing over the rocks beneath its surface. It sounded like a stream or river. Hopefully the Witchfoot. He picked up his pace slightly and Kinn was happy to keep up. The trees began to completely clear out and the boys found themselves on the banks of a wide river. Ard looked to Kinn expecting to see a huge relief-ridden smile, but he was frozen with a frightened look on his face.

"What is it now?"

"That's the Witchfoot, that is," Kinn breathed.

Ard shrugged. "So? You and your dad caught fish from the Witchfoot. You said it yourself."

"Yeah, but not this part of the Witchfoot. People always said it turns to blood in the Bardenwood and they were right. I'm not going anywhere near it. You already got me into these awful woods and my heart can't take much more."

Ard looked at the water as it rippled under the moonlight. He could see it was dark red like a goblet of wine. He stepped over to the bank and dipped his hand in. The water was cold, and he could feel the current pull at his fingertips. When he pulled his hand out, the water trickled down his arm clear as glass. Realizing what was happening, he reached his hand back into the river and pulled a rock from its bed. Turning it over in his hands, he could see that the rock was red as a candied apple. He threw the rock at Kinn and said, "You need to stop believing everything you hear. It's just the rocks, mate. This is the same water you and your dad fished salmon out of."

Kinn walked cautiously to the edge of the river and peered into the ripples. He dipped his hand below the surface and pulled out one of the red rocks. He ran his fingers over the stone. Even in the dark Ard could see him blushing from embarrassment. "I guess it's safe," he admitted.

"And the forest didn't eat us, did it?"

"No," he said bashfully. "I guess I don't really know that much about this stuff."

"It's not your fault, Kinn. You didn't know. Sometimes things aren't what the stories tell you and sometimes they are. Take our kelpie friend for example. I don't think you've ever been more right about anything in your life."

"Ha! I guess that's fair. Stupid river."

"It is a stupid river," Ard agreed. Before Kinn could respond, he splashed some water onto him and pretended to panic. "Lords, it *is* blood!" Kinn let out a squeal that rang out through the forest, echoing off of the trees. He clutched and pulled at his shirt as if the water was acid burning his skin. He was too busy being wrought with fear to notice Ard wheezing from laughter.

"You filthy tosspot!" he spat, walking toward him with clenched fists. "I could have woke every creature in the entire wood!"

Through the laughter, Ard choked out, "I think you might've woke the entire kingdom!" But then, he stopped moving. Stopped breathing. Frozen to the spot. His eyes widened and his ears tuned themselves to the vicinity. Something in the air was making his hair stand on end.

Kinn stopped in his tracks, scoffing, "You play another joke on me, Ard, and I swear..."

"I'm not," he whispered.

"What is..."

"Shhh!"

The smell was something he knew, but before he was able to recall it, the scent began crashing through the forest behind a pair of reflective eyes and snarling white teeth. Another scream exploded from Kinn as Leonora's hound hurdled toward the boys across the bank, hauntingly transfixed on its long-awaited quarry. Ard suddenly thought of Mr. Brinkley standing there in the field between a burning Pipton and the Bardenwood. He ran that day. He knew he couldn't save himself from the gnashing teeth of Leonora's beast, but he would save Kinn. He wouldn't run this time. He grabbed Kinn by the shirt and threw him onto the ground behind him, facing the charging hound head-on. His face faded instantly from fear to calm focus as if he were back in the Grandpit. The great hound leaped in for the kill.

Ard could see its arctic blue eyes widen with hunger as it closed in, but before its jaws could clench themselves around his throat, a deafening boom and blinding light knocked him to the ground and his vision began to blur. His body went limp with numbness as he tried to recover from the fall. He could feel himself passing out again, but Kinn's muffled voice kept him awake as he shouted over the ringing in his ears, "Ard! Ard, get up! Come on!" As his sight returned in a hazy kaleidoscope of stars, the feeling in his limbs started returning. He could feel Kinn's hand slapping against his cheek. The sting and the alarm in Kinn's eyes forced him to look around. They were right on the bank of the river and Leonora's hound was several feet away stumbling to stand. It was whining from pain, but its eyes were locked to Ard's. He couldn't explain it, but even though the beast was in pain, he could tell its hunt for him was not over. Its whines turned to growls as it rose shakily to its feet. Suddenly, Ard felt himself being dragged backward into the icy water of the Witchfoot. The cold jolted his senses back and drove the last of his bizarre haze away. He looked up and saw Kinn using all of his strength to pull him by the collar into the river. Through his grunts, gritted teeth, and furrowed brows, Ard saw something different in his face. This wasn't the scared Tailton boy caught in a hunter's trap. This Kinn was a hero. A fighter. For a sliver of a moment, he realized why he made it out of Tailton. Kinn was a survivor.

The water of the river was getting deeper and he could feel himself being tugged by the current whose pull was growing stronger and faster. Kinn's grunts turned to gurgled coughing as he struggled to stay above water while hauling Ard into the middle of the river where the current was strongest. He took one final look into the starry night sky before the white water of the river rushed over his face. All the feeling in his body was back and he was able to get himself above the water, but he couldn't feel Kinn's hands on his collar anymore. As the water began to carry him faster and faster downriver, he looked around but couldn't see Kinn anywhere. "Kinn!" he called out. "Kinn, where are you?" The icy water made it hard for him to yell, but before he could cry out again, he saw Kinn's head pop up from the water downriver.

"Ard!" he cried. "Help! Someone help!"

"I'm coming, Kinn!" Ard shouted back as he swam with the current. He could see the hero in Kinn was gone. His face was painted with real terror. The river had turned to rapids and bobbed him up and down like a ragdoll. Ard could feel his strength begin to surge as he paddled faster. Within a few seconds, he had Kinn locked in his arms. "I've got you, mate. Hold on!" He could feel Kinn's body trembling from the cold, but he held onto him tightly. As soon as the rapids weakened, Ard steered them to the bank opposite of where they were attacked, careful to keep his legs toward the surface and avoid any rocks. As the water shallowed, he tried to get Kinn to stand, but he wasn't moving. "Kinn," he said, struggling with his arms. "Come on, stand up."

No response.

"Kinn," he repeated. "Hey, you alright?"

His body had stopped shaking and his eyes were closed softly. The same soft way that Gran's were when he found her strewn about in her garden. "No," he said out loud. He pulled Kinn onto the rocky bank, feeling the water slosh around in his boots. His clothes stuck to his skin and steam started to swirl around them from the cold. Kinn's body was limp. He leaned him against a tree and grabbed hold of his face. "Hey!" he called. "Kinn, wake up. Wake up!" Kinn's eyes blinked as he tried to open them. A frail breath quivered over his lips. His skin was a pale blue and his body barely trembled. The cold was slowly eating him alive.

"Kinn?" he said, turning his chin to him. "Hey, you're freezing. We've got to warm you up. I'm going to build us a fire. I'll be right back!" He let Kinn's cold face lean against the tree. His already short breaths were starting to slow. He had to move quickly. As he stood up, he could feel the weight of the water in his own clothes. It reminded him of what it felt like before his new abilities made him feel light as a feather. He tried wringing out the water as best he could, but it was no use. He had to get dry. He took off his shirt and tunic, letting the bitter cold seize his skin, and set them next to Kinn. Wrapping his arms around his middle to keep warm, he ran to find firewood. Thankfully, this part of the Bardenwood didn't see as much rainfall as the parts near the Cluster, so he was able to find a decent pile of dry wood to burn. Once he'd grabbed all that he could carry, he sprinted back to where he'd left Kinn.

When he got back to the bank, Kinn had fallen onto the ground from his spot on the tree and his eyes were shut again in that same peaceful way he hated. Dropping the sticks, Ard rushed to his side. "No, no, no, no!" he cried, clutching his face. "Kinn! Hey! Kinn, look at me."

Kinn's eyes opened slightly and he heard a groan roll across his frozen lips.

"Hey!" Ard shouted again. "Stay awake, Kinn! Stay with me. I'm going to get you warmed up." Ard built up the firewood into a triangle and placed a bit of kindling in the center. He saw that Kinn still had his bag strapped to him. He wrenched it from around his back and dug through it. Just as he hoped, he was able to find his fire starter, but it was soaking wet. He bent over the firewood and desperately struck the flint to get a spark, but nothing was large enough to sustain a flame. "Come on," he willed. "Light. Light!" He tried striking the flint again and again, over and over.

Nothing.

His body tensed. "LIGHT!"

A small flame burst wildly over the kindling and the fire was lit. Ard fell back onto the bank in shock. He couldn't tell if the flame had come from him or the fire starter. Regardless, the campfire was blazing perfectly. The light from the flames danced against the trees mixing with the early morning twilight. Still stunned, he crawled over to Kinn and dragged him to the fire with ease. He stripped his soaked shirt off of him and threw it next to his own. He could feel his skin was glazed with frost. He started to rub his shoulders to warm him up. "Come on, mate," he cheered. "Come on, Kinn, you're alright. Wake up."

To his shock, he watched as Kinn formed some words. "You... y-you stopped it w-w-with a l-light."

"What?" Ard asked, still rubbing his arms. "What are you

on about?"

"A l-light," Kinn repeated.

"You're not making sense," Ard said, trying to hush him. He remembered being on the bank. He remembered some type of explosion. *Was that...me?* he thought to himself.

Kinn coughed, sputtering a bit of water from his mouth. "Ard?" he managed, opening his eyes, "Am I d-d-dead?"

"No," Ard laughed with relief. "You're not dead, Kinn. You're just cold."

"Are you sure?" he asked. "I c-can't feel m-my toes." Ard realized his boots were still on. He reached down, untied them, and pulled them off, letting the water empty out onto the riverbank. He placed Kinn's feet near the fire and began rubbing them.

"Can you feel that?"

"Yeah," Kinn said with a weak smile. "Yeah, I can f-feel it."

Ard let out an immense sigh. Realizing his own boots were still on, he took them off and placed his feet by the fire which was crackling nicely now. His feet were tough to move about, but he wiggled his toes back and forth, letting the droplets of freezing water vanish from his skin. He looked over at Kinn who was now rubbing his hands together near the flames. His eyes were still shut but he was shivering now which was a good sign. Ard felt tears starting to pool in his eyes. The thought of losing another person close to him was gut-wrenching. He didn't know whether it was the fire or the fact that Kinn was alive making him warm inside. "Kinn," he said, "you saved my life."

"You saved m-m-mine," he replied. "G-guess we're even."

Ard smiled. Now that Kinn was talking, he wanted to know what he saw. "Kinn, what happened back there?"

Kinn cleared his throat and opened his eyes, still rubbing his hands together. "It's like I said," he explained, "you stopped it with a light. The hound."

"What do you mean? What kind of light?"

"I-I don't know," he said with a puzzled look on his face.

"Th-the hound was there. I mean right there, he was. He w-was so close to us I could see straight down his gullet. Then this... light passed between you and it. The beast's head hit it like a s-s-stone wall, and it fell on the ground next to you. Then the light was gone. V-vanished! Just as quick as it came. You weren't moving and I couldn't get you to come t-t-to, but the hound w-was starting to get back up, so I grabbed you and pulled you into th-the river."

Ard smiled at him. "Maybe having you around wasn't such a horrible idea after all," he relented.

"I told you I'd be worth having by your side," he said through a half chuckle.

Ard edged closer to the fire, letting the heat from the flames warm his face. He wondered about what was happening to him. Had the fire come from him or had the fire starter worked? If it worked, it worked better than it had ever before. Something felt different about it. Ard felt like the flames came straight from his fingertips. He wondered about the light Kinn spoke of, trying hard to remember it. The only thing he could seem to remember was the gleaming fangs of the hound, and the more he thought of that, the more chills shot down his spine. What kind of light could stop an animal of that size dead in its tracks and where did it come from? Maybe it was one of Emagora's spells. Ard began to wonder if maybe she cast some sort of protection spell around him before leaving her garden. It wouldn't be that surprising after everything else he'd witnessed her do. She was able to enter his dreams from miles away and disappear into thin air only to reappear feet away. He had so many questions.

"So," Kinn said, breaking the silence, "you really are a...what was it again?"

"A Thorn," he explained. "Or so Emagora says."

"And Emagora is?"

"A witch."

Kinn made a confused face. "Right. Lives in the woods. I don't know about you, but aren't witches living inside creepy woods a no-no?"

"Well," Ard explained, "she's...different. She's a bornwitch."

"A bornwitch?" he asked, scooting closer to the fire. "What's that?"

"It means she was born a witch, obviously," Ard laughed. "She was chased out of her village when she was little. They tried to kill her for what she was. So she ran into the Bardenwood and never looked back."

"How terrible," Kinn said. Ard could tell he was still confused. He turned his head to the side like a puppy and asked, "So...what's a Thorn exactly?"

"Apparently, I'm some sort of protector. I can do things like see in the dark, jump really high..."

"Break padlocks with your bare hands?" Kinn finished.

"I swear I didn't know that would work."

"Did you know you'd be able to toss that dining table?"

Ard laughed again. "Not really. I sort of just reacted. I don't know. I get these...feelings."

"What kind of feelings?"

"I have no idea," he admitted. "They just happen. Urges or something. My muscles tense up and my face tightens. My body just knows what to do and it does it. Sometimes I don't even remember it."

Kinn nodded his head, seeming to understand. "So, if you're a Thorn and Thorns are protectors, what are you supposed to protect?"

"According to Emagora, someone called the Child King."

"The Child King?" Kinn repeated. "Never heard of him."

"They call him the Bringer of Magic. Years ago, he was imprisoned by Queen Leonora and the rest of the kingdoms out of fear that he would grow and overtake the Settled Lands. The only thing that can free him from imprisonment is a Thorn. That's why Leonora is after me. She knows that as long as Thorns exist, there's a chance this Child King can return."

Kinn's mouth gaped confusedly. "Well are there more

protectors out there?" he asked. "Thorns like you I mean?"

"They're rare now," Ard said. "Leonora and the other kingdoms hunted most of them down to make sure that no one could bring the Child King back. What they don't know is that we need the Child King."

"Need him?" Kim asked. "What for?"

"Emagora showed me that magic is a part of nature," Ard explained, "just like plants and animals. Without it, all the lands of Gylem, Settled and Feral alike will just wither away and die. That's why the Bardenwood is so gray and dark all the time. Without the Child King, it's dying. Our fields will follow next, then our animals, then us. That's why I need to free him."

"I thought you were freeing him so he could stop Kolbran and his riders."

"That too. That's if this Child King is feeling generous."

Kinn grabbed his soaked shirt and held it in front of the fire to dry it. "What could the Child King do about King Kolbran?"

"Well," Ard sighed. "I figured that this so-called 'Bringer of Magic' would be able to do something about the Ashen Horde. He must have been quite a force to be reckoned with for six kingdoms to decide on locking him up and killing off all the keys, right?"

Kinn nodded, agreeing. "That makes sense, it does. So that's why you needed blackstone?"

"Yes, it's part of the...the blackstone," he realized. "Where's the blackstone?"

"Don't brown your skivvies," Kinn said, waving his hands. "I grabbed your bag too when we went for our little evening dip." He tossed Ard the bag and let him tear through it. He pulled out the small chest Leonora had given him at the winner's banquet. Water poured out of its sides as he opened it up. All the blackstone coins were there. Soaked, but they were there. Locking it back up and putting it in his bag, Ard let out a huge sigh. "See?" Kinn said. "I told you."

"Skivvies remain untarnished," he joked back. Kinn laughed

through his belly, nearly dropping his shirt into the fire. As Ard noticed the sun starting to rise, he realized how tired he was. They had marched through the Bardenwood all night long with no stops. With a huge yawn, he went to make himself comfortable. He wrapped the chest of blackstone in his wet shirt and placed it next to the fire. "Alright, mate," he said through a stretch, "I think it's time we got some rest." Kinn's response was a light snore. He had fallen over onto the ground next to the fire and almost instantly fell asleep.

"Well, I'll take first watch I guess," Ard whispered to himself. He leaned comfortably against the trunk of a tree and watched as the sun burned the dark sky to a brilliant tangerine, suddenly realizing how long it had been since he was able to watch an actual sunrise. All the early mornings he could remember were spent in the stables tending to Hook and the other horses or preparing some tedious prank. He imagined a sunrise to look like Gran's smile or a wink from behind Mr. Brinkley's spectacles. Even though he was away from the fire and the chilly bite of the early morning still nipped at him, both of them were there to keep him warm.

16

The Huntress

The huntress crept from the trees and crouched silently behind a boulder, tightening her ponytail against her head. Beaded braids weaved wildly in and out of her ebony hair, but she always kept them high and tight, a typical practice of Vargynian hunters. Hair in the face can distract from a target and loose braids can get caught on branches. Her deep-set, chocolatey brown eyes were painted with a black mask to shield her snow-white skin from being spotted among the trees.

The Lushlands were different from what they were accustomed to in the insufferable heat of Ashar, but the Ashen Horde had no problem making themselves at home in the ruins of Passton, another Clustertown destroyed by their unquenchable flames. The frequent rains of the Cluster during this time of year made it difficult for things to burn, but this was just another challenge to the pyromaniacal riders. As their tattered banners hung among the smoke-blackened buildings, a pile of charred bodies smoldered into the evening sky, something the riders left in every town or village they ravaged. Any who lived were taken as slaves, but survivors were rare during their notorious flamelettings. The last rain choked out their massive fire pile in Passton's square, leaving a horrid smell of burned flesh, mud, and smoke permeating the night air. This mixed with the filthy, sweating bodies of the riders and their horses made it very easy for them to be detected—much too easy for her.

One of her comrades snuck quietly to her side and peered over the boulder. Some of the riders were sitting around the fire, gnawing on turkey bones, spitting and laughing. "Kella, who are these strangers?" he whispered.

"Riders from Ashar, Terik," the huntress said. "From the east. Have you not heard the stories?"

"No, huntress," he answered. "The only thing I know that lies east are the Sunlands."

"Yes," she whispered, "ruled by the scorned King Kolbran."

"The Burnt King," he said knowingly. He peeked his camouflaged face over the boulder again. The vermilion of the riders' rusted armor glowed blood-red in the smoldering embers of the burn pile. "You think he has sent them?"

"Who else, hunter? They bear the Crimson Pyre. That is his mark. I know it."

"What are they doing here?"

"From the look of things? Whatever they wish. It looks to be another uprising. If these riders made it here to Passton, the other Clustertowns south of here are surely ash. All they need to do now is brave the Pale Road and our lands will be no more, our people enslaved or butchered. We must do something."

Terik peered carefully over the boulder once more. "I count twenty, huntress," he whispered. "We can put these pigs down quietly."

"Twenty we can see, hunter," she pointed out. "How many do you smell?"

He sniffed the air subtly. "I do not know," he relented. "The smoke. It is too strong."

"There are over eighty soldiers here, hunter. I can smell their stinking skin and rotting teeth." She pressed her fingers into the dirt. "I can feel the stomping of their horses. I can hear them snoring in Passton's homes. Homes of the precious blood they have spilled. Their homes." She pointed to the pile of burning bodies.

Terik bit his lip sadly. "Eighty, huntress? Forgive me, you are a strong warrior, but that is too many for us."

"Too many for us," she repeated conclusively.

"What do we do?" he asked, rubbing his shaved head.

Kella pointed toward the trees they emerged from. "Assemble the others," she commanded. "Astakalla must know of what has happened here."

"The khetef? You know the law, huntress. He will do nothing. We will be punished for interfering."

"We have not interfered," she scoffed. "Not yet."

"Huntress..."

"Hunter," she cut him off. "Assemble the others."

Terik nodded obediently and crept back into the woods. Kella took one last look at the riders while they reveled in their horrors. She imagined taking down all twenty of them before the others would even know where she was. It would be easy for her, but Vargyn's strict non-involvement law was something she was not prepared to break. The grip on her elk bone bow tightened in frustration. She knew her penalty would be inescapable if she attacked. She would also risk the lives of her fellow hunters. Going back to Vargyn was a logical move, but she couldn't help imagining herself sending the monsters to the coldest depths of Nuvílda to answer for their atrocities. Few Vargynian souls ever descended to the "Endless Ice" and it was an unspeakable curse to wish someone there. She didn't care. If anyone deserved the torture of enduring the eternal blizzards of Nuvílda, it was the Ashen Horde. Unable to bear their cloying smell and deranged laughter a moment longer, she moved toward the trees but stopped when the pounding of hooves approached the boulder.

The riders' laughter died as a snarling voice boomed, "Having fun are we?" The riders remained silent, looking down at the dirt. "Huh?" the voice yelled again. Kella could tell it was coming from the other side of the boulder. Her body went rigid with silence as she pressed it against the rock, praying she would not be seen by the speaker. She heard the man hop down from his horse and scatter the mud from under his feet. "I thought," the man continued, "you dogs had a job to do."

One of the other riders spoke out now. Their Gylish was difficult to understand with their thick Ashari accents chipping away at every word, but Kella was able to hear him say, "It is getting dark, torchmaster. The day has been long."

"Not nearly as long as a day in the Sunlands," the man snapped. "You believe your work is finished when the Greatflame sets? Is my work as your torchmaster done now as well?"

The rider remained silent along with the others, gritting their teeth.

"You are dogs. Dogs do as commanded," the torchmaster growled, climbing back onto his horse. "A flameletting is a privilege. A sacred reward, not work. Dogs only get rewards when they have done their work."

The riders groaned and spit angrily on the fire, but none challenged the torchmaster's words. Torchmasters were chosen directly by Kolbran himself. Defying them meant defying him and no one dared disobey the Burnt King of Ashar. Even Kolbran's own men were no exception to his twisted punishments.

"I want that road blocked by nightfall by any means necessary," the torchmaster commanded. "Those filthy Vargynian savages have nothing we need. Their lands are shunned by the Greatflame. Cursed with cold. Kill anyone who approaches...and burn them." The sound of the torchmaster's horse galloped away and Kella peeked carefully from behind the boulder. The riders were all beginning to stand up. She had to make it back into the trees to tell Terik and the other hunters before she was noticed. The Pale Road was the only safe path through the Paasian Peaks to Vargyn and without it, the

Bitterlands would be cut off from the rest of Gylem. Kolbran wasn't planning on overtaking Vargyn—he was going to seal it up. The Bitterlands would become a tomb for their own people. Silent and swift, Kella crawled back to the tree line and sprinted to where her comrades awaited her, hidden from the soft glow of the burn pile embers. When she reached them, Terik had the rest of the hunters grouped, ready to return home.

"Hunters," she announced. "We cannot leave."

"What is wrong, huntress?" Terik asked.

"The riders are blocking the Pale Road to cut Vargyn off from the Settled Lands," she explained. "We cannot let them. We cannot leave. We must do something."

"Kella," Terik protested, "that is not our fight. Our law says—"

"Not our fight? Did you not hear me? If they close this pass, Vargyn will suffer. You have stopped others from doing harm to our people before, Terik. What makes this any different?"

"This is the Ashen Horde, huntress. Not the Kanungák, not a pack of wolves, nor a stampeding herd of goliamoth. This is war. Astakalla will punish us. There are other ways out of the Bitterlands. You use them yourself. We all have."

Kella stepped toward her fellow hunters, making sure to look each one of them in the eye. "Not all are us," she said softly. "What of our children? What of our elders? The paths we take can be made by no others. Without the help of the Cluster, our people will starve. What good will these paths be if there is no Cluster for them to lead to? We stood by and watched as these monsters butchered innocent people. We watched as they burned, pillaged, murdered and we did nothing. Arrows did not fly. Spears did not splinter—a shaking breath barely crossed our lips. These people were our friends and we failed them."

Terik argued, "We must not interfere, huntress. The khetef will not have us. You know the law!"

"You have already broken our country's law, Terik, do not forget," she fired back. "We all have. You know this. We have fought the Kanungák for years in spite of that law. You believe there is a difference between cannibals and the Ashen Horde? There *is* no difference. We oppose those who would try and harm us, we protect those who cannot protect themselves, and we stand and fight where others recoil in cowardice. That is what we do. That is what we have always done for the good of our people—for Vargyn!"

Terik looked down in chagrin. "You are right, huntress," he admitted. "Forgive me. I should not have spoken against you. We cannot let our people suffer while we still draw breath. We stand with you, Kella."

The other hunters nodded in agreement. "Terik," Kella said, placing her hand firmly on his upper arm and pounding her opposite fist against her chest, "you are my friend. There is nothing to forgive."

Terik grabbed hold of Kella's arm and pounded his own chest in a similar fashion, the Vargynian handshake, and asked, "What will you have us do, huntress?"

She looked back toward the riders then met the eyes of each hunter. "There are many of them and few of us. We will have to be silent. The night is still, so the wind will not mask our footsteps. There are twenty riders heading this way to begin blocking the Pale Road. We will take them out first. We will use the trees as cover and attack them from both sides. Terik, take some men across the road and strike first. When they have turned their backs, the rest of the hunters and I will take them from behind."

"Yes, huntress."

"We must be quick," she advised. "If any of them shout or alert the other riders, we will be overtaken. Terik, you and your men await my signal. Do not stop firing until they have all fallen. Red the snow."

Terik nodded obediently. Pointing to ten men, he commanded, "Hunters. With me."

Kella looked at the five men left with her. Seventeen Vargynians against almost one hundred deadly barbarians.

The odds didn't seem very promising, but they knew something had to be done. All of the men looked to their captain, ready to fight beside her. Years spent under the command of a warrior like Kella had fortified their trust in each other, cementing an unbreakable bond that made them a force fiercer than any army in the Settled Lands. She drew a deep, focused breath and signaled quietly for the other hunters to follow her into the trees. With a tight grip on her bow, she vanished into the foliage like a ghost.

17

The Whipping Town

"I got one!" Kinn shouted excitedly. "I got one, Ard!"

Ard clapped happily. "Great!" he exclaimed. "Only took half a century, but let's have a look at it!"

Kinn held up his long-awaited catch only to receive a frown from Ard. "Kinn," he sighed. "That fish is barely four inches long! That's not supper."

"It's an appetizer!"

"You can't even spell appetizer."

"A-P-A...agh...piffle! Who cares if I can spell it? I know what it is!"

"Clearly not," Ard laughed. "That's no appetizer, it's a morsel."

"Well, if you're going to complain I can just eat it myself. There's no fish in this part of the river. The current's too strong."

Ard stood up from the bank. It was a bit past noon. He was so exhausted from the night before that he'd fallen asleep on his watch. Thankfully nothing tried to eat them while they slept. After a much needed deep snooze, the boys were starving, and fish were becoming scarcer and scarcer in the rushing parts of the Witchfoot. "To Ferals with your stupid fish," he said. "We need to hunt."

"What are you going to do?" Kinn laughed. "Catch a wild animal with your bare hands?"

"I have a sword. I'll manage."

"Isn't that neat?" Kinn said, tossing the fish back. "I had no idea forest critters knew the art of swordplay. I'm learning more and more about these woods every day!"

"Very funny," Ard replied, grabbing his sword belt. "Keep watch and don't move until I get back. It's already past noon so you won't have the light for much longer." Kinn nodded his head, happy with his joke, then plopped down on the ground next to the fire. Ard knew they had to eat something, but truly he'd never hunted anything in his life. Even if he managed to kill something, he had no idea how to skin or cook it, but he had to try. Sword in hand, he began traipsing through the woods, secretly hoping he came across some fruit trees or berry bushes. That would be a lot less work than trying to kill a rabbit with a sword.

Hours burned away like twigs in a campfire. The sun was going down quickly and there was no sign of a single animal. As the rays pierced the thinning canopy of the autumnal Bardenwood, Ard could see everything in immense detail. His eyes were becoming attuned to even the smallest of movements. He noticed things like bark breaking from tree limbs and beetles shifting underneath dead leaves on the ground. He even stopped as he noticed a moth trembling to emerge from its cocoon. Hundreds of pollen specks glinted in the sunbeams like a golden snowstorm frozen in midair. The forest had never looked this way to him before. Even as the day whittled away, he couldn't help stopping every now and then just to take it all in.

Several yards away, he heard the satisfying snap of a twig followed by a shuffle in the leaves. His body reacted and he crouched low to the ground without a sound. As he looked toward the noise, he realized he could push his vision deeper into the forest, zooming in like an owl perched at the top of a tree. "Incredible," he whispered to himself. His abilities were becoming more and more manageable, yet still, he was amazed. As he pressed his eyes further, he was able to spot the source of the snap. Yards away, a lone buck grazed in a small clearing, completely unaware of his presence. Perfect.

Ard's constant pranking had made him stealthy, but with his new abilities reaching full control, he was nearly undetectable. Homed in on the deer, he inched foot by foot through the trees, careful to freeze when it looked in his direction. His feet may have been lighter, but not enough to muffle the crunching of leaves. Still, a few yards away, he had to stop. He was getting too close and the trees he was using to hide behind were thinning. If the buck heard anything above a whisper, the stalk would become a chase. Even though he was getting stronger, he didn't think he could match the speed of a frightened deer bounding through the woods. Now he had to figure out how he was going to kill it. Lobbing a sword at a fully-grown deer seemed a bit unorthodox, but what else could he do? He slowly unsheathed the sword, never taking his eyes off of the deer. As he drew his arm back, the sun reflected off of the blade and bounced right into the animal's eyes. He hurled the sword at it, but it was too late. The blade soared past the spooked buck and sunk into the trunk of a tree. He didn't have a choice now. He pounced into action, feeling his muscles surging again. Wrenching the sword out of the trunk with ease, he sped after his prey—the chase was on.

The buck was incredibly surefooted as expected. Ard struggled to keep up as it leaped through the forest, diving through brambles and around saplings like a fish through a stream. It had the home field advantage and knew exactly where to run. Ard swung from branches and slid under fallen trunks, trying desperately to get a clear shot. Every time he thought he had one, the buck would disappear behind another tree or boulder. He could feel himself start to sweat, but he was still able to go a bit longer. His breathing seemed different. He could feel his lungs take in extra air, making him run farther and harder. He was picking up speed he'd never experienced before. As the air rushed past his face and over his ears, it carried the deer's scent right into his nostrils. Even if it disappeared from sight, its trail stayed fresh and he could keep on target. He looked ahead to the buck and smiled triumphantly. Its mouth was agape and panting wildly. The beast was tiring.

Transfixed on his prey, Ard failed to notice the snare loop directly in his path. As his foot came down, the trap triggered almost instantly. The snare whipped around his ankle and jerked him upwards, knocking his head against the stony ground. Hanging upside down was not a pleasant sensation, especially after a decent crack to the skull. The blood rushed to his head and flushed his wincing face to cherry red. Before his head could explode from the pressure, he heard a pair of boots approach him. He looked up to find a man clothed in a camouflage suit wearing a sinister smile that cracked its crooked way across his dirty face. "Well, well, well," the man said. "Lookie what I caught m'self."

Ard wasn't in the mood for jokes. "You want to get me down, Toothless?" he barked.

The man squatted down and put his face close to Ard's, brandishing a gnarly blade with a club on the handle. "Shhh," he hissed. Before Ard could retort, the man flipped the blade to the club side and struck it against his temple. The pain was the worst he'd ever felt in his life. His vision blurred and he grunted from the sting of the blow. He felt his body fall to the ground and his neck crunch under his own weight. He yelled from the pain, trying hard to stand and defend himself. Another blow to the head and he hit the ground, scattering leaves into his mouth. He passed in and out, struggling to get control of himself to fight back, but before he knew it, the man had his hands and feet tied with some rope. As his vision started to return, it went black as the man tied a cloth blindfold around his head. The pain from the blows had his head ringing. He fought to struggle but the pain was so intense, he could do nothing but utter muffled grunts. He felt himself being slung over the man's shoulder and his head lolled upside down. As the blood rushed to his head once more, he felt the world around him fade away.

The ground was wet. His clothes were wet. He could feel the water droplets run down his face in trickling rivers. A roar of thunder rumbled endlessly overhead. He blinked through the downpour, trying hard to keep his eyes open. Looking around, Ard could see he was in some sort of cage. His skull felt like it was going to explode. He reached his hand up and felt dried blood on the back and sides of his head that had grown sticky from the rain. Groaning, he grabbed hold of the rusted bars of the cage, trying to see through the downpour. It was nighttime, but the rain fell in sheets so heavy that not even his new night vision allowed him to see. He looked around the cage. Through the downpour, he could see a small figure curled in the corner.

"You know," the figure said, "you really ought to get this fainting business under control."

"Kinn?" he said, ignoring his jab. "Where in the Ferals are we?"

"Where do you think?" Kinn said sarcastically. "There's only one place in the world I can think of where people get put into cages and forced into a lifetime of servitude, ain't there?"

Ard didn't want to know, but he knew. Barden's Belly. The place every Clustish child knew well from spooky tales told around a fire. A town nestled in the heart of the Bardenwood full of thieves, murderers, and lost souls. When kids misbehaved, their parents would threaten to send them on a boat down the Witchfoot into Barden's Belly to be whipped for all eternity. Once Ard got older, he stopped believing in the tale of the "Whipping Town" like every other kid, even though a small part of him always remained secretly afraid of being sent there.

"How did you get here?" Ard asked, still rubbing his head.

Kinn was sniffling and coughing, probably catching his death in the cold rain. "They came for me just as I was about to go looking for you. Three chaps dressed in plants and stuff. The next thing I know, I was blindfolded, gagged, and thrown into this cell. A few hours later they tossed you in, limp as a sack of potatoes."

The cold didn't affect him as it did once, but it was hard to deny the sharp chill of the incessant rain. He tried again to peer through the sheets, trying hard to get his bearings. "Lords Above," he gave up. "I can't see a thing. It's all black...*black*. Where's the blackstone?"

Kinn looked down at the mud. "Gone," he lamented.

"You're joking," Ard pleaded. "What do you mean gone? Where did they take it? Where, Kinn?"

"Don't know, sir," he said sullenly. "They took it all, they did. Everything and anything. Even my coat."

"No, no, no!" Ard cried. With an angry thrust, he swung his fists into the bars of the cell, rattling the whole cage. Over and over he banged his fists and arms against the bars. He'd never been so angry. As he continued to swing, the bars shattered with a humming clang. He looked at his unharmed fists in shock as the shards of metal pieces lodged themselves into the mud.

"Lordly fish lips!" Kinn exclaimed with laughter. "Ha! I should lie to you more often!"

"What?" Ard said, confused. "Lie to me? What are you talking about?"

Kinn reached into the side of his pants revealing a hidden pocket and pulled out a gleaming blackstone coin. "Thought it'd be a good idea to keep one for myself," he said, tossing the coin to him. "But I guess if it's the last one we have, you can finish your quest."

Ard caught it and inspected it. The Mossa Castille insignia was printed on each side and the metal shined even in the faintest light. This was definitely one of the blackstone coins. His mission was still safe. "I'll get you for that," he said, pointing a finger. "And 'lordly fish lips'?"

"My dad used that one a lot. Sorry. At least now we have a way out thanks to you and your fists of fury! Let's go before someone sees."

"Wait," Ard said. "No one catches me in a snare, knocks me unconscious, steals all my stuff, locks me and my friend in a rusty cage, and gets away with it." Kinn laughed, nodded, then hopped through the broken bars, splashing his feet in the mud. The rain was beginning to let up. Ard could see torches in the distance lit under shabby tin roofs and wooden shacks. The Whipping Town was definitely living up to its macabre reputation. There were other cages around his own filled with other prisoners. He could hardly stand the sight of them. Drenched, freezing, and malnourished, they huddled together in the cages, trying desperately to keep warm. He had to do something. The rain had eased enough to where he could see through the night. The cages sat overlooking a large shantytown nestled on either side of the Witchfoot, hidden beneath the canopy of the Bardenwood. Torches were lit all throughout the dirt roads and pathways. It looked to be early evening.

"What do you see, Ard?" Kinn asked.

"Looks like the good folks of Barden's Belly are turning in for the night," he answered. "We need to get everyone out of these cages, Kinn."

"Right," he agreed.

Ard walked over to the other cages and met eyes with one of the dark figures huddled inside. Gripping the handle, he pulled the cage door open, snapping the lock. The figure lunged at the door and pulled it back shut. Ard was confused. He tried to open the door again, but the figure held it in place. "What are you doing?" he asked. "I'm trying to help you."

"No," the figure said. It sounded like a woman.

"Why not?" he asked. "Don't you want to get out?"

Ard could see the figure shake its head and grab hold of a smaller figure in the back of the cage. "Nowhere to go," the woman said.

Kinn chimed in, "Anywhere's better than here, miss."

The woman stepped forward. Ard could see her face was hidden by a hood. "There is no place for us in these lands," she said. The woman pulled her hood from around her face to reveal herself. Her hair and eyebrows were dark as the night sky and her pale skin was covered in intricate raised scars that formed markings around her eyes and chin. The smaller figure next to her did the same, revealing a girl with the same features and similar markings. No doubt this was the woman's daughter. The markings seemed familiar to him. Before he could recall them, he felt Kinn tug at his sleeve.

"They're from Ashar," he said under his breath.

Ard took another look at them. The tattooed scars on their faces were the same ones adorned on the skin of the riders who attacked Pipton. For a moment, all he felt was anger and hatred, but as he looked at the woman, whose face tried in vain to mask pain and hardship, something stopped him in his tracks. This woman had done him no harm. She and the rest of the prisoners were just as much victims as he and Kinn were moments ago. He knew he had no right to judge her, yet the anger at the markings on her skin still boiled.

"Let's get you out of here," he decided.

"Ard," Kinn whispered. "What are you doing?"

"I won't hold the crimes of Kolbran over his people," he answered. "Not moments ago we were in the exact same cages. I used to think I was better than the people in my own village. I was wrong then, and I won't be wrong now."

The woman spoke to Ard, "You are very brave, child, but you know very little."

"I know enough," he said with unbroken sureness. "I know that all of you will catch your deaths in this rain, that you'll be whipped, tortured, or worse if you stay here, and that I can get you out of this town."

"There are many guards," the woman said. "Even some

hidden in the forest. Angry men with swords and crossbows. Horrible men. There is nothing you can do, child. This is the way things are for our people. Leave us before you suffer our fate."

"Angry men with swords don't scare me anymore. If I can clear a path for all of you through the woods, will you take it?"

The woman looked down at her daughter and to all of the other prisoners, but they gave no response.

"Will you take it?" he asked again.

The woman nodded her head with a broken smile. He could see the glint of possible freedom glaze over her eyes in the form of tears.

"Right then," he said, gripping the cage lock. "I'm going to get you all out of these things. Keep quiet, stay low, and follow me."

Ard began breaking the locks on the row of cages. He looked back to see Kinn smile as he helped an elderly man walk. There were about two dozen prisoners. Most of them being women, children, and elderly. He needed to get some bearings. "Kinn," he commanded, "I need to scout ahead. Get these people into the trees and keep them quiet until I get back. Can you do that, mate?"

"Yes, sir," he answered. "You watch your back. Oh, and don't faint."

For a short moment, he was reminded of Gran. How she and he always made playful jabs at one another no matter how serious the situation. He missed her more than anything, but instead of feeling sad, he let himself smile. "I'll try not to. Now go."

He moved into the trees like a shadow. The rain was still trickling down through the leaves, pattering the ground with a soggy chorus of frogs and crickets. None of the guards would be able to hear him approach. His eyes had adjusted and were able to see through the darkness with ease now. This patch of the Bardenwood was much less dense. Although that made it easier to move around, it made it much harder to hide a group of escapees from the eyes of guards. As he moved through the forest, his new hearing detected the sound of a conversation between three men. As he approached them, making sure he stayed hidden, he could see they were all perched on a rocky outcrop lit by a few torches overlooking the area in his direction. Probably in case any prisoners tried to escape. He'd come as close as he could. Any further and they would see him. In the low light, he was still able to see the glint of their crossbows, loaded and ready to kill. The spot on his ear where he first felt the slice of a crossbow bolt suddenly started throbbing. He didn't want to be pierced by another bolt, let alone be skewered by one. Knowing he could get no closer to the men, he started looking around to see where he could make his next move. The trees were so sparse, any movement from his position would—

The trees, he thought. Looking up the trunk, he noticed that he could easily reach the first branch. Silent as a cat, he leaped into the top of the tree hidden by its drenched foliage. The men would never suspect an attack from above. After climbing all the way to the top, he could reach the branches of the neighboring trees. With ease, he was able to leap from branch to branch without a sound. He was close now. He could smell them through the rain. They reeked of smoke, sweat, and pine needles. They'd been stationed here for quite some time. One final leap and he was in a pine right above them. He lowered himself slowly branch by branch, eyes fixed on his targets. The rain continued to drip through the leaves, soaking his clothes. The weight from the water betrayed him and a branch snapped beneath his foot...he was spotted. The men looked up into the tree, but he was already on the way down. His feet shoved the first man's head down into the ground with a hard thud.

One.

The two remaining guards shot their loaded bolts, but he dodged them effortlessly. Flipping backward, he planked in midair, kicking both feet into the chest of the second guard. With a shout of pain, he careened off of the outcrop into a tree and fell to the ground unconscious.

Two. He was getting good at this.

The third guard began loading another crossbow bolt, but before he could, Ard snatched it from him and smashed it to pieces on a rock with a grunt. The man drew his sword. "Stay back, devil!" he cried.

"Let's not kid ourselves, mate," Ard said with his hands up. "I don't want to hurt you. I simply want to get me and a couple of new friends out of Barden's Belly without a fuss. What are the chances you're going to let that happen, hm?"

The man hesitated, but he must have had some seriously full pockets. "Slim, wretch!" he spat. "Those were my friends. You're gonna pay for hurting them with your life."

"Figured." The man swung his sword and Ard dodged it without fail, throwing a vicious counter punch into his face. The man fell backward into the mud and stayed there.

Three.

The path was clear. Now he needed to get back to Kinn and the others. As he ran through the mud, the same smell of the guards drifted into his nose. There were more of them. He silenced himself, taking a hard look all around him. Seeing no sign of more guards, he followed the smell to where he left Kinn and the other prisoners. Peeking from behind a tree, he could see another group of men had apprehended them. Their leader held Kinn above the ground by his collar. "Who helped you, boy?" he growled. Ard knew his voice. This was the man who had beat him senseless after catching him in the snare trap.

Kinn wiggled his feet desperately. "I'm not telling you anything, pig!" he spat.

The man threw him into the mud and kicked him in the face, hard. He drew his sword and balanced it under Kinn's tiny chin. "I'll ask once more, you pissing little cuss. Who helped you release my property?" Kinn was breathing hard and trying not to cry. A trickle of blood ran from his nose and mouth, dripping onto the ground.

Ard wouldn't have it proceed further. Without thinking, he plunged out of hiding and knocked the man over, grappling him into a headlock. As he rolled to stand, Ard grabbed the man's sword and put it to his throat. "Doesn't feel so good on this end does it?" he growled. The other guards stood still, fearing for the life of their captain. Ard continued, "Option one. You tell your men to drop their weapons, walk away, and let us go free. Option two...well, you take a guess."

The man struggled, but Ard's strength had grown and he was able to hold him despite his larger size. With Ard's arm tight around his neck and his own sword beneath his chin, the captain struggled to say, "You're pretty strong for being s'tiny. What say you come and work for me eh, lad?"

"Can't say I quite enjoy the business of kidnappers, thieves, and cutthroats," Ard rejected. "Did I stutter? Tell your men to drop their weapons and let us go free. Kinn, count to five for the nice man."

Kinn wiped the blood from his chin and glared at the man. "One..."

"Look..." the captain started.

"Two."

"Just wait a m—"

"Three."

Ard pressed the blade harder against his throat, letting the razor-sharp edge do the gentle work of slicing into his skin.

"Alright!" the man relented. "Have it your way, boy. You heard him, idiots! Drop your bloody weapons."

The thugs' swords hit the ground with a reluctant clang. The second they did, an enormous black shadow crashed through the trees near where they were standing. Leonora's hound tore into the now defenseless guards. Their screams erupted from everywhere. Ard watched in horror as the hound ripped the men to shreds. He couldn't wait. Once the beast was done with them, it would be coming for him. He looked at the Ashari woman he had freed from earlier. "Go!" he commanded. "I cleared the way!

It's after me. Not you."

The woman nodded gratefully, grabbed her daughter and escaped into the woods with the rest of the prisoners. "Kinn!" Ard called. "Go with them. I'll draw it off!"

"No!" Kinn defied him. "I won't leave you, sir!"

The hound was finishing off the men like a scythe through wheat. There was no time for arguing. "We have to head upriver! Come on! Follow me!"

As fast as he could without leaving Kinn behind, he sped off toward Barden's Belly. Maybe if he stirred a commotion he could slow the hound down. When they reached the main road he started yelling frantically, channeling Lord Herman. "Beast! Beeeaaast!" he cried, trying anything he could to get people out of their homes. A horrid howl erupted from the hound. It had finished its appetizer. Ard could almost feel its fangs sink into his skin as he and Kinn made it to a small dock on the bank of the Witchfoot. He looked around for a boat. Without one, they'd have to risk the cold of the Witchfoot again – an option he did not want to relive.

"There!" Kinn said, pointing to a small rowboat among a row of river barges.

"Get in!"

Kinn wasted no time in clambering into the boat and nearly flipping it over. "How are we supposed to head upriver in this?" he asked.

"I don't know," Ard admitted, gripping the oars, "but Emagora's garden is northward. We can't go south. We'll waste time and the hound will just circle back for us anyway."

More screams, this time from the people of Barden's Belly, cut through the night. The hound was close. Ard pushed off of the dock and rowed upriver with all of his might. Easier than he expected, but his arms still burned feverishly with every stroke. With a scraping slide, the hound reached the dock and let out a snarling bark that echoed across the water. They had escaped it a second time—or so they thought. To the boys' horror, the giant dog leaped into the water and started paddling upriver after them. This time it wasn't losing them to the Witchfoot.

"Faster, Ard!" Kinn cried. "It's gaining on us!"

Unable to argue through gritted teeth, Ard rowed harder and harder, each stroke putting more feet between them and the monster that swam close behind. Kinn reached his hand into the river and started splashing water into the hound's eyes trying to slow it down. "Get!" Kinn shouted at it. "Fetch! Sit!" Panting and unable to keep up against the current, the mongrel gave up and turned back to the dock. It scrambled out and shook the water from its shaggy fur. Looking back at the boys with an icy glare, it howled once more before bounding off into the night, resuming its hunt on land. The river was wide and its banks grew more treacherous and sparse near this part of the Witchfoot. There was nowhere for the beast to follow. They were safe for now.

Thankfully the current had slowed and Ard was able to resume a regular pace of rowing. His arms stung, but he knew stopping was out of the question. Kinn let out a huge sigh. "That thing doesn't quit, does it?"

"Apparently not," Ard grunted between strokes. "We definitely haven't seen the last of it."

"How much further up river to this garden?"

"Not sure," he relented, straining. "A day? Maybe two? Three?"

"Here. Let me help you," Kinn offered, gripping one of the oars.

"Thanks, mate. You took a decent hit from that fellow back there. You alright?"

"Yeah," he sniffed, rubbing his nose. "Yeah, I'm alright. It'll take more than that to keep Kinn Sturly down."

"Ferals," Ard laughed. "Maybe try not to be so mouthy next time. Lucky you didn't lose any teeth."

Kinn chuckled, trying to wipe the bloodstains from his face. "It's going to be a long night, isn't it, Ard?"

"Yeah, mate," he strained. "No doubt. We'll keep going a bit more, then anchor to rest. We can't risk getting back on land so we'll have to camp on the river."

"Right. Well, at least the rain's let up!"

As soon as he said the words, an ironic roll of thunder tumbled overhead. Ard sighed, "You had to didn't you?"

18

Red the Snow

Kella signaled for the hunters to cross the Pale Road and hide among the trees. She felt a light sleet begin to fall to the ground, melting into the dirt. Hopefully, this would not affect her comrades in battle. Her trained ears could detect the sound of the riders moving down the road, twenty strong. She could see the masked face of Terik across the path nod assuringly. He pulled his furred hood over his face and practically vanished. She did the same. All hunters now patiently awaited her signal.

The boisterous riders approached now, reeking of rusted metal and mud. Sloshing through the sleet, not a single one of them took notice of the seventeen hunters keenly camouflaged within the trees. The riders were immense men, each of them capable of taking out a dozen assailants in combat, but unaware, the giants would fall like timber. They were carrying large pots of a bizarre smelling substance. Its heavy scent clung to the air and made Kella's nose crinkle, but she would not let their cargo distract her. If anything, it would just make them easier to take down. She carefully drew an arrow from her quiver and nocked it, gripping her fingers around the bowstring. The riders were right where they needed to be. She raised her fist slowly, sure the other hunters could see it—then spread her fingers wide.

A nearly silent rain of owl feather fletched arrows sailed into the riders, dropping almost half of them with lethal accuracy. As the remaining riders turned to draw their swords, Kella and the other hunters released another deadly volley of arrows bringing all of them down like a flock of spooked fowl. Their aim was so true, not a single arrow endangered their fellow hunters even though they were down range. As the last of the brutes fell, Kella and her comrades emerged from the trees to retrieve whatever arrows they could. The pots of powder the riders were carrying had fallen to the ground and shattered. The dust blackened the ground and had a terrible smell. She scrunched her nose at it. Just as she was about to congratulate Terik and the other hunters, she heard the beating of footprints further down the road. Looking back toward Passton, she could see her mistake sprinting to alert the other riders.

A rear scout. She'd missed him.

Stupid.

She'd have to cut him off through the woods or he would bring the wrath of the other riders down on her and her men. Without pause, she tore off through the trees after him, leaping over boulders and fallen logs to gain momentum. These trails were as close to her as the blood that sped through her veins. Her speed grew so much that the scout could now hear her drumming footsteps closing in on him. Frantic, he ran as hard as he could, but Kella had never lost a quarry before and she wasn't planning on starting with him. She intercepted the scout at the top of an outcrop that overlooked the Pale Road. Without hesitation, she leaped into the air. Flipping upside down, bow drawn, she sunk her arrow into the base of her quarry's skull with a sickening thud. She landed with an effortless roll and disappeared back into the trees, pulling her hood over her face. She was back at Passton. The scout had almost ruined everything. How could she be so careless? *Never again*, she promised herself. Mistakes happen once, then they are failures. Her father taught her that.

She quickly scanned the area, making sure no enemies saw her stunt. Everything seemed quiet. They had succeeded. Now the rest of the invaders would be their prey.

Terik and the other hunters regrouped with Kella on the wooded edge of Passton. With a slight bow, she congratulated her men. "Good work, hunters."

"Did you expect any less, huntress?" Terik boasted.

"I did not," she laughed. "But your work is not done yet, my friend. Gather the men and your spears. This will not be easy."

"Yes, huntress," he obeyed. "Hunters. The huntress commands spears." The hunters all strapped their bows to their chests and unsheathed deadly spears that swung from their backs, bone spears made from the tusks of goliamoth, enormous beasts native to the Bitterlands that supplied Vargyn with many resources. These bone weapons were sharp enough to pierce through the toughest armor but light enough to carry with ease. A Vargynian hunter was not complete without one.

Kella spoke to her group, "We must spread out here. Passton is not a large town, but we must sweep the whole village from here to the main road. The sleet has iced the ground so your feet must be sure. If you are made, do not give away the group. Use it to your advantage. Work together. You have trained for this. I have made you ready. *You* have made yourselves ready. Be strong and do not fear. We must not fail, hunters. Ika nojek!" *I am the drum*, it meant. A saying she and her hunters coined themselves. Vargyn was known for its animal skin drum music. Their deep beating could be heard from a mile away even through the icy rock and stone of the Paasian Peaks. Being a hunter meant keeping Vargyn's people safe and fed. They were what kept their people's hearts beating. What kept their rhythm of life steady. The drum was everything they represented. It was everything they were.

"Ika nojek!" the hunters repeated, pounding their fist to their heart. Kella never saw herself as their leader, despite the fact that they would do whatever she commanded of them. She saw herself as their equal. The relationship between her and her huntsmen was based on a mutual desire to do good in spite of their country's ways. A desire to be better than their ancestors. This was the Vargyn that she believed in. Ridding Passton of the Ashen Horde had now become their greatest mission together. They weren't just protecting Vargyn. They were protecting something more. They may not have been able to save Passton's people, but if they succeeded, they might be able to save a piece of the Cluster and drive the riders out of the Settled Lands. Moving silently as shadows with arrows nocked, the seventeen hunters crept through the streets of Passton.

Kella and Terik took to the rooftops. With a bird's eye view, they were able to see through the now torchlit village without a single obstruction. Smoke still smoldered through the sleet from the burned down buildings of the town. The riders were an unstoppable force during a flameletting, but now that they believed to be victorious, they were almost too easy to overtake. Drunk on Clustish wine pilfered from the pantries of Passton's fallen citizens, and without a soul on guard, the riders were picked off with ease. Kella's arrows flew without fail, taking down as many unsuspecting riders as her quiver would allow. Below, cloaked in the darkness of nightfall, she could hear her comrades taking out more riders as they slept. They had already made decent work of the barbarians when she heard the stomping of hooves approaching.

Peeking from behind a chimney, she could see the torchmaster had returned. In the street, he stopped a group of five riders. "Is your task complete, dogs?"

"Sir?" the riders asked, confused.

"Is the Pale Road blocked?" he asked with an irritated tone. "The Greatflame has set. Night has come. Where are the others?"

One of the riders answered nervously, "I do not know, sir. They took some jars of blackblaze to blow the pass. They have not returned."

Blackblaze. Kella had heard of the substance. A black,

odorous, powder that made a lethal explosion from even the tiniest amount. Blackblaze was an evil too great to be wielded by men, yet here was the worst of humanity using it to kill and destroy at will. She listened further.

"I wanted that pass blocked by nightfall," the torchmaster spat. "It is nightfall, is it not? Find out what keeps them from obeying the will of their king and report to me immediately."

The riders groaned, but turned and did as they were commanded. Many of them still remained in Passton. If they were alerted even now, the hunters would have to retreat. There was no room for more mistakes. Across the street, Kella could see Terik perched on the neighboring rooftop. He had been listening as well. She signaled for him to follow her and cut down the group of riders. If they discovered what happened to the first group, the whole horde would be put on alert. The hunters would be overwhelmed.

Once the torchmaster was out of sight, Kella nocked two arrows and watched as Terik drew his spear. Being second in command to her was something he'd rightfully earned. The two grew up beside each other as best friends and were the fiercest combative force in Vargyn. All of their years growing together were spent reading each other's strategies and training as a unit. Without hesitation, she leaped across the street to the neighboring rooftop, releasing her two arrows mid-jump.

Two down.

Before the other riders knew what happened, Terik descended upon them, silent as an owl. With blinding speed, he took out another two riders on his own, covering their mouths to stifle their final screams of pain. As the last rider raised a warning horn to his lips, a third arrow from Kella's bow shot it out of his hand, just in time for Terik to deal a final, devastating strike.

The group of riders was downed and all hunters were still undetected. They were winning. Climbing back to the rooftops and regrouping with Kella, Terik spoke, "Nice shot, huntress."

"You act surprised, hunter," she replied sportively.

"This seems too simple," he complained. "Perhaps we should alert them. Let us give these hunters a real challenge."

"No," she disagreed. "I will not risk my brothers' lives for sport, Terik."

"Come on," he goaded. "Even you cannot resist a good challenge, huntress."

"Stay focused, Terik," she commanded. "Uka nojek. You are outside your head."

"Maybe," he admitted. "But you know I am right."

"Stay focused," she repeated. "We need to eliminate the torchmaster. If he escapes on horseback, we will not be able to stop him. Are you with me, hunter?"

"Ika, huntress," he answered. "Until death claim me."

Kella nodded and began moving to follow the torchmaster. As they closed in on him from both sides of the street, she met eyes with Terik to confirm their plan of attack, but the sleet had made the roofs slick with ice. Her foot slipped and a roof tile fell to the street, shattering with a loud crack. Knowing her position was revealed, she leaped in for an attack.

The torchmaster turned and looked up in her direction, but she was already soaring toward him. Sending the full weight of her jump into his shoulders, she toppled him off of his horse as it whinnied with fear. He recovered and drew his scimitar. Toe to toe and no longer unaware, she was unable to take him out quickly. Before she was able to silence him, he called, "We're under attack! Riders, to me!"

Her eyes widened. They were too far into Passton now. On foot, the hunters would be run down by the riders before they made it back to the trees. They had no choice. They had to fight. Terik made it down to the street and plunged his spear into the back of the torchmaster, tossing his stiff body into the mud. "We are made!" he exclaimed.

"You wanted a challenge, hunter," Kella said, unsheathing her spear. "Your wish has been granted. Hunters! Red the snow!"

From the homes and rooftops, the rest of the hunters emerged like lethal shadows to regroup with her. Thankfully the immense riders were still in a sleepy, drunken stupor, otherwise, the Vargynians may not have stood a chance. Working together, the hunters made short work of the rest of the barbarians. Their bone spears knocked against the rusted steel of the riders' scimitars, refusing to bend or break. Using their own bodies as launch pads, Kella and her comrades cut through the brutes like hot water through ice, seemingly never tiring. Their finesse frightened some of the riders so much that they tried hopelessly to retreat, but archers on the rooftops made sure none of the villains escaped. Within minutes, Passton had become a bloody graveyard rather than a smoldering victory camp. Grinning from ear to ear, Kella cheered alongside her huntsmen with relief as the last of the riders fell to the sleety, blooded ground. They had survived the night and rid Passton of Kolbran's plague.

"You fought well, huntress," Terik congratulated, smiling.

"As did you," she replied, pulling arrows from corpses. "That was our greatest challenge yet."

"Yes," he agreed. "It was. What do you suppose the khetef will have to say about this?"

The cheering from the other hunters subsided. They knew what they had done was right, but the laws of Vargyn were sound. They would be banished and shunned by their people for what they had done here. All of the hunters had acted on their own will and none of them questioned their captain, but they all knew the punishment for their actions and it was hard to swallow.

Kella spoke to all of them, "What happened here tonight was an act of history. Make no mistake, hunters. We have done what is right. Whatever happens to us, Khetef Astakalla must know of Kolbran's uprising. We must convince him, no matter our punishment, that Vargyn's borders must be protected against what is to come. Vargyn's people must be made safe. I do not ask that you stand with me. I ask, as I have always asked, that you do what you feel in your heart to be right. You have fought bravely, but the punishment for what you have done tonight is exile. You will not be welcome in the borders of our country if you admit to your actions. You will be shunned by the people you saved. Some of you may lose the love of your own families. If you do not wish to stand with me, know that I understand and do not blame you."

The hunters all looked at each other then back to their young leader. Smiling they all pounded their chest and said in unison, "Ika nojek!"

With a grateful smile, Kella struck her chest. "Ika nojek."

19

Beneath the Blackened Oak

"Ard sat up from where he was sleeping. He was back in Pipton at the edge of the Bardenwood, where he always was when Emagora visited his dreams. He looked back at Pipton where everything seemed normal again and took a deep breath. He'd missed this view. From here he could see the rickety sign of Sore Swallow, swaying in the breeze. Maybe if he stayed here long enough, he could see Gran again. Maybe she'd walk down the front steps of the inn and look out to the Bardenwood like she did sometimes. Ard knew she was fearful of the forest, but when she looked across the fields at its graying edge, she didn't seem scared. She would look at it with worry. Like something between its trees awaited her. Or maybe she was the one awaiting something. Ard closed his eyes, trying hard to remember her face. He sniffed the air for a scent of rosemary, felt the ground with his fingertips for her tugging at the weeds in her garden, anything to feel her one last time. *No*, he thought. She was gone. Gone, but not forgotten. He knew his mission to avenge her was almost complete. Shaking the thoughts away, he looked back to the Bardenwood where he knew she'd be waiting. "It's been a while," he said, smiling. "How are you, Em?"

Emagora sat crouched just out of reach of him, staring longingly into his eyes. "Em?" she blushed. "Hm...I like that."

"I'm so glad," Ard said smoothly.

"My, my!" she said with a raised brow. "One journey to Mossa Castille and you're sweeping me off my feet with charm? And using my favorite phrase against me no less." She levitated off the ground placing her hands coyly behind her waist. "I suppose I should consider myself a lucky witch." Her shimmering red hair swayed in the wind just like it had the first time Ard laid eyes on her. Before, she seemed so ominous, like the dark loom of a storm cloud ready to burst. Now, as she swayed suspended in midair, he could feel his heart flutter and blood begin to race. A fluttering that only occurred when she was near.

"You should consider yourself a very lucky witch," he said. "I'm almost back to your garden."

"Truly?" she exclaimed. "Oh! I'm so glad! Just remember to follow the toadstools. They won't lead you astray, I promise."

"I will," he assured her. "I've missed you, Em. You're not going to believe what I've been through."

"Me?" she said shyly. "You've missed me?"

"Of course," he laughed. "Why wouldn't I?"

"Sorry," she said. "It's a strange feeling. Peculiar...feeling."

"What is?"

"To feel...wanted."

Ard frowned. "I'm sorry that's a strange feeling for you. I hope it's a good kind of strange."

"It is!" Emagora said excitedly. "Oh, truly it is. I must say, Arden Ford of Pipton, my garden has not been the same since you've been gone. I feel as if you might've taken something with you when you left."

"Really?" he asked. "Well, hopefully, I get the chance to return whatever I took."

She looked up at him with a velvety smile. "Can one return a stolen heart?"

He froze, unable to speak. His cheeks flushed red and his

heart pounded against his ribs. Why couldn't he talk? He was always so quick to respond. Why couldn't he say anything? *Speak,* he thought. *Speak, idiot!*

Emagora blushed embarrassingly. "I'm sorry," she said. "How forward of me. So, so rude."

"No!" he finally managed. "It's fine, Em. Really. I'm forward too. I mean, I would be if I was...no, what I mean is you're welcome to forward be me. I mean be forward me..."

She chuckled as he fumbled helplessly over the phrase. "I'll see you soon, stableboy," she said delicately. "Be safe."

Another moment slipped through his fingers as a crackle of thunder woke him from the dream.

***

More storms. Ard knew they were definitely near the Cluster now. Practically everything grew in the Lushlands and there was one reason for it—rain. Rain, rain, and more rain. Especially during this time of year when the cold winds blew in from the Paasian Peaks and clashed with the warm winds of the lower fields. The thunderclap that woke him rumbled in the distance. Kinn woke from his side of the rowboat too. Through a yawn, he asked, "How much further, Ard? It's been two days almost."

Stretching his arms wide, he answered, "Nearly there. Storms are worsening and the current is slowing. We should continue on foot." Ard reached into his pocket and twirled the blackstone coin around his fingers, a nervous habit he'd developed since their first escape from Leonora's hound.

"You sure that's a good idea?" Kinn asked nervously. "What if the hound comes back?"

"Don't worry," he said, pulling up the anchor. "If we make it to Emagora's garden, she'll keep us safe."

"Right," Kinn worried. "About that."

"What?"

"Are you really okay with her being a witch?" He squinted his eyes, hoping the question didn't offend him.

"As a matter of fact, yes," Ard retorted. "I am. What do you know about witches anyway?"

"Nothing good," he argued. "Nasty stories about stuffing children in ovens come to mind. Mind you, I could use some color, but I don't fancy being baked alive to a crispy, golden brown."

"And the man-eating trees?" Ard reminded him. "Or what about the bloody Witchfoot River? They're all just tales of the Bardenwood. Nothing more. I told you she's not like that. She's a bornwitch. She can't help what she is. She's no different from you or me."

"Aside from living in a garden in the middle of the woods, of course," Kinn snarked. "And the whole magically entering your dreams bit. There's that too."

"Oh, shut up. You listen to too many stories. Emagora's—"

"Different. I know, I know. What does the miss look like anyway? Is she covered in warts? Can she fly on a broomstick or turn into a cat?"

"No," Ard said flatly, rowing to shore. "She's nothing like that. She's got long hair that's red as a rose. She loves flowers and plants so much that they cling to the strands just so. Her skin is white like a first winter frost and she—"

Ard noticed Kinn was holding in a laugh.

"What?"

"You like her, don't you?"

"Of course, I like her. Why shouldn't I? She's better company than you, that's for sure. And she doesn't stink of fish."

"I don't stink of fish!"

Ard laughed as the rowboat grounded itself against the sandy riverbank. The storm loomed overhead now. He could feel the rain getting ready to burst from the clouds. The woods looked more familiar here. The pines were gray just like the forest edge behind Sore Swallow. Even the smells seemed familiar. The soaked wood of the tree branches, the muddled foliage on the ground. Most importantly, he could smell flowers. Flowers that could only grow one place in a dying forest. Emagora's garden had to be nearby. He could remember the luscious fruits and the effervescent greens that seemed to pool from the ground. They'd be a welcome reprieve from the black shade of the Bardenwood. "Come on," he commanded. "It's not much farther."

"How do you know where you're going?" Kinn asked, hopping from rock to rock.

"I don't."

"You don't? What do you mean you don't?"

"Will you keep your voice down? We need to keep heading upriver. Keep an eye out for toadstools."

Kinn scrunched his face confusedly. "Toadstools? What in the Ferals for?"

"They'll lead the way to Emagora's garden," Ard explained.

Kinn shrugged. "Ah, of course. Magical toadstools. I hope this doesn't take long. I'm starving."

"If only there was enough food in the world for you, Kinn Sturly," Ard patronized. "So am I. Emagora will take care of us. Don't worry. There's plenty of fruit and vegetables in her garden, you'll see. There's apple trees, pear trees, peach trees—"

"Does she have a salmon on rye tree?" he joked. "Or maybe a nice turkey leg tree? Lordly fish lips, I'd be muchly grateful."

"Again with the lordly fish lips?"

"You'll get used to it, you will."

Suddenly, a breeze picked up from behind them carrying a familiar scent. Ard sniffed, tensed, then grabbed hold of Kinn, throwing him to the ground behind his legs. Had it not been for the breeze, he would never have known Lenora's hound was there stalking them in silence through the underbrush. Now that it had been spotted, it lunged at the boys, closing in fast. As it leaped into the air, Ard instinctively raised his fists above his head and watched as a beam of silvery-white light flashed around his arms, forming a blinding, spherical wall in front of him. The hound's enormous body crashed face-first against the light and it rebounded feet away to the forest floor with a ground-shaking thud. Ard looked at his hands in shock.

"See?" Kinn exclaimed.

Ard picked him up off the ground and threw him forward. "Run, you idiot!"

As they sped upriver, they could hear the hound recovering from the blow. They would never be able to outrun it now. As he leaped over a log, Kinn noticed a toadstool sprout from the ground. "There!" he cried. "Ard, look!"

"Follow it! Go, go!"

Kinn ran as fast as he possibly could, but he wasn't gaining much ground. A howl echoed through the trees as Leonora's monster bounded into chase. It would be on them at any moment if they didn't pick up speed. Ard knew he could run faster but he couldn't leave his friend behind. "Kinn!" he commanded. "Get on my back!"

Kinn wasted no time. As soon as he clambered onto his shoulders, Ard darted through the Bardenwood with him in tow, sure to keep his eyes on the toadstool path. Even over his own heavy breathing, he could hear the giant hound crashing through the trees behind him. The dog's frenzied panting was the most terrifying sound he'd ever heard. He dared not look back. Ahead of him through the branches, he could see the wall of trees that surrounded Emagora's garden. They were almost there. Pressing as hard as he could, he sprinted toward the garden door. "Emagora!" he called. "Em, open the door! Hurry!"

Kinn screamed into Ard's ears. He could feel the heat of the hound's breath on his back as it closed in. They weren't going to make it.

He shouted for her once more. *"Emagora! Open the door!"*

The hound opened its jaws to clamp around Kinn's back, but before they snapped shut, Ard dove through a tangle of vines. As if they sprung to life, the snares entangled the beast in their grip. The hound snarled with rage, snapping and scratching at the vines, trying desperately to get free. The tree trunk door cracked open just as the boys were slowing to a stop. "Get inside!" Ard said, dropping Kinn to the ground. "Those vines won't hold it for long."

Kinn jumped inside as Ard slammed the door shut. The garden was still as beautiful as he remembered. Emagora's evening lanterns were lit throughout the trees just like when he first met her. *It's dreadfully dark during storms here*, he remembered her saying. Out of breath, he called, "Em? Emagora, are you here?"

No answer. Just a flash of lightning and roll of thunder. Before he could begin looking around for her—

BANG!

The tree trunk door cracked with the weight of the charging hound. It rammed its body against the door over and over. It was trying to get through the tree wall and into the garden. It was free of the vines and not ready to give up. Its sharp claws scratched maniacally at the door, scraping away the bark to get inside. Ard was running out of time. He had to get to the oak tree in the middle of the garden. Grabbing Kinn once more, they made their way past the fruit trees and flower shrubs that grew like fountains through her garden. The blackened oak sat gnarled and bent in the shade of the storm clouds surrounded by its muddy soil. This was where he had first met Emagora face to face, but she was still nowhere to be seen.

Kinn stared at the tree with wonder. "What is this, Ard?" he asked fearfully. But, before Ard could answer, the garden door burst open and the hound squeezed through, speeding straight for them.

"Run, Kinn! It's not after you, mate!"

"No!" he said bravely. "I'll draw him off. Do what you came here to do, sir!"

"Wait!" Ard pleaded. "Don't, Kinn!"

Before he could grab him, Kinn ran straight for the monster, screaming wildly trying to distract it. But the hound was too well trained. Staying on target, it jumped clean over him, knocking him down with its back legs. Ard was its quarry and it was ready to die for it. Why was this beast so determined to kill him? It had traveled miles away from its mistress and home, seemingly never tiring. How was Leonora capable of training such an animal to do her bidding? None of it mattered now. He knew he wasn't going to live to see his family avenged. At least before he was mauled to death he could save Emagora, her garden, and the Bardenwood, a place that at one time filled him with paralyzing fear. He remembered Emagora's instructions. He had to do this now before it was too late.

He knelt down on the ground and plunged the blackstone coin into the muddy soil. He grabbed a bramble of thorns near the tree roots, the only sharp object around him. With all his might, he clenched the thorns with both fists, wincing with pain. He heard the hound leap in for the kill behind him. He could smell its horrible breath. The blood dripped from his wrists onto the spot where the coin was buried and the ground beneath him quaked with an echoing boom.

Ard turned to meet his death head-on, but the hound fell to the garden floor in midair sliding to his feet. He watched in horror as it began contorting itself and snarling in pain. Writhing on the ground, he could see its bones breaking underneath its skin.

No...Not breaking.

Changing.

Its fur fell to the ground and evaporated into a gray smoke while its howls of pain turned hauntingly into human screams. Its claws shortened and paled to finger and toenails and its gray skin paled to a fleshy white. Lightning flashed, revealing a shaking, bearded man gasping for air. The only thing that remained from Leonora's ravenous dog was the man's icy blue eyes that stared into Ard's with otherworldly shock.

Kinn rushed to over. "Ard!" he exclaimed, hugging him tightly. "What's happening? What was that noise? It shook the ground, it did! Who's this guy?"

Ard couldn't speak. He was trying to figure out what he just witnessed. The ritual was supposed to release the Child King, not turn Leonora's hound into a naked, trembling man. What had he missed? What had gone wrong? Was it not enough blood? Was it too much? His hands stung from the thorns which still clung to his skin. The blood continued to drip from his fingers as he looked around the garden, trying to make sense of it all.

The shapeshifting man stood up, legs trembling. He looked at Ard then to the blackened oak tree. His eyes widened with horror as he stammered, "What have you done?"

20

Emagora

Thunder. Horrible, monstrous thunder shook the ground. The storm above began to churn into a menacing vortex. Leaves and branches peeled away from the garden's trees, whipping and snapping in the gusting wind. The clouds spiraled directly above the blackened oak where Ard, Kinn, and the hound man stood. A bolt of lightning struck into the soil where he had buried the blackstone, knocking all three of them to the ground with a deafening crack. As Ard sat up, he saw a pair of eyes gleaming from behind the oak tree.

"Emagora!" he cried. "Thank Lords. What's going on?"

She crept from behind the tree, her dress whipping about in the wind. He could see in her eyes that she was frightened. Another bolt of lightning hit the blackstone spot and the ground rose up and fell down with a shudder. Emagora screamed and ran to him, leaping into his arms.

"Em," he repeated, holding her head to his shoulder, shielding her from the flying debris. "What's going on? What's happening?"

Her heavy breathing turned into whimpers as she began to

sob against his chest, shaking her head back and forth.

Ard was confused. "Em?" he said, holding her tightly. "What's wrong?"

She sniffed and placed her dirty hands gently on his face. They smelled like freshly picked flowers and nectarines. Her head was facing the ground as she continued to sob. As she fought through tears, she stuttered, "D-do you remember all those s-stories about witches in woods?"

Ard tried to look her in the eyes, but she refused to look up. "Em," he said. "Look at me."

She sniffed again, stammering, "Do you r-remember how they kept you awake all night? H- how they turned your blood to ice?"

His breathing began to quicken. "Emagora? Why won't you look at me?"

Her soft sobs began to morph. Her whimpers turned to wheezes. Her tears dried like morning dew to sun. Something was wrong. Ard tried once more to look at her face but it was hidden beneath her crimson cascade of hair. She twitched as an odd sound worked its way from her gut and across her lips. Her shoulders started to shake up and down as she began—cackling.

Her face was still turned to the ground, but there was no mistake. Emagora was laughing. Not her usual cheerful chuckle. Not the laugh Ard loved where her lips pressed tightly together like a flower bud ready to bloom. This was something else. She wheezed and twitched back and forth nightmarishly, unable to control herself. Before he could pull her together, her hand moved from his face to his throat, squeezing with incredible strength. For some reason, he couldn't move. His body wouldn't cooperate. He was paralyzed.

"Agh!" he choked. "Em! You're...ch...me...sto..."

Emagora pulled him close and finally raised her head, locking her ghostly eyes with his. Her face looked the same but somehow completely different. Her snowy skin was there. He could even see the flower petals entangled in her hair's scarlet strands, but she looked nothing like the witch he'd left behind weeks ago. In an unrecognizable voice, she hissed, "You should have listened to them."

The next thing he knew, he was soaring backward through the air into a tree trunk, shaking the leaves from every branch. Before he could recover, something fell from the branches and wrapped around his head, blinding him. Clutching the object, he tore himself out from under it. It was a blue cloak, one with an unmistakably horrible stench to it. He looked into the tree above him and gasped. An old man was gruesomely strapped to the trunk of the tree in a twisted position. He had bloody, red wounds etched into odd shapes all over his chest and arms and his head drooped, lolling from side to side. The man looked up, groaning painfully and wheezing for air. As Ard met eyes with him, he knew exactly who he was looking at.

"Gell?"

Before the old man was able to respond, vines shot from the shrubs of the garden and pinned Ard to the ground. He tried to fight, but the snares would not break or loosen their terrible grip, no matter how hard he pulled at them.

"Ard!" Kinn screamed. Turning to Emagora, who stood beneath the blackened oak with a horrible smile, he yelled, "Let him go you—"

"*Witch*?" Emagora finished with delight, widening her foggy eyes. Before Kinn could reply, roots exploded from the ground trapping him in a gnarled cage. It was like the garden had turned into a waking nightmare that awaited her every command. Another wheezing cackle erupted from her chest, echoing through the trees. Ard was in shock. He looked around for the hound man, but he was nowhere to be seen. Emagora didn't seem to care as she pranced over to Ard like her usual cheerful self.

"Hello, Arden Ford of Pipton," she snickered with a flip of her crimson hair. "Miss me? Ooh, how silly you must feel."

Ard struggled confusedly against the vines. They were

beginning to cut his skin. "Emagora, you're hurting me!"

The witch looked down on him with a cruel smile. "I'm so glad," she mocked.

Never in his life had he felt so stupid. "How can you do this to me?" he cried. "I'm your friend! Let me go! Please!"

Instead of responding, Emagora pounced onto his chest, straddling her legs around his waist. Her eyes were cold and inexpressive, unlike the ones he'd grown to adore. To his horror, she dug her nails into her cheek and began peeling away her white flesh like a snake. Beneath her perfect, alabaster skin, he could see slimy wrinkles. A guttural laugh began to creep its way from her lungs as she continued to tear everything away, letting the pieces fall beside his face. With a sickening tug, she pulled her scalp back and the dazzling strands of her auburn hair dulled to a frizzy gray, falling to the forest floor. Her real hair dropped against Ard's cheek with a slap. The strands had turned to wet pond reeds that hung sparsely from her head. From her face, all the way down to her arms, she continued the gruesome shedding as he watched on in absolute terror. The only thing left of his precious Em was her swirling, foggy eyes. Eyes that no longer held a kind or loving gaze.

He could find no words. This was some evil imposter. Some horrible doppelgänger here to thwart their mission. No. Emagora was good. He knew she was. He'd felt her touch. He'd grown to know her heart, her soul. This couldn't be her. It couldn't be. As the last piece of her skin tumbled to the floor, the witch let out a grisly, clicking shriek.

The bone-seizing cry was cut short as a gleaming blade glinted against her throat. Ard looked down the hilt and met eyes with the hound man, only this time, he was not naked and trembling. He was fitted with a matchless suit of armor that clung to his body like bark on a tree. It was an armor that looked forged by nature itself, silver and green as the dew-soaked fronds of a fern. It weaved itself around his chest, legs, and arms in perfect fashion, like it was built for him and him alone.

"Release the boy or die, witch," he commanded in an icy voice.

Before the conflict could continue, another deafening blast of lightning hit the blackstone spot. The ground rose and fell like the breathing chest of a giant, tossing Emagora off of Ard and into the trees. The hound man, who had held onto the vines for balance, began cutting them away fluidly. His sword was slender and elegant as if the blade itself was made of fabric. The shining steel cut through the vines like a sickle. As soon as Ard was free, he rushed over to Kinn.

"Ard!" he pleaded. "Please, sir! Get me out!"

"You're alright, mate," he calmed him. "Move back!" As Kinn moved to the other side of the cage of roots, Ard gripped it with all his might. With a strained pull, he snapped the roots open, making a hole just big enough for him to crawl out of.

Hugging him tightly, Kinn cried, "Where did she go?"

Ard scanned the garden for any sign of Emagora, looking closely at every tree and shrub. He knew how good she was at vanishing. It was only a matter of time before she reappeared. "I don't know," he replied. "Come on. We have to leave!"

As the boys ran for the tree trunk door, a boom from deep beneath the blackened oak stopped them in their tracks. The wind slowed to an eerie halt and a chilling quiet fell over the garden. The forest went still – stiller than it had ever been. Not even a single blade of grass or fallen leaf dared a tremble.

Ard was told tales of the Bardenwood all his life. None of them spoke of what he was seeing. A sight that he would come to remember for the rest of his life, despite how hard he' would try to forget it. A sight that froze him to the spot like the forest around him. A sight that could only be described as the birthing of darkness itself.

21

An Evil

K ella and her hunters were nearing the icy walls of their city. The Pale Road was now covered in a white blanket of fresh snow that crunched under their feet like thin sheets of glass. Worn from the battle in Passton, the hunters were much slower than usual. Traveling on foot was not easy, especially through the frozen hazards of the Paasian Peaks, but this was their way. Horses did not do well in the frigid north of Vargyn and they weren't ideal when hunting. Fire was a hunter's best companion in the Bitterlands. That morning, Kella had snuffed out what was left of, hopefully, their last campfire. As they marched through the snow, she turned to Terik.

"When we meet with Astakalla, let me do the talking," she commanded.

"As you wish, huntress," Terik replied. "What fate do you think awaits us? Do you really think we will be banished?"

"That is the law," Kella said flatly. "But I do not know. I wish I did. I wish I could send these hunters home after a hard month's work of protecting our borders. I wish them to be with their wives, their children. I wish them to be safe in their homes, warmed by firelight with a full belly. Instead, they blindly follow me into exile."

"Not blindly," Terik corrected. "They follow you because they believe in you, Kella. *We* believe in you. You have given us purpose. You have given our lives meaning. Does that mean nothing?"

"It means everything," she said with love. As they continued trudging through the snow, they reached the top of a hill. Faint sunlight broke out across their faces as they reached the top, their skin soaking the warmth gratefully. The sun's rays were a rarity in the Bitterlands and it took being high up on a hill to feel their touch. Deep below in the valley, they could see smoke rising from stone chimneys and hear a faint whisper of voices. They were home.

"Vargyn means everything to me," she continued. "These people mean everything to me. I wish that was what counted when it came to breaking our ridiculous law."

Terik pursed his lips. "Perhaps today the khetef will change his mind," he tried. "Perhaps he will see the error in the ways of our people."

She gave him a look.

"Or perhaps you will be shunned by Vargyn for the rest of your days," he laughed nervously.

The rest of the group reached their two leaders, sighing comfortably in the sun. Out of nowhere, Kella felt a monstrous boom beneath her feet. Alarmed, she drew an arrow and nocked it instantly, ready for anything. The other hunters looked at her with confusion. "What was that?" she asked.

Terik slowly moved closer to her, avoiding her lethal arrow that awaited its next kill. Looking around, puzzled, he asked, "What was what, huntress?"

"Did you not feel it?"

"Huntress, feel what? Nothing has happened. Are you alright?"

Kella knew what she felt. The shudder was enough to cause

an avalanche. How could they not feel it? As she looked at their confused faces, she realized how silly she must have looked. She was breathing hard and ready for a fight, but none of her comrades heard or felt anything. Placing her arrow back into her quiver embarrassingly, she replied, "Yes. Forgive me, hunters. I am alright."

"It seems the huntress has been away from her bed for too long," Terik joked, trying to defuse the tension. "Some rest would do her well!" The hunters laughed then began making their way down the hill into Vargyn. As the last of them passed Terik, he turned to her. "Huntress, are you sure all is well?"

She was not quite convinced herself. She knew she felt the ground shake. Now everything around her felt—wrong. She couldn't put her finger on it. "Yes," she breathed, unsure. "Let us go home, hunter. There is a warm bed and bath with your name on it."

Terik smiled at her then began making his way down into the valley. Kella took one last curious look down the Pale Road toward the Cluster. The sun was out in full, with barely a cloud in the sky. But for some stirring reason, she could hear the distant rumble of thunder. A thunder that seemed to call to her in a way she couldn't describe in words. The rumbling tugged at her very soul, beckoning her to heed its desperate plea, but the answer was lost to her. She stared into the trees waiting for the unknown summon to reveal itself, but when it didn't, she turned back to her home dreading a crisis— an evil— she knew absolutely nothing about.

22

The Child King

Fingers rose from the muddy soil beneath the blackened oak. Two hands emerged and clawed voraciously against the twigs and wet foliage. Ard could see they were green and translucent, similar to a frog. Slowly, a rack of velvety antlers appeared. They were fuzzy and short, like a springbuck. The antlers were attached to the hairless head of a boy, no older than Kinn, who gasped for breath as soon as he surfaced. The soil clung to his skin like mud as he crawled like a living nightmare from the ground. Ard could see that his eyes were as black as the gnarled branches of the oak.

No whites.

No color.

Just an unending...*black.*

As the boy continued to pull himself out, coughing and gulping for air, Ard saw a dark smoke emanating from his skin. It furled around his lanky body like a cloak. As it settled, the smoke solidified into cloth robes that hung down to his bare feet, which were dirtied similarly to Emagora's. The boy with green skin stood shakily, looking around with a bewildered gaze. Ard's hair stood on end. All of his senses were telling him one thing. Not to run. Not to fight. All they kept screaming was—*danger*.

"Ard," Kinn whispered. "Is it him? Is that the Child King?"

He was frozen. He couldn't answer. This looked to be the Child King Emagora spoke of, but something about the antlered boy made his blood run cold. Something was terribly wrong. He could feel a horrible, unseen fire burning in the black of the boy's eyes. A fire he felt burning beneath his own skin. Before Ard was able to answer, the hound man stepped in between them, sword in hand. As the antlered boy noticed him, his face tightened with intense hatred.

"*You.*"

The boy's voice was beyond anything heard in the most horrific nightmares. It resonated like hundreds of echoes layered on top of one another, each fighting for which could sound more like a blade against rusted iron. The echoes chimed through the Bardenwood like the haunting toll of a broken bell. Kinn gritted his teeth at their ringing.

The man looked afraid but held a brave stance. "Here we stand again, Grymling," he said to the boy. Rather than let him respond, the shapeshifting man ran his hand along his blade from hilt to tip. To Ard's bewilderment, the sword cracked away with a million wooden snaps, transforming into something else. Within seconds, the strange man now held an ornate spear. He hurled it at the boy with incredible speed. Unable to dodge in time, the spear plunged deep into his chest, dropping him to the forest floor.

From behind one of the trees, Emagora flung herself into the fray. "No! My king!" she cried, falling beside him. She turned her eyes upward and met the hound man's with a glinting, fiery hatred. "Diiiiieeeeee!" she shrieked. Fog began to swirl around her in a whirlwind of twigs and leaves, shrouding her from view. As she disappeared, the man knelt to the ground, grabbed hold of a mossy, broken branch and squeezed hard. As he did, the branch exploded into wooden pieces and in an instant, he held a dazzling shortsword that fit the curves of his hand like a glove. The swirling fog moved behind him with blinding speed and Emagora reappeared in a terrifying form. Her nails were extended into long claws and her jaws were filled with rows of sharp teeth. But before she could attack, the man ducked low and spun around, thrusting the dagger directly into her unprotected chest. Her face melted into shock as she looked down at the blade wedged between her ribs. The man's face was poised, completely unfazed. As Emagora choked on her last breaths, a trickle of blood escaped out of the corner of her mouth. Her monstrous form slowly shrunk back to that of an old woman. Ard watched in horror as her body twitched and grabbed at the blade, trying to stave off death for just another moment. As the last of the light in her foggy eyes vanished, she looked at Ard. "Stableboy," she sputtered, "what...have...you...done?"

The man tossed her body onto the ground in a bed of her garden flowers. He did not waste time. He turned to Ard and Kinn, spitting, "Run if you wish to live!" Without waiting for a response, he dashed through the garden. Ard looked at Emagora's lifeless body. *This is just a nightmare,* he told himself. *None of it's real. It's not real. It's not real.*

Kinn snapped him out of it. "Ard!" he said, shaking him by the collar. "Let's go!" He nodded then pulled Kinn onto his back, sprinting after the man as another enormous thunderclap shook the ground. He was incredibly fast, even against Ard. By the time he caught sight of him again, he was slashing through Emagora's wall of trees like it was nothing. Who was this man? Or more importantly—what was he? Just minutes ago, he'd been the most fearsome beast in the Settled Lands, ready to devour Ard alive. Now he was...Ard didn't even know. His mind raced with endless questions. Questions he knew he wouldn't get answers to while sprinting through the Bardenwood. He suddenly felt an awful despair wash over him. He didn't know who to trust or what to think, yet he couldn't stop his legs from running. He wanted to be free of the Bardenwood. Free of the garden. Free of this man. The trees around him felt like the bars of a cage. Bars he couldn't break through no matter how hard he thrashed. Even as his legs burned, every sensation in his body was telling him to keep running. *Get out,* they begged.

Get. Out.

Mind whirling with thought after thought, Ard didn't even realize they'd sprinted all the way back to Pipton. He could see the charred remains of buildings through the forest edge. The smell began to choke him all over again. Even though it had been weeks, he could still taste the smoke rising from the burn pile in the square. All the faces of his fellow villagers flooded back to him, each passing by like ghosts. He tried to fight them, but the tears began to roll. *Keep running,* he thought. *Keep running. Get out.*

As they passed into the field, Ard started to cough violently. Kinn slid off of his back to help him. "Ard! Ard, you're okay, sir! You're alright, you are."

The hound man stopped. "We cannot stay here in the open," he said. "We must find shelter."

As if he summoned it, a flash of lightning crackled overhead, and the rain finally started to pour. Ard felt the droplets hit his skin like falling needles. Crying out in pain, he clawed at his skin like the drops were biting him. The sound of the thunder was deafening. He was losing control of his senses again, but this time, it was excruciating. Everything hurt. Convulsing, he fell to the ground, twitching and writhing in agony. His teeth ground together so hard he thought they might shatter into pieces. Kinn tried desperately to calm him, but every small touch felt like a blow shoving him back and forth on the ground.

"What's happening to him?" Kinn yelled at the man. "What did you do?"

"I've done nothing," the man said over the rain. "He's—"

Ard tried to focus on the stranger's words, but his body was beginning to shut down. He couldn't hear anything but a humming ring deep in his ears. His head suddenly became very heavy, falling against the grassy ground. His shaking slowed to a stop as he once again started slipping into total darkness. He could have fought it. He could have tried to stay conscious. Instead, he let it all fall over him like a comforting blanket, hoping this time he never woke up.

23

The Thorn

Rosemary.

The smell of wood and mothballs. Garlic. Charred pieces of bread. More wood. More garlic. Apples. Berry...blackberry jam.

Rosemary.

Dirty apron. Wet mud on the threshold. More mothballs. Fireplace. Sooty chimney. Drying mop.

Rosemary.

Sore Swallow. He was home. She was—here.

"Gran!" Ard screamed, sitting straight up from the floor. All the smells vanished. He was in Sore Swallow's kitchen. Right where Gran used to cook and serve the inn's guests. The ceiling was almost completely burned away, letting the rain patter against the wooden floors. The old inn had put up a good fight, but only enough to provide one last bit of shelter for a stableboy, a terrified stripling, and a mysterious, shapeshifting man who stood in the corner of the kitchen looking out into the storm.

"Ard," Kinn said softly. "It's just us, sir."

Ard looked to the hound man. "Who's us?" he said coldly.

The man turned his face to him. He was slender, middle-aged, barely taller than Ard himself, but he looked incredibly strong. His beard was brown and long like his hair, a stark contrast to his crystal blue eyes. His armor was gone. Now he wore a wet, tattered cowl and black trousers that must have been dug up from Pipton's remains. "Can you travel?" the man asked.

"What?" Ard asked, rubbing his head.

"I did not mumble, boy. Answer my question."

Ard clenched his teeth. He was not feeling particularly patient right now and he could feel himself growing angrier. "Yeah," he said low. "Yeah, I can travel."

"Good," the man said. "You and the child must leave. Now."

Ard let out a tired, uncaring laugh. "And go where? For what? Why should I even trust you, huh? You tried to eat me not long ago. Remember that?"

"You have no idea," the man said, stepping forward. "You have no idea the events you've set in motion."

"Yeah?" Ard said, standing up. "Well, why don't you tell me? Go on then. You can start with who the Ferals are you?"

"Of all the pressing things you have to worry about," the man pointed out, "you wish to know my name?"

"I don't want to know your name," Ard corrected. "I want to know *everything*."

"You are losing time, boy," he groaned.

"Does it look like I care? To Ferals with you and everyone else as far as I'm concerned! I'm not doing anything for anyone, least of all a complete stranger that could turn into a giant hound and kill me at any moment."

The man looked at Ard as if he was battling whether or not to trust him. "If I tell you everything," he bargained, "you must pledge to me that you will do exactly as I say. No options. No excuses. Your pledge and your word. That is what I ask."

"How do I even know I can believe you, mate?" Ard argued.

"You don't." The look on his face was that of a man who got what he wanted. It was stern, determined, as if he knew exactly what Ard's response would be and he was just asking out of courtesy. Gran was like that.

"Perfect," Ard sighed. He looked at Kinn to see what he was thinking. He looked white as fresh linens, probably only able to think of witches and ghouls crawling out from the ground. With no words to say, Kinn simply shrugged his shoulders.

"Your pledge and your word," the man repeated.

Ard took a deep breath. "Fine," he agreed. "My pledge and my word. But, you're answering every question I have. Come what may."

The man sighed, relinquishing, "My pledge and my word."

Ard wasn't wasting a second. "Your name."

"Cedar," the man answered.

He continued, "Why were you hunting me?"

"Because Leonora bid me to," he answered.

"But *now* you have a conscience? Why disobey orders now?"

Cedar realized he would have to do better. Leaning against the charred walls of Sore Swallow, he patronized, "Let's start here. Were you ever told *not* to trust witches hidden inside a forbidden forest?"

Ard gritted his teeth and tried to ignore the I-told-you-so look he knew Kinn was giving. "That thing was not Emagora," he said defensively. "She's a bornwitch."

"Still under her spell, I see," Cedar sighed. "There is no such thing as a bornwitch, boy." Ard went to retort but he continued over him. "Witches come about one way and one way only. Dabbling in Grae or Grym holds binding consequences over humans. Dark consequences."

"You're talking about magic," Ard said, unsure.

"Magic," Cedar scoffed. "What the fairy tales call it, yes. Grae and Grym are two parts of an element known as Dül. Grae being the good, Grym being the bad, for lack of a better explanation. To mankind, Dül is sometimes called 'spirit' or 'soul'. It's within us all. Not just people, but animals and plants. The ground we walk upon, the water we drink, and the air we breathe. But, humans were never meant to harness Dül. Any who try become slaves to it in a horrible way."

"So, she was right," Ard said. "Magic is a part of nature and it's not meant for humans."

Cedar nodded. "Emagora may have told you truth, but only truth that held a benefit for her lies."

"You know her? Emagora?"

"I *knew* her, yes," he corrected. "That witch has prowled the Bardenwood for decades, serving the Grym in whichever way sees her the most reward. Her evil far surpassed that of any other Grymling. You are not the first boy she has tricked but you're certainly the last. You're lucky to be rid of her."

Ard's head spun. It was all a lie? Or was this the lie? How did Cedar know all of these things? How did he know Emagora? Ard had known her for much longer than he'd known this shapeshifter. It seemed right at first to believe her over him. Yet still, a thick embarrassment flushed his cheeks to red. Had he really been so foolish to trust a witch? Despite all of the stories he'd been told? Maybe he had, but the last thing she said to him felt so real. It wasn't the beautiful girl he'd known before saying it, but it felt the same somehow. "You really killed her," he said, looking down.

"You're lucky to be rid of her," Cedar repeated straight-faced and pitiless.

"And the Child King. You killed him too. Why?"

"Oh, I didn't kill it, dear boy" Cedar laughed. "I merely injured it so that we could escape."

"So," Kinn interrupted timidly, "he's still out there?"

Cedar nodded.

"That's comforting," Ard sneered.

"All the more reason for you to hurry up with your questions," Cedar pointed out. "You're wasting time."

"Alright," Ard said, "so if that...thing...was the real Emagora, what was she doing to Gell?"

"The man in the tree?" Cedar asked. "I suppose he didn't

look like that the last time you saw him."

"No," Ard said sadly. "He didn't. He lived here in Pipton. He was barely fourteen."

Cedar went on, "To maintain her alluring appearance, she would've had to slowly drain the boy of his youth. A painful practice. But then, Grymor is never pleasant. Even you still feel the effects of her perversions."

"Will he...die?"

Cedar's unapologetic face endured as he answered, "She would have kept him alive as long as she wished to retain her beguiling persona, but yes. It will most likely claim his life in the end. As is the way of witches."

A cold realization sent chills beneath Ard's skin. The screams at the gathering—they *were* Gell's. Emagora used an innocent child to lure a dumb, naive stableboy into the forest. Horrible guilt wrapped around him, tightening in his throat and gut. "We have to go back and help him!" he panicked.

"No," Cedar ordered. "You will be killed as soon as you step foot through the woods. You are not prepared to face the Grymor that has awakened."

"You keep saying that word," Ard said angrily. "What is that? Grymor."

"Witchcraft," Cedar said. "Evil. Darkness. It has many names. Grymor and Graemir are the works done by using either part of Dül. Two faces on the same coin."

Kinn interjected, "I get it! Grymlings are creatures that serve the Grym. And those that serve the Grae—"

"Graelings," Cedar finished.

Ard didn't care so much about Dül or magic or witches anymore. He pressed further. "So what's been happening to me? My senses. They're overwhelming."

"All Thorns are born as simple humans," Cedar explained, "but during adolescence, they experience something called the Waking. Many creatures, Grym and Grae alike, can sense a waking Thorn. Like bees to a blooming flower. That is how the witch found you. All she needed to do was wait patiently for you to start morphing so she could sink her teeth into you. As a Thorn's new senses and strengths develop, their former selves will sometimes have difficulty keeping up. Hence the fainting."

That made sense. Now Ard knew why certain smells, tastes, or sounds sent him reeling into a frenzy. His body couldn't handle the sensory overload so it would just shut itself down. He continued with, "So, are you a Thorn? Is that how you know all of this?"

"That I am," Cedar admitted.

Ard was finding it hard to grapple with. Dül, Grae, Grym, Thorns, and witches. He tried hard to fathom it, but the weight of it all was growing impossibly heavy. He took a deep breath. "So it's true then," he concluded. "I really am a Thorn. Like you."

"Only a Thorn could have released the Child King from imprisonment," Cedar said. "That much of what Emagora told you was true."

The thought of the rose-haired witch made Ard's blood boil. How could he have been so naive as to think she could be trusted? That she possibly loved him. All his life he'd been warned of witches and their gingerbread houses, their empty promises, their tricks. His mind filled with more questions, just like it had when he first met her in the garden. He needed more. More information. More explanation. More truth. Breath quickening, he commanded, "Go on then. Tell me what a Thorn really is."

Cedar remained quiet. Ard could see him thinking of how best to answer, but he could wait no longer. "Let's have it!" he yelled. "Tell me the truth!"

"Keep your voice down," Cedar hissed. "There are men nearby."

"It's the Ashen Horde, Ard!" Kinn warned. "They're still here."

He had forgotten about them. The real reason he set out on this quest in the first place. Kolbran's pigs. The filth must have taken up residence in Pipton's ashy corpse. Terrible anger began rushing over him. It lit him up like a white-hot bolt of lightning. All of a sudden, he could feel the heat of the flames that burned Sore Swallow to the ground. He could see Gran's eyes, smell her hair, feel the soft wrinkles on her cheek. He could hear the sound of Mr. Brinkley laughing, see the glint of his spectacles, feel his hand upon his shoulder. He could feel his body surge as he walked out of the inn into the rain. He would kill them all this time. Every last one of them.

Cedar grabbed him and threw him back onto the muddy floor of the kitchen, pouncing on top of him. "You think of no one but yourself!" Cedar spat.

"I think of *everyone* but myself!" he fired back. "I see all of their faces every night. I still hear their screams, feel the heat of the fire...I can still taste the smoke. You don't know what they took from me! You don't know!"

Cedar ignored his grieving, arguing, "Should you not survive a fight with those men, what will happen to your servant boy? Am I to care for him? You think you can just get tricked by a witch into raising a long-imprisoned evil, off yourself, and leave us all to clean up the mess? You gave me your pledge and your word, boy. You do exactly as I say, I answer your questions. That was our deal. Do not break it again."

Ard shoved him off, brushing the mud off of his trousers. "Fine," he growled. "Have it your way."

Cedar calmed himself and leaned against the wall out of the rain as another thunder roll cracked across the sky. Continuing, he asked, "What did the witch tell you about the nature of Thorns?"

"I thought I was the one asking questions."

Cedar repeated angrily, "What did she tell you, boy?"

He sat up. "She said I was a protector."

"A protector of what?"

"The Child King," Ard said. "'The Bringer of Magic', she called him. She said he'd been imprisoned by Leonora and the other kingdoms years ago and that only a Thorn could set him free. But, all of the Thorns were killed off so that he could never return. She said that him being gone was the reason the Bardenwood looks the way it does, all gray and dead. I'm guessing all of that was a lie."

"Not all of it," Cedar said. "The Child King is not the Bringer of Magic nor was it imprisoned by the kings and queens of man. You were never meant to protect it. Thorns were meant to fight it."

"You keep calling him 'it'," Ard pointed out. "What is the Child King? Where did he come from?"

He paused and looked out into the Bardenwood as if he was waiting for something to come bounding out into the storm. "Humans destroy," he said softly. "Wherever they go, trees become timber, water becomes sewage. They burn, chop, and hunt with no regard for nature or her gifts to us. Well, after so many years, nature responded. 'It' was her reply."

Ard gulped. He remembered the black eyes of the Child King staring through to his soul. He could remember their blood-curdling darkness that seemed to go on forever. He could feel them sending icy shivers through his bones even now. Another crack of thunder roared overhead. "What does 'it' want?" he asked.

"The end of us all," Cedar breathed. "Graeling and human alike. To rid the world of man and extend the Bardenwood to the farthest reaches of Gylem and then beyond. Far from any king, it is a purely Grym spirit born of raw hatred for mankind. It represents nature's sheer destructive force and nothing else. Its power is unlike anything you've ever seen, and it's only just begun."

Ard was still perplexed. "But, what does all of this have to do with me?"

"It has nothing whatsoever to do with you," Cedar said harshly. "You are selfish to think so. Had you not been so foolish, evil itself would have never been set loose in the first place.

Its poison upon the world will now start to spread, turning the Bardenwood into the real nightmare we all fear it to be. Grymlings all across these lands will now awaken from years of deep slumber and descend upon the kingdoms of mankind. Their devilry will spare no one. I liked to believe we Thorns were intelligent creatures, but with you, I'm beginning to doubt it."

"Look," Ard said defensively, "it's not like I had someone around to tell me these things. How was I to know what was lie and what was truth? I still don't know what's real, but now I'm just expected to trust you and everything you say?" He shamefully felt himself begin to cry. The feeling burned in his nose as the tears tried to fall.

Cedar laughed, "You would trust witches in woods but draw the line at someone who just saved your life? Someone who showed you what you are? What I tell you now is truth, boy."

"I don't even know who or what *you* are, mate!" Ard retorted. "Can all Thorns randomly turn into giant monster dogs or is that just a neat party trick you do?"

"No," Cedar said plainly. "It was the cost I paid."

"Cost? What cost?"

"All Grymor comes at a cost," Cedar brooded. "Years ago, when I failed, I cast a Grym curse on the Child King, imprisoning it beneath the oak. Upon performing the curse, I was transformed into a giant mongrel. Shortly after, Leonora found me and had me brought to her kennels, where I replaced all of her prized hounds by devouring them at her command. I have obeyed her every whim since. Even the whim to find you and bring you back to Mossa Castille alive. From her first request, I was hers to command forever, bound by an unshakable fidelity. Dül is oftentimes unpredictable and it has a sickening sense of irony."

"How do you mean?" Ard asked.

"The price the Grym demanded was 'eternal loyalty'. I had no idea what it meant at the time, but what creature in this world is more loyal than a dog?" He forced a smile, an attempt that concealed vile deeds Ard could tell he had yet to forgive himself for.

How horrible that must have been. Killing and consuming against your own will. He imagined what it would be like to be forced into obeying every command you were given without hesitation. But then to remember those commands, no matter how gruesome, that would be worse than horrible. He tried not to let his empathy get the better of him though. After all, his empathy was what made him trust the word of a witch. "So the kingdoms didn't imprison him," he realized. "It was you. That's why you changed back in the garden. I broke your curse by freeing the Child King."

"Yes," Cedar said callously. "Now you see what the witch's lies have accomplished. Looking back, I should have known the trees would soak its poison. *That* is the reason the Bardenwood suffers the way it does now. The Child King has made the forest ill, even in its imprisonment."

Ard looked across the field to the grayed tree line of the Bardenwood. He could almost hear the sickly moaning of the pines longing to be lush and green again. He turned back to Cedar. "What did you mean when you said you failed?"

Before Cedar could answer, the clopping of hooves approached the inn. The three of them pressed against the walls, hoping the shadows and the rain hid them well enough. After a few moments, the hooves made their way around the corner. Ard sighed with relief as he looked upon a familiar long face. A sweet friend he had nearly forgotten about trotted up to him with a grateful whinny. "Hook!" he cried as the horse rustled his wet mane.

"You know this beast?" Cedar asked.

"Yes, I do," Ard said, stroking Hook's nose. As he looked closer, he could see the stallion was wearing a strange bridle. It was blood red and trimmed in a fiery, golden design. His heart began pounding as he looked on the seat of the saddle.

"The Crimson Pyre!" Kinn exclaimed. "He's one of the rider's horses!"

Ard gaped at the emblem painted on the saddle. It was even gruesomely branded onto Hook's bare chest. The barbarians must have broke him to use in their savagery. Ard stroked his neck lovingly. "What have they done to you, Softy?" he said to the horse. Hook replied with a reassuring toss of his head. Suddenly, Ard's body froze. He could hear the sound of footsteps heading down the road toward the inn.

Kinn noticed him trying to listen and whispered, "What do you hear, sir?"

The footsteps turned to voices. Voices Ard hoped he'd never hear again. A group of Kolbran's men were searching the streets for a horse that had thrown its rider into the Witchfoot. He could hear them whistling and whooping for the horse to come out. They were looking for Hook.

Ard looked at Cedar, who had also been listening. "You must leave," he said quietly. "Now!"

"Where will we go?" Ard asked, grabbing hold of Hook's reins.

"You must head east," Cedar instructed. "There is nowhere else for you to go. You must not venture into the Bardenwood for any reason. For any reason, you understand? As the Child King regains strength, the wood will come alive with all manner of Grymlings. Grymlings that won't take kindly to a young Thorn like yourself."

Ard swung his leg onto Hook's back, petting his neck to keep him calm. "Are you not coming with us?" he asked.

"The flames of Kolbran will spread," Cedar said, lifting Kinn onto Hook behind him. "The other kingdoms must be warned. There is a greater threat brewing than they know."

"What do you mean?" Ard asked. "The Child King?"

"That and more," Cedar said gravely. The footsteps of the Riders were getting closer. They had mere seconds before they were caught. "I'll draw them off," Cedar said. "Ride east. Stick to the road as far as it leads you, then take Frystakall Pass to Thenderland. No matter what happens, tell no one what you are.

Not a soul. Understand? When you reach Thenderland, speak with the queen. Above all else, *speak with the queen.*"

"The Silver Sorceress?" Kinn gasped fearfully. "Haven't we dealt with enough witches already?"

Even Ard had been told tales of the Silver Sorceress, the Thendish queen rumored to possess magical powers beyond belief. Some stories spoke of her conjuring storms to wreck traveling ships or twisting the minds of her own people to be her willing slaves. None, however, spoke fondly of her.

"Ard," Cedar repeated, "our deal must not be broken. Speak with the queen above all else. After you have spoken with her, head south and meet me in Pyce. It is imperative that you wait for me there. Is that clear?"

Ard nodded shakily. Everything was happening so fast. Thenderland? Pyce? Those were in two separate parts of the Settled Lands. Cities in kingdoms he'd never even dreamed of seeing. These were not light journeys. He had no supplies, no food, just the clothes on his back and boots on his feet. His heart pulsated through his chest so hard he could hear it in his ears. The beating was so intense, he almost didn't feel Cedar grab hold of his arm. "Ard," he urged, "there's something else you must know. When nature birthed the Child King, she never knew the horrors it would commit. To correct her mistake, nature birthed a solution. A balance. A savior. The one you were truly meant to protect."

The footsteps drew nearer. Even Kinn could hear the riders now. Their whistling made Hook stomp nervously. Cedar tried to continue quickly, whispering, "The Rose—"

They had been spotted. The group of riders charged at them, flailing their blood-rusted scimitars above their heads in a wild frenzy. Cedar picked up a piece of wood and ran his hand down its length. As he did, it splintered and chipped away like a hundred tiny axes to a tree trunk. Within seconds, Cedar held a beautifully crafted sword similar to the one he used in the Bardenwood. Its blade was a gleaming silver but the hilt and handle were wooden. Just like his armor, the blade fit in the curve of his hand with a perfection only nature could have crafted. Bounding toward the riders, he called back, "Find the Rose! Find her!"

Ard kicked Hook's sides and clutched the reins. Kinn held tight against his back as the horse galloped eastward through the fields of Pipton with incredible speed, kicking up mud and grass. The rain beat against Ard's face, washing away the tears that fell for his home. The home he was leaving for a second time. The home that he was leaving for a final time. He could hear the clanging of metal as Cedar's sword clashed with the scimitars of the riders. Over the rain, he could still hear his final instruction replaying in his head.

Find the Rose! Find her!

Find her.

Find her...

⚓

Hook had carried them as far east as he could. Since stopping to make camp, the poor horse hadn't moved from the spot where he'd collapsed, panting for breath. Ard scratched him lovingly as he watched Kinn attempt to make a fire. The storm had stopped a few miles back giving them dry ground to rest on, something they'd never been more thankful for after enduring miles of being pelted by pouring rain on horseback. Ard knew the road to Thenderland was going to get colder and harder. He feared the fire might be the last one they saw for a while. As soon as he saw the kindling ignite, he let out a grateful sigh.

"There we are," Kinn said. "And no wind to snuff it out. Can't ask for much more, can we?"

Ard said nothing. They had barely spoken a word since leaving Pipton. He stared into the tiny flame, unable to piece his thoughts together.

Kinn sat next to him, leaning against Hook's hip. The exhausted horse took no notice of him as he said, "Ard, are you alright?"

He was barely listening to him. He raised his eyes above the fire and stared at the hazy border of the Bardenwood that stood still against the darkening sky across the fields. He hadn't taken his eyes off of it since they'd stopped. Thankfully the road to Thenderland kept the forest edge at a safe distance, but Ard still couldn't bring himself to turn his back on it.

Kinn followed his eyes. "The woods seem different now. Darker somehow, don't you think?"

Ard relinquished a slow nod.

Kinn pulled a few blackberries from his pocket that he'd picked from the side of the road and popped them into his mouth. He offered some to Ard, but he turned them down with complete silence. Hook swung his head around, grateful to accept Kinn's offer in substitution. "What do you think he meant?" he said through chews. "Cedar I mean. Going on about a Rose and whatnot. You think the Silver Sorceress will know?"

Still nothing.

Kinn swallowed the berries and put a hand on Ard's back. "Ard, listen. I don't know what's coming or what happens next. Ferals, I don't even know what day tomorrow is. But, I promise you that I won't let you face it alone. The way I see it it's like you said. It's all just tales of the Bardenwood. Only now the story's ours. It's our very own tale. You know?"

Ard broke his brooding gaze and looked at Kinn. His freckled eyes crinkled into a cheeky grin mottled with blackberry seeds. Something about his smile this time squeezed a tear from his eye. He put his arm around Kinn's back and pulled him into a tight hug. "Our very own tale."

The fire had grown now, thanks to the dry sticks and leaves. They let its warmth touch their faces as the night set in. The hazy border of the Bardenwood had disappeared into the dark, but they knew it was still there. Waiting there still as stone. Where it would be for a while. The woods stretched east for miles and the boys couldn't afford to head north out of its sight. There'd be no road to guide them and they'd risk losing time. Kinn stretched his arms up and let out a yawn. Ard knew it would be difficult for him to get to sleep, so he offered, "Why don't I take the first watch? Get some rest, mate."

Kinn nodded gratefully then tossed him a branch he'd picked up while gathering sticks for firewood. Ard caught it and looked it over in his hand. Puzzled, he asked, "What's this for?"

Kinn shrugged. "I figured if that Cedar chap could turn one into a sword then so could you." He smiled then rolled over away from the fire, almost immediately starting to snore.

Ard took another look at the branch. It was just a regular pine bough that had somehow found its way to the road. Maybe Kinn was right. He'd already made an impenetrable wall of light out of thin air. If he was a Thorn like Cedar, maybe there were other things he could do. He held the branch out on his left palm and ran his right hand across it. Nothing happened. He tried it again, starting from the opposite end. He moved his hand slowly, but still, nothing happened. He tried moving his hand quicker, but all he did was come close to smacking himself in the face. He gripped the branch with both hands and squeezed it gently, but after everything he tried the branch remained a branch. He took a deep breath and held it out one last time, focusing hard on what he wanted.

Branch to blade, branch to blade, branch to blade...

As his hand moved across the branch this time, he felt it heat and vibrate, chipping away at itself. Within seconds, he held a dagger in his palm. Shocked, he dropped the blade and watched it explode into dust as soon as it touched the ground. The faint breeze gathered the dust and swept it across the field toward the woods like they were calling it home. Like the remnants of the branch itself were running back to the open embrace of the forest. And though Ard knew what awaited him between the darkness of the trees, he felt the Bardenwood itself beg him to take one more step inside.

Glossary & Lore

Dazmos (DAZ-mus) - one of the high deities in Gylish religion. He is High Lord of the Sky and is described as a giant four-armed blacksmith who forges mountains. Lightning, thunder, and rain are said to occur when he is forging.

Dül (DOOL) - an elemental force within the biology of Gylem; known as "magic" by common folk, it can only be yielded by Graelings or Grymlings.

Ferals - an area of unexplored territory outside of the Settled Lands; an expletive among Clusterfolk

Galexia (Guh-LECK-see-uh) - the highest deity in Gylish religion. She is described as a woman with aurora hair who lights stars in the names of those who have died and lived a respectable life. Her children and grandchildren make up the divine Lords Above and Below.

Goliamoth (Guh-LIE-uh-muth) - Giant, aggressive beasts with long, sharp tusks that roam the Bitterlands. They are a necessary resource to the people of Vargyn.

Grae - one of two "faces" or components of Dül. It encompasses the positive aspects of nature like growth, light, birth, life, and nourishment.

Graeling - a being that serves, benefits from, or harnesses Grae.

Graemir (GRAY-meer) - acts performed using Grae

Grym - one of two "faces" or components of Dül. It encompasses the negative aspects of nature like destruction, death, darkness, decay, and strife.

Grymling - a being that serves, benefits from, or harnesses Grym.

Grymor (GRIM-or) - acts performed using Grym

Gyle - the lesser known third face of Dül that encompasses the human aspect of nature, mostly described as love, hope, and emotion

Gyling - human

Gylar (GUY-lar) - acts and nuances of human nature, condition, and emotion

Ika (Uka) nojek - A Vargynian phrase coined by a small group of hunters which translates to "I am (you are) the drum."

Kanungák (Kah-noon-GAHK) - a wild group of cannibals that roam the Paasian Peaks

Lords Above - the deities that reign in the trees, sky, and heavens under the rule of Dazmos.

Lords Below - the deities that reign in the layers of the Gylish underworld and alongside humans under the rule of Uxos.

Metals - the currency of the Settled Lands in the form of coin. Each kingdom has their own unique metals with their own insignia on each.

Nuvílda - the Vargynian underworld described as a frozen wasteland

Pesculos (PESC-you-lus) - one of the high deities in Gylish religion. He is High Lord of the Sea and is described as an old sailor on a small boat. He was cursed to eternally wander the seas by his mother Galexia after making them undrinkable for humans out of jealousy.

Verdamaïn (Vare-duh-MINE) - the holy name for the Lushlands often used by Queen Leonora

Uxos (OOK-sus) - one of the high deities in Gylish religion. He is High Lord of the Soul and rules over the Lords Below in the Gylish underworld. He is responsible for the judgment of souls after they pass on and the fate of souls brought into the world. He is described as having no physical body, just a voice that presents itself as human conscience.

Acknowledgments

To my beloved wife, my muse, my inspiration, my love. The world I built within these pages could never compare to the world I'm building with you everyday. Thank you for every piece of wisdom you offered, every bit of light you shed, and every late night you spent making sure this tale was a real priority. I owe you a debt I'll never believe is paid. I love you.

To my parents, whose names gave life to my own, I love you so much. Mom, you were right.

To Patrick Munnelly, my editor, without whom The Bardenwood would surely wither. Thank you for believing in me and my story, thank you for keeping the wind at my heels, and most importantly, thank you for being my friend.

To Susan Brooks and the rest of the team at Literary Wanderlust for making sure my book became a real and beautiful thing. Thank you for being so fluid and willing to work with any vision I presented. You're a rarity and I'm so thankful to have found my home with you.

To Gabi, who spent so much time and precision bringing my book to life with her dazzling cover art. I am so lucky to be a partner to you and I hope I can always be a small part in your incredible career wherever it may lead you. You are a goddess among us.

To the High Ladies of Fae Crate Brittany, Meagan, Lyss, Michelle, Taylor, and Kayce for sending my book to faraway lands and countries whose inhabitants I never imagined would be reading it. I owe you so much.

To Brittany Frazier for all your love, support, and assistance with designing my type and graphics. The Blackstone Ritual owes a lot of its fashion sense to you. Thank you for everything.

To Kathy Ver Eecke and the crew at Pitch To Published for helping me and countless other writers curate my query and for teaching me the importance of knowing the industry. I wouldn't be here without you.

To Michelle Reyes @berrybookpages for being my ultimate cheerleader and the sweetest of friends in the #bookstagram universe. You make me feel like a star and I'll never forget you for it. I hope the Bardenwood is your new fave.

To the Barden Betas, Autumn, Azizza, Cassie, Dara, Denise, Duane, Eddie, Emilee, Forrest, Hannah, Jackson, Jenny, Jordyn, Kailey, Kailyn, Kat, Sarah, Shana, Tamara, and Tim, thank you for all the support and encouragement you gave me. Your genuine reactions to the events in this book filled me with indescribable joy. I love all of you!

To Madison Zaine for being the first person to ever animate my characters and bring them to life for me. You will seriously never know how important it was to me. I hope your art takes you to heights beyond the clouds because you deserve it. Never stop.

To Donna Van Oss, Elise Leblanc, Shannon Donze, Ann Clement-Kemp, Lisa Bezet, Monica Alford, and all the English teachers out there who make their classrooms a place for creativity, love, safety, and expression. You're all heroes.

To Jon Bellion, James Newton Howard, Hans Zimmer, Ramin Djawadi, Bear McCreary, and Alan Silvestri for teaching me that music is storytelling.

Lastly, to you, dear reader. I hope I brought a tear to your eye, a smile to your face, or a raise to your brow. Always remember the importance of sticking your nose in a book...and always beware the Bardenwood.

About the Author

From Lord of The Rings to Jurassic Park to X-men, Swearingen is a fan first and author second. He believes the key to being a good storyteller is to adore stories. His love of characters and adventure found him writing his first works in grade school (even if those works were handwritten and bound with craft yarn). He loves music, animals, and just about anything that involves a stroll through the woods. An avid hiker and environmentalist, Swear often uses any time outdoors as inspiration for his writing. Although originally from Baton Rouge, Louisiana, he currently resides in Portland, Oregon with his wife and their three fur-children Merry, Pippin, and Weasley.